Big Bad Wolf

WOLF DUET, BOOK ONE

DIANA A. HICKS

HMG, INC.

Copyright

Publishing History

Print ISBN 978-1-949760-38-5

Digital ISBN 978-1-949760-37-8

Credits

Cover Model: Dominic Calvani

Photographer: CJC Photography

Cover Designer: Veronica Larsen

Editor: Becky Barney

Recommended Reading Order

The Crime Society World

Beast Duet

Lost Raven - Novella

King of Beasts (Beast Duet #1)

King of Beasts (Beast Duet #2)

Wolf Duet

Wolf's Lair - Prequel

Big Bad Wolf (Wolf Duet #1)

Big Bad Wolf (Wolf Duet #2)

Once Upon A Christmas - Bonus Epilogue

Raven Duet

Dark Beauty - Prequel

Fallen Raven (Raven Duet, #1)

Fallen Raven (Raven Duet, #2)

Knight Duet

Wicked Knight (Knight Duet, #1)

Wicked Knight (Knight Duet, #2)

Cole Brothers World

Stolen Hearts Duet

Entangle You

Unravel You

Steal My Heart Series

Ignite You

Escape You

Escape My Love - Bonus Epilogue

Provoke You

Cole Twins Duet

Unleash You

Defy You

Praise for Diana A. Hicks

"Hicks' first installment of her Desert Monsoon series is confident and assured with strong storytelling, nuanced characters, and a dynamic blend of romance and suspense."

— KIRKUS REVIEWS

What makes any romance a great read isn't the fact that two hot people meet and fall in love. It is the episodes that bring about the falling in love and the unexpected places the experience takes the characters that make it an enjoyable read. Diana A. Hicks knows just how to make this happen.

— READERS' FAVORITE

About the Author

Diana A. Hicks is an award-winning author of dark mafia romance and steamy contemporary romance with a heavy dose of suspense.

When Diana is not writing, she enjoys kickboxing, hot yoga, traveling, and indulging in the simple joys of life like wine and chocolate. She lives in Atlanta and loves spending time with her two children and husband.

Check out my bookstore!

Don't forget to sign up to my newsletter to stay up to date on my latest releases, free content, and other news.
Subscribe to my VIP List now!

SINFULLY DARK ROMANCE

Dear Reader,

I'm so excited to share the next installment in my Crime Society world. Santino and Luce's forbidden love story is finally here in the Wolf Duet.

Please note that Big Bad Wolf is book one in the Wolf Duet. It ends in a cliffy.

Over the summer, I released Wolf's Lair, a long prologue to the Big Bad Wolf Duet, which provides a bit of background on the gang war brewing between the Irish and Italians.

If you haven't read it, that's okay. Like I said, I've included those chapters in Part I of this book. If you're familiar with how it all started, go ahead and skip to Part II.

One last note: I write dark romance with questionable situations that might be triggering (i.e kidnapping, dub-con, BDSM, etc.). I trust you know yourself and will proceed with caution.

Happy Reading and welcome to the Society!
Diana

PART ONE

Wolf's Lair

WOLF DUET, PREQUEL

CHAPTER 1
A Virgin Wife

LUCE

Beverly, South Chicago

Though we still had plenty of summer days left, the Sassafras trees in our expansive front yard had the distinct bark scent that signaled fall was coming. The warm breeze rustled the treetops, and a few orange-brown leaves fluttered to the ground like burning pieces of paper.

Growing up, this was my favorite time of year—when the foliage around our Chicago home turned a deep red. I always felt like the change happened overnight. But I knew that wasn't the case. The change was gradual. We had plenty of warning.

It happened with Mom, too. She died on a night much like this one. Her passing felt so sudden, though it took years for the lung cancer to eat away at her body.

I pushed off the thick tree trunk, ambled to the next one about twenty feet away, and glanced up at the sky. White clouds crowded the swaying tree limbs high above us. Another optical illusion.

"I should be there with them." I rubbed my bare arm, wishing Dad had let me come.

"And do what, Luce? Get killed?" My best friend Kayleigh squinted at me then followed my line of sight. When she didn't find anything worth noting, she picked up a stick and threw it across the way.

Dad and my twin brother Ronan had gone out to, literally, fight for our family and left us here to do nothing but twiddle our thumbs—or as it were, throw sticks and scowl at the heavens. I wanted to be with them and do something worthwhile, make a difference. Dad and Ronan were not the only ones willing to make a sacrifice for our crew.

The Irish gang, my family, had been around for a long time. We prided ourselves on offering our community protection and solvency. Something the Italians had made extra hard recently.

In the past few months—or maybe the gang war had been brewing for longer than that—the Italians had declared open season on our territory. Dad, as the oldest surviving O'Brien and leader of the Red Wolves, had tried to improve our relationship with the Chicago Outfit. He had no interest in their human trafficking business. We weren't about that. We ran guns to the people who needed them, and yeah, sure, when times were rough, we even dipped our toes into the drug-dealing pool.

Apparently, the filthy Italians thought that lack of excessive greed meant we were weak. And now they were killing us off one by one.

"No, Kay. To help. I can help. We can help."

"I know. But someone had to stay home and deal with the fallout. You know this."

We didn't exactly know this. In the twenty-five years I'd been alive, I never had to deal with gang wars over territory. The Italians came out of nowhere and had been ruthless and relentless in their pursuit for expansion into the south of Chicago.

I turned away from Kay, and then I saw it. A slight movement toward the back of the house. "Kay," I said under my breath.

"I see it." She nodded, reaching for her handgun tucked in the back of her waistband. As usual, she stepped in front of me as if I were the one that needed protection. We were both in danger. But sometimes Kay liked to play my bodyguard. With her dad being my dad's lieutenant, we grew up together. We were more than best friends; we were sisters.

"Let's split up." I gripped the handle of my weapon.

"We never split up," she hissed. "This isn't some recon mission, Luce. We assess the danger and then take cover."

"Are we seriously having this conversation right now?"

"You started it."

"Fine." I put up my hand. "Left side has more trees in the way."

"One, two, three," she counted fast then bolted.

"Dammit." I darted after her, keeping my weapon aimed at the ground. The last thing I needed was my gun going off because the adrenaline rushing through me made me trigger happy. Kay's dad had trained us both since we were twelve. Kay had a knack for guns, but not me. I hated the things. If I kept one, it was because Dad begged me to do it for my own protection.

"Oh, fuck." My heartbeat spiked as soon as Ronan's face came into view near the kitchen door that led to the back yard.

"It's them." Kay stuffed her gun back in its place and took off.

I did the same, taking in big gulps of air. I needed to still my trembling hands. In the kitchen, I followed the trail of blood. Weirdly enough, the sight calmed me down. I set my gun on the counter and went straight to the sink to wash my hands. Nursing school had been Mom's idea. She was a registered nurse—something that came in handy more than once while I was growing up. In the mob, the thing about playing with guns was that someone always got shot.

By the time I walked into the living room, Dad was already resting on one of the cots I had set up for this very purpose. "What's the damage?"

"Three wounded." Ronan nodded once and stepped aside to let me get to Dad. "Connor and Sean didn't make it."

"Jesus." I cut open Dad's shirt. "Where are they?"

"Two of our guys stayed behind to get them back." He pursed his lips, exchanging a meaningful look with Dad.

I furrowed my brows, putting pressure on Dad's shoulder wound. Something had happened between them. Did they fight on the way here? "What did you do?" I glared at Ronan.

"Nothing."

"Don't give me that. I know that look." I rinsed Dad's shoulder wound and took the time to assess the damage. The lump in my throat bobbed, and I swallowed to keep the tears from coming. Dad was wearing a bulletproof vest and had a dish shaped bullet lodged in it. "You're gonna need X-rays to be sure there's no internal damage." I used my nurse voice because, right now, I couldn't be his daughter. I would fall apart and that would help no one. "Help me with the vest."

I stood and let Ronan lift Dad so I could work the straps off the garment that saved his life tonight. As expected, the area was already turning purple and spreading below his rib cage. Dad was built like an ox, but he wasn't young anymore. "You can't keep doing this, Dad."

"Tell that to the Italians," he mumbled in his smoky voice and waved Ronan away.

"Bring the other two. Why are they not inside? They need to be triaged."

Ronan nodded toward the back of the room, and our wounded magically appeared. They had stayed out of sight so I would work on Dad first. It wasn't fair. All life was valuable. But they needed Dad alive. When I met their gaze, they blurted out their injuries. We'd done this more than once in the past few months.

"Blade to my side. It feels squishy."

"Dog bite. Don't ask."

"Lie down," I ordered, looking at the two of them. "Let me have a look. You too, Ronan. That eye looks nasty."

"We were ambushed, Luce." Ronan stepped into my line of sight.

"Ronan." Dad practically barked his name.

"The Italians never had any intention of calling a truce." He clenched his jaw and swallowed. "They were there for Dad and me."

Dad closed his eyes and dug his head into the flat pillow. I couldn't tell if he was tired from the night he'd had or if he was just done with all this bullshit with the Italians. At this rate, our crew would be decimated before winter was over. Our people and everyone I grew up with would have to live under the threat of the Italians, running drugs for them, paying for protection and...I stopped my train of thought because I didn't want to think about how bad things would get if our crew didn't exist.

"Tell her, Dad."

"Tell me what?" I stopped midway through my stitching. Honestly, in all my training, I never had to do sutures while the patients were fighting amongst themselves.

"We need outside help." Ronan crossed his arms over his chest. "I mean, everyone can see that." He gestured toward the bloody scene around us.

Both Kay and I nodded because Ronan was right. If we could get one of the other Irish gangs to pitch in, we could kick the Italians out of the South—for good. No more shootings. No more vandalism. No more break-ins. Our entire community would be safe.

I looked to Dad, but he didn't turn to me. Instead, he kept his gaze glued to the light fixture on the ceiling.

"Does this have something to do with me?" I asked.

"Yes." Ronan stared at Dad while he spoke. "Liam Walsh has offered his help. But Dad refuses to accept."

"Um, what?" Kay stepped in. She had managed to keep quiet and out of the way because she hated blood. Fighting ruthless assholes was more her speed. Liam Walsh being the ruthless asshole in this case. "We can't get into bed with that creep. Who the hell knows what he'll ask for?"

"Watch it." Ronan turned his furious gaze to Kay.

Ronan wasn't normally the angry type. In fact, I had never seen him act like this before. What the hell did the Italians do to piss him off?

8

"This is Red Wolves' business. You don't get a say."

"Sorry." Kay cleared her throat.

When she stepped back, she quickly scanned the room—no doubt looking for her dad, who, as Dad's lieutenant, would have some say in who we asked for help. Or at least Dad would take his opinion into account. Though judging by the stern look in Dad's eyes, he had already decided. And he wasn't proud of it.

"Luce." Dad reached for my hand and squeezed it tight. "This contract does involve you. Liam has the men and resources to get us out of this hole the Italians dug for us. He can get us back on our feet."

"What does he want?" I had a pretty good idea. It couldn't be money because the Italians had made sure to sabotage all our latest dealings. They were starving us out. It also couldn't be guns or drugs. The New York Irish had their own suppliers.

"A wife." He winced in pain.

"Not a plaything?" Wasn't that what he liked? At least, those were the rumors.

"I'm so sorry, Luce. I've tried to handle this on my own. But what choice do we have?" He rubbed the creases on his forehead, looking a decade older than he did just this morning when we had breakfast together. "At least this way, you'll be safe. He wants children. He's ready for a wife."

More specifically, a *virgin* wife.

Dad didn't want to embarrass me with that small detail. It would make this whole transaction too dark and twisted. But just because he wasn't saying the word didn't mean that it wasn't an understood requirement. A big boss running a crew in New York would never settle for less than a virgin with ties to another boss. Dad knew this because twenty-six years ago, he made a similar deal for Mom.

I did appreciate that he'd shown some remorse, and I rather liked the illusion that I had a say in this.

Swallowing my tears, I rose to my feet and headed back into the kitchen to wash my hands. Two more of our men needed my help. One of them had a nasty dog bite that was already turning colors. Really? They were using dogs? I hated the Italians now more than ever. Tears stung my eyes as I rubbed the sticky, dried blood from my hands and forearms. Before I knew it, I was in full-on sobbing mode.

What was it they said? Be careful what you ask for, you just might get it. I wanted to help in a more significant way. Now Dad was telling me I could end this war. And all I had to do was marry a heartless monster.

Liam Walsh was the boss of the Irish Crew in Harlem, New York. He was well-known and feared by everyone, including me. *Especially me.* By the way Dad hesitated with every word, I'd say he was scared, too. Liam was rich and powerful. He could marry anyone he wanted. What else was he getting out of this deal?

I'd always considered myself a pragmatic woman. Mending people was never my passion, but I was good at it, so I went to nursing school after I finished my undergrad at Barnard College. Same with my virginity. I didn't save myself over some romantic ideal. I knew one day; I would need it. I never thought I would marry for love. That was for normal people, not people like us.

My parents' marriage had been an arranged contract between their families. Over the years, they learned to cherish each other. Were they soulmates? No, not really, but they were content and respected each other. In the end, their union made our crew stronger.

Early on, Mom had explained to me how, one day, my virginity would be a highly sought commodity. I didn't save my virtue because of some religious ideal. I did it because I was a realistic woman. In my world, my virginity had value, as in men were willing to pay money for it. Or in my case, with a small army. My marriage to Liam Walsh could save our lives and ensure our longevity. With the Italians out of the way, we could resume our gun business.

"Fuck me." Kay stomped into the kitchen. "You're actually thinking about this? It's insane. He's *insane.*"

"He wants a wife." I lifted my gaze to meet hers. "Obviously, he's thinking about a family. He needs an heir. So who knows? He might be decent to me."

"He wants you because you're gorgeous and you check all the boxes. You're the big boss's daughter in Beverly. And, well, you're a virgin. Apparently, he wants one, and those are hard to come by these days." She braced her hands on the marble counter, taking in a deep breath. "What the hell am I saying? I'm so sorry."

I inhaled too to ease the pain in my chest. Liam wasn't called the "butcher" for nothing.

"Isn't he like sixty years old?" Kay asked.

"Fifty. And you're not making this any better."

"Sorry." She put up her hands.

"I hate this." I splashed water on my face. "I don't have a choice, Kay. Imagine saying no. He might even retaliate by helping the Italians finish us off."

"Honestly, that sounds like something he would do. How did we get here?"

"The Italians. That's how." I fisted my hands and leaned over the sink.

My stomach clenched at the idea of what I had to do. Even though I was ready for a marriage of convenience, I had hoped I'd get to stay in Chicago. There were plenty of suitable men here, where my family was. Accepting Liam's help and marriage contract would mean I would have to move to New York. I glanced up to look at Kay. She nodded as if saying, "you're doing the right thing."

I blamed the Italians for all of this. "I hate them all."

CHAPTER 2
Every Goddamn Time

Mia

Hell's Kitchen, Manhattan, New York

"Where the hell is Tyler?" I pressed my back to the brick wall in the alley and peeked around the corner.

A block away, the machine gun smoke still lingered just above the asphalt. The scent of blood mixed with burning fuel shot up into my brain. As tired as I was, as scared as I was, that small detail kept my senses on high alert.

"Shh." My second in command, Vic, stepped out of the shadows.

The old man practically raised me. Now that I was the Rogue River Boss, he never left my side. I trusted him implicitly. But when it came to Tyler, my husband and the father of my one-year-old son, I couldn't stand idle while he was out there risking his life and getting shot at.

My body jerked when it dawned on me why the old man had shushed me. I'd said Tyler's name out loud. The one word we had all agreed never to utter again—not in public anyway.

To me, my husband would always be Tyler. Chase Rossi was someone who overdosed a long time ago. Chase Rossi was Tyler's fake identity. The one he used to infiltrate the New York faction.

"He keeps playing the hero, he's bound to get shot one of these days," Vic deadpanned, in his usual pragmatic tone.

He wasn't wrong. Wasn't that how Tyler got caught up in my world of criminals? How he ended up being the leader of the New York faction when he was supposed to bring them down? He did it all for me and to keep our unborn child safe.

"We have to go back and get him. Now."

"He told you to go home."

I turned around so fast that Vic put up his hands in surrender. "First of all, I'm still the boss. Tyler...Chase doesn't get to tell me what to do. Husband or not, I'm in charge."

"You got it, boss."

Vic could imply a thousand things with just his tone. Tonight, his tone implied that the men, *my men*, were confused. Part of the deal with the Society, with Rex Valentino, was that the Jersey crew would become part of the fold. Rex wanted everything under his command. That meant my crew now answered to the New York faction, who in turn, answered to Rex. Tyler was in charge of this run. But that didn't mean I was going to sit pretty and let the fucking Irish kill my husband.

I missed the days when we stayed on our side of the Hudson, ran our gun business with the Mexican cartel and lived a happy life. It all changed when the late Jac Rossi decided he wanted my crew to advance his standing with the Society. But I couldn't be too mad about that. Because of him, I met the love of my life, Tyler Cole, who, at the time, was undercover with the FBI playing the part of Jac Rossi's grandson, Chase.

I didn't care about any of it. How it got started or how much of our time and effort it required to keep Tyler's true identity hidden. I cared about my family. I would do anything to keep them alive. If that meant killing the Irish to send them back to Harlem, I was more than prepared to do that tonight.

"What do the Irish want in Hell's Kitchen?" I said through gritted teeth. "The Italians own this territory. We always have."

Vic grunted with a soft click of his teeth. "Peace never lasts. It's been too quiet around here. I'm sure the assholes thought we were prime for the picking."

"It's getting worse, too." I peeked around the wall again, hating that I'd stayed in my hiding place for so long. "It's a war zone out there. You know what that means."

"Yeah, the Feds are bound to take notice. Come knocking. Ask Tyler for favors."

That was exactly the problem here. The Irish, with their greed and thirst for power and territory, had created a huge problem for my family. If the pigs came looking for Tyler, they would have no qualms exposing him to get what they wanted. They'd done it before. And it ended with Tyler almost dying from a shot to the chest. *Not this time.*

"There's only one way to keep the FBI away." I checked my AK-15, a model I'd outfitted myself. A little something I had to do to appease the Mexican cartel last year.

"We handle this business ourselves," Vic finished my thought.

"Let's go."

With my heart thrashing in my ears, I darted out onto the

street. The cacophony of guns shooting from every direction had died down. Either we were all out of bullets or both sides had decided to take a reprieve to strategize and advance. I used the small window of time to try and find Tyler in the cloud of smoke.

Instead, I found one of my men, Manny. "Where's Chase?"

"He's trying something." He stood at attention.

"I told you to stay with him."

"I know. But he ordered me to stay put." He dropped his backpack to the ground and pulled out a laptop. Manny and his brother, Tom, were my hackers. They were good. I could only hope Tyler's plan was as good.

"What did he ask you for?"

"Simple hacking job. Security cameras, and then he said to cut the lights." Manny punched a few codes into his screen. "Their boss is here, too. Why would he show up?"

"Because he thought this was it. He thought we would concede tonight." I lifted my head toward the end of the street and the warehouse where most of the shooting was happening. "That's not one of our sites."

"It's theirs. Fully operational distribution center. Mostly nose candy." Manny switched to another screen to show me.

The assholes had settled in. They knew Hell's Kitchen was Italian territory. "They have some balls."

"Not for long, boss."

"Jesus. Tell me he's not planning to blow up the place."

"Um. He's not planning to blow up the place." Manny rubbed the back of his head. "But he is. He sent everyone home. I stayed behind to be his eyes. Tom and me, we flipped for it. I won."

"This is a suicide mission. God, I'm going to kill him." I moved Manny's screen to face me. My gaze darted from one dark image to the next. Now it made sense why the blaring of the guns had gone silent. Tyler had ordered our crew to retreat. "Which way did he go?"

"The alley to the right. It has a door with a code."

"A code you disabled?"

"Yes, boss." He beamed at me. "Just like old times, huh?"

"Yeah. I guess a year of peace was too much to ask for." I tapped him on the shoulder and bolted for the dark alley he had indicated. Without having to ask, Vic covered me, following close by.

When I reached the entrance, I tripped over a body. As I scanned the dark corridor, extending to the street over, I counted five more bodies. I scrambled to my feet and faced the door.

"Don't hesitate. That'll get you killed." Vic stood behind me. His words were an echo of my own thoughts.

Ever since I had a baby, I'd had this compulsion to overanalyze everything; every angle, every possible outcome, every stray bullet. I didn't want our baby to grow up without parents, like I did. But Tyler was on the other side of this door. *I had to do it.*

I turned the doorknob, peeked inside, and immediately spotted Tyler in a standoff against the Irish. I counted a dozen men on the opposite end of the warehouse. Had they not yet figured out Tyler was alone? Of course not. Who in their right mind would face a bunch of angry Irishmen alone?

Vic tapped my shoulder, pointed two fingers at his own eyes then gestured toward three different spots along the wall. Homemade explosives. When my gaze settled back on Tyler, I realized his plan wasn't entirely done. He still had two more pipe bombs on either side of him. Without missing a beat, Vic started shooting at the Irish. I used the distraction to make my way to Tyler.

"We'll talk about this later." I picked up one of the bundles. Up close, I could tell the thing was poorly assembled, which wasn't surprising, since Tyler only had about half an hour to come up with this plan and then execute it. I had to admit, his criminal methods were improving. "Where do you want it?"

"I told you to go home." He gritted his teeth.

"And I told you I wasn't leaving without you. You're wasting time."

"Jesus fuck, Mia." He raked a hand through his dark hair.

His intense blue gaze shot daggers at me for a moment. And then something else—he had wanted me to go home because he wanted at least one of us to survive this ordeal for our baby.

"Behind those pallets." He pointed. "I'll cover you."

"No, you take that one. Vic's got it."

"The old man should know better than..." He puffed out a breath. "Go."

The heat of his anger bore through my skin, sending tendrils of heat directly to my veins. But we would deal with that later. First, we had to get to safety by blowing up the place. As I darted to the spot Tyler had said, I realized the device in my hand had a long wire attached to it. How were Tyler and Manny planning to detonate all the devices? I had to trust Tyler—trust that he would want to stay alive for us.

As soon as I started to make my way back, Tyler's voice boomed over the intercom. I could only assume Manny had hacked into all their systems. Thank God for those boys, Manny and Tom. "Hell's Kitchen doesn't belong to you. Go home. You have thirty seconds to get yourself out. We have eyes everywhere. If I see any one of you trying to save the product, my men will shoot you dead."

I swallowed the lump in my throat, hoping the Irish didn't know Vic and I were the "my men" in this scenario. The reaction to Tyler's words spread in a domino effect. First, one guy's creepy laugh rumbled in the back of the room, then another and another. They were calling his bluff because a proper criminal would not have given them a way out. But Tyler was a good guy. He didn't belong in my world. My worst fear was that one of these days his kindness would be his downfall.

Shots pelted around us as we headed for the only way out. Over the loud roar of the guns, the familiar sizzle of a burning wire made me pick up the pace. Blood pumped hard and fast through me as I darted toward our only exit. Within seconds, the fuse had ignited, and the first pipe bomb went off. The eerie quiet that followed compelled me to look back. Tyler grabbed me by the elbow and rushed me away from the compromised building.

A street over, Manny had the SUV ready for us. We jumped in the back seat, and as soon as Vic's body landed on the passenger seat, Manny slammed on the accelerator, and the vehicle careened away from the scene.

"Jesus." I shifted my weight to face the now burning warehouse. "We're lucky the police didn't catch wind of the shooting."

"It wasn't luck." Tyler reached for me and pulled me into his arms. "I called Rex."

"What?" I made to face him, but he held me tighter. "You

called the guy who could snap his fingers and make all your guys shoot you on the spot?"

"Yeah, I called that Rex."

"What now?" I fully relaxed my body against his solid muscled frame. Not because I thought calling Rex was a real solution, but because Tyler's scent and his energy always had a calming effect on me. He was home. He was everything I ever wanted in a man—strength, brains, and yeah, even his kind heart.

"It's not ideal." His deep voice broke the rhythmic dance of the car tires against the smooth asphalt. "In this case, Rex is the lesser of two evils. We can't have the FBI interfering again."

"Clifton is no longer our problem. Rex saw to that."

Special Agent in Charge, Clifton, had been the mastermind behind a plan to expose Rex and his secret organization and bring them down. Because of him, Tyler had to turn double agent for the FBI and the ATF. Clifton was a madman.

"Plenty of other agents still know who I am. They'll let us be. But the minute they need a favor from me..." He stopped to inhale, and his chest rose and fell. "Don't think they're above using you and the baby as leverage."

I had to agree with him. Even someone as ruthless as Rex was better than the FBI. If the Society backed us up, we had a chance at surviving the hostile takeover the Irish were hell-bent on carrying out sooner rather than later. Tonight, they came at us with everything they had. Mounting a fully operational warehouse in secret, this fast, took resources and a shit-ton of motivation.

Tyler fished his phone from the back pocket of his pants and tapped the screen. "Rossi, here." He used his business tone, which meant Rex was on the other side of the conversation. "It's done." He waited a few seconds, then replied, "Yes, we're in." He ended the call.

I wrapped my arm around his torso and held him tight. I didn't want to think about tomorrow and the implications of everything that happened tonight. Manny pulled into the private garage of our building and stopped in front of the elevator bay that led straight into the Rossi penthouse.

"Go home. Get some rest," Tyler ordered when Vic and Manny made to exit the SUV.

When they both froze, Tyler grabbed my hand and climbed out. I did my best to keep up with him until we reached the safety of the elevator car. Two seconds after we started our ascent, he hit the emergency button. I opened my mouth to ask what he was doing, but in that moment, his lips collided with mine.

His kiss was urgent and erratic as he undid the straps of his bulletproof vest. I helped him out of it, then he helped with mine. A moan echoed in the small space, and I couldn't tell if that was me or him. In the next breath, he turned me to face the mirrored panel. His hands were all over me—kneading my breasts, my butt cheeks, and my pussy. Every rough stroke was a reminder that he owned me, body and soul, that he had already conquered every inch of me, that I was his.

Another sound echoed between us. This time, I was sure it was my own desperate groan that escaped my throat—a plea to not make me wait, a promise of surrender. He pulled down my pants without preamble and entered me from behind. I reached back, taking handfuls of his sweaty hair as he pumped hard into me. This wasn't lovemaking. Tyler was fucking me as if trying to teach me a lesson, teach me to obey him. Or maybe he meant it as punishment for staying put.

Gripping my hip with one hand and my breast with the other, he plunged into me harder and harder until an orgasm ripped through me with the same urgency as his rough strokes and the engulfing flames from the warehouse. The heat I had felt on my back now moved down to my core. I squeezed my eyes shut and saw the building burning down. "Tyler." I clung to him as my walls clenched around his hard cock, aching for more. "Tyler," I repeated, over and over, while he continued to claim me, filling me until he found his own release.

"Fuck, Mia. How many times are you going to save my life?" He panted in the shell of my ear.

"Every goddamn time." I fought back tears. "You can't leave me, Tyler. I can't do this alone. I can't keep my family safe without you."

"I was hoping not to start a war tonight." He nibbled on my neck and then my shoulder, still digging his long fingers into my skin.

"I know." I turned around and pressed my lips to his. "We're not gonna let the bastards win."

CHAPTER 3
And Yet They Have To

SANTINO

Manhattan, New York

My father's office fit me. The high ceilings, the expensive, one-of-a-kind art, the bookcases filled with first-edition books, and a bunch of other crap that screamed power and old money.

When I was a kid, I could sit on Dad's gray leather sofa, facing the tall windows, and get lost in the city view. The shape of the buildings, the tiny people beneath me, and the gentle hum of the AC offered an odd sense of comfort. The entire setup was nice when it wasn't my own gilded cage. Yeah, my father's office fit me—that didn't mean I liked it.

I paced the length of the room, keeping my gaze on the passing clouds, feeling like a caged animal. For the past couple of years, my father's health had been—diminishing—to say the least. Don Buratti needed a successor. As the eldest of five, the honor—or the curse—fell upon me.

"Sir." Lia's small voice stopped me in my tracks. Actually,

it wasn't her voice that caught my attention, it was the scent of whiskey that now lingered in the air. "Your drink, sir."

"Took you long enough." I took the glass tumbler from her and sipped. "What the hell is this?"

"Pappy Van Winkle, sir. Your favorite..." She framed her answer as a question.

A five-thousand-dollar bottle of bourbon should please me. I supposed I understood her confusion. "It tastes like water."

"I could remove the ice." She offered me the small silver tray in her hand, so I could return the drink.

"No, leave it. It's fine." I knocked the rest of it back.

In truth, my lack of taste buds, or overall numbness, had nothing to do with the Pappy and everything to do with my father's visit. He liked to keep himself relevant by showing up at my office once a month. Today was that day.

I glanced toward the hallway, past my office doors. My employees were buzzing with excitement, mixed with terror, as they rushed to their positions. That could only mean one thing. Don Buratti had entered the building.

"Show him in as soon he gets here. And Lia?"

She made to leave, but promptly turned around when I called her name. "Yes, sir."

"No phone calls and no interruptions of any kind."

"Of course, sir."

I crossed my arms and faced the city again. Two seconds later, I reconsidered my stance and decided to try and be less hostile toward the old man. I sauntered toward the chair behind my desk and sat, bracing my hands on the armrests. This meeting would be over soon. And then I could go back to doing things my way.

"Ten million dollars in tax deeds?" The double doors busted open, and Don Buratti strode in with Lia on his heels.

"Leave us." I motioned toward the hallway. When she didn't move, I sat back in my chair. "What is it?"

"Don Valentino is here to see you as well." She meant Rex. Outside of our tight group, no one was allowed to use his name.

I chuckled at her predicament. Who had higher standing, my father or the king of the Society, a one-hundred-year-old enclave that managed all criminal activity in the country? Rex Valentino was the sitting king, whether we liked it or not.

"Show him in," I said to Lia, then turned to Dad. "We'll double that money by the end of the year, Dad."

"It's not about the money, and you know it." He tossed the manila folder on my desk.

I chuckled. Dad was an old school mobster who thought if his money wasn't covered in blood, it hadn't been earned. Times had changed, and he refused to see it. If the Society wasn't careful and didn't keep up with the times, they too might become obsolete.

"Well, would it make you feel better if I told you I bullied my way into the real estate auction and bought all the deeds and the properties that came with it? Also, many people will lose their homes in the process. Better?"

"Watch your tone with me, boy." He lowered himself into the leather club chair across from me. "This is still my company. We run the firm my way."

Buratti Investment Research Advisors, Inc. was founded shortly after the market crash of nineteen-twenty as a front for the Society. The era was our golden years. Booze, money laundering, and racketeering activities was how Dad built this company from the ground up.

I was here merely to make sure the engines were well-oiled, and the money kept flowing. Being CEO was an easy gig. What the Society required of us took a bit more effort on my part. As Don Buratti's second-in-command, I oversaw investments and real estate, but also, whenever Rex needed to take care of someone, he would call upon my crew—which was all a bunch of nice words to say, I was the Society's assassin. My crew and I, we took out the trash. We were the best at it.

From the beginning, since I was barely a teenager, I had a knack for tracking down those who'd done us wrong. I could smell our enemies' fears and guess their next move, their next hiding place. My guys nicknamed me the Punisher. I didn't mind it. The name suited me.

"Yes, Dad. This is still your company. Shall we get started with our monthly review?"

The meeting tended to go a lot smoother when we were focused on business matters and not my personal life.

"We could've been done with these meetings a long time ago." He reached into his coat pocket and retrieved a Cuban cigar, cut off the tip, and lit it. After a few long draws from it, the tobacco ignited, and Dad settled in. "You're ready to take it on, son."

"I'd like to point out that I've been doing this job for two years now."

"I mean all of it. The firm, the Society, our family."

"Don't let him talk circles around you." Rex entered the room with his usual pompous air.

Behind him, Lia rushed in with a tray, carrying three more glasses of whiskey. She set them on the coffee table facing the windows and then left. Dad stood and hugged Rex. A year ago, he would've left my office. Or punched Rex in the face. How Rex became king didn't sit well with him. But a lot had changed in the past year since Rex officially took over the Society.

Dad eventually saw the benefit and the need for the five original families to band together. Correction: four original families. After the FBI came after the Society last year, the entire Gallo family was executed. They came after us, too. But Rex managed to find a way out and handled the pigs. Dad appreciated that. So now Rex had our full support.

"Good to see you, old man. The last time I spoke with Santino, he acted as though you were on your deathbed." Rex sat on the club chair in the living area and sipped his whiskey.

"My death has been highly exaggerated." He chortled at his own joke—a stolen one from Steve Jobs.

"Not that I don't appreciate your visits, Rex, but what the fuck are you doing here?"

"Don Buratti invited me."

"Oh, fuck me." I grabbed my drink and perched myself on the sofa armrest. "Is this some sort of intervention? Is it my drinking?"

"You're not taking your birthright seriously." Dad's deep voice had a sad tinge to it.

The Society and this mobster life were his legacy. He was afraid it would all fall apart when he passed. "You're strong as an ox, Dad. I have years before I need to take anything serious."

"You're thirty years old. At your age, I was well on my way to taking over from my father."

I chose not to point out the fact that Dad had stabbed

Granddad in the back to push him out of his role as Don. The man sitting across from me looked like a decent man, a concerned father. But he was as ruthless as they came.

"If I didn't know any better, I'd say you're disappointed I haven't killed you in your sleep and taken over."

He grunted. "All you have to do is get married."

Rex sat forward and watched me intently. So that was why Dad had invited Rex to our monthly meeting. He wanted to talk about succession, marriage, and children—lots of children. Dad liked big families. But I would never do that to another human being. The women in the Society tended to die quickly. In our mafia world, the innocent always paid the sins of the wicked.

"I don't see what one thing has to do with the other."

"I'm done asking, Santino." Dad shot to his feet. Ten years ago, the boom in his smoker's voice would've sent me running from the room. "You will find a wife and take your rightful place as the head of this family."

I opened my mouth to ask, "Or you'll do what?" but Dad beat me to it. It started with a cough. Then a gurgling sound like he was choking. And then, he collapsed. I heard my own voice calling for Lia, but every sound was muffled by the fast thumping of my heart. Rex got on his phone and walked away from me while I worked on undoing the knot on Dad's tie. Was he having a heart attack? Dad was in his late sixties. He was technically too young for that. Wasn't he?

"Come on, old man. You can't leave me just yet." I did short compresses on his chest, just to get some air into his lungs or to jump-start his heart. Who the hell knew? This small act felt better than sitting on my heels and watching my only parent die. "Come on."

Dad was never what one would consider a loving father. He was brutal with his teaching methods. Life was pain. Trust no one. Shoot to kill. I learned that from him. Whatever he was or wasn't for me though, I needed him alive. Why couldn't we stay the same? Why did things have to change?

"Santino." Rex squeezed my shoulder. "Let the paramedics do their job."

I blinked fast to bring the scene in front of me back into focus. Sure enough, two guys dressed in blue uniforms stood on the other side of Dad, waiting to take him away. I conceded with a nod, and they quickly got to work.

"Did you call his doctor?" I asked Lia.

"Yes, sir. He's on his way to the hospital. He'll meet you there." She stepped back to make room for the other men pulling in a gurney.

Five minutes later, everyone but Rex was gone. After the big commotion, the silence I usually found comforting felt eerily still.

"I'm sorry." Rex finally spoke.

"For which part?" I met his gaze. "Because Dad might die tonight or because you don't have a successor like you wanted."

"Because we still need to talk business." He downed the rest of his drink. "Then you can go see him."

"I'm not a doctor. I'm not needed at the hospital. I'm needed here." I sat on the edge of the sofa and braced my forearms on my knees. "I don't like it when things change."

"And yet they have to."

"What's going on?"

"The Irish mounted a hostile takeover last night. They want Hell's Kitchen. They almost had us too." He unbuttoned his suit jacket and took the chair across from me. "I promised Caterina we'd have peace. This is the fucking opposite of that."

"Wait. The building that blew up last night. That was us?"

He nodded once. "Rossi was ambushed. He had no choice."

"The New York police are easy to control. But explosions? That's candy to the FBI."

"That's why we need to handle this in-house." He sipped from his glass. When he realized it was empty, he made his way to my desk, where Lia had left a bottle and ice for us. "Last thing I need is the FBI in our business. A gang war will definitely get their attention."

The Irish made a move on Italian territory. That was ballsy or incredibly stupid. Though I couldn't blame them. They thought they were going against the New York faction. They had no idea the Society was here to back them up. The board, the five original families, controlled every industry, and that sometimes extended beyond this country. So much time had passed since the Society went underground, we were no more than a scary bedtime story to keep intruders at bay. Until they came for us, of course. Then they quickly found out we were more than the monster under the bed.

"The Society has become an old allegory. It's no surprise the Irish aren't afraid of us anymore." I wasn't opposed to getting my hands dirty.

"I've considered becoming more than that. But then we would lose a great advantage—right now the Irish are celebrating their almost victory. They have no idea I'm coming for them." Rex had a plan.

"If you don't handle them soon. They'll assume the Italians are cowards. We can't have that." I was itching to punch something. "It just so happens I'm looking for something to keep my mind off things. What do you need?"

"First, we need to make sure we eliminate anything that might look like a pattern, or the beginning of something bigger." He took a big gulp of whiskey. "I need you to send a message to our Chicago crew. Seems they made a similar move on the Irish on the South side."

"As retaliation for what happened here?"

"Nah. Two mutually exclusive events. But that's just it. I don't need the FBI making that connection, thinking that the Irish and the Italians are starting a national feud. Can your crew manage that?"

"I'll fly to Chicago myself. Consider it done." I raised my tumbler to him. Work was what I needed right now. Anything to keep my mind off of family matters. "What about the Irish in Harlem?"

"I have a different kind of war planned for them."

"I like the sound of that. Count me in."

"I appreciate that." He patted my arm, then his smile faded. "I hope you understand that sooner rather than later, you'll have to step into the role of Don, get married, and do your part."

"I am doing my part, Rex. I'll go to Chicago and deliver your message just like you want. But don't ask me to tether my life to a woman because that will never happen. My sister has three boys of her own. I can train any one of them to follow in my footsteps."

"What?" He raised his hand to stop my ranting.

"I'm assuming that's what the marriage requirement is for. Dons need successors, heirs."

"I never said anything about kids." He chuckled. "What is

this aversion to marriage you have, anyway?" He furrowed his brows as if he were confused by my dissent. "Look at me. I've been married to Caterina for almost a year. We're happy. We're allowed to be happy."

"You've been thinking with your dick for so long, you can't see straight anymore. And that's exactly my point." I dug my index finger on my temple. "Women mess with your head and your ability to think."

"Caterina is a smart woman. I'd be a fool if I didn't listen to what she has to say."

"See what I mean?" I threw my arms up in exasperation. "I can't have that. I don't trust women. And I never will."

CHAPTER 4
Are You Lost?

Luce

Beverly, South Chicago

"Tomorrow night?" I bit my lip the second I heard the whiny tone of my voice.

I had made this choice for myself. No one pushed me into doing something I didn't want. Technically, I didn't want to marry Liam Walsh, but I hated the alternative even more. Our crew in Chicago needed help. Since the attack from two weeks ago, they had come back several times, killed two more of our men. We were weaker than before. Something needed to be done sooner rather than later.

"Yes. He's sending his private jet." Dad met my gaze for a split second before he turned his attention back to his phone, as if all the answers to our problems were written on the small screen. I supposed they were. In the form of my trip details to travel to New York to meet my future husband. "The contract." He released a breath. "You can read the contract he sent once you get there."

"Why not now?"

"I think it's best if you focus your attention on getting your things together."

"Would you be there for the wedding?"

"Of course." He reached for my hand. "I need to stay for a few days and make sure Liam makes good on his end of the bargain."

My breath hitched, and Dad's cheeks turned red. I was the bargain. "I chose this."

"Not much of a choice."

"A choice nonetheless." I plastered a smile on my face to make him feel better. "I'll go start packing."

He squeezed my fingers, fixing his gaze on them. When he opened his mouth, my chest filled with hope. I have no idea why. If he hadn't come up with a different solution in the last two weeks, I had no reason to think anything would change in the eleventh hour. Still, it would've been nice to hear him say, "Thank you," or "I'm sorry."

"Go on." He released me.

I strolled into my room, feeling numb and disconnected from reality. Though I knew with certainty that the entire situation with Liam, the help he was sending and my marriage to him, was one hundred percent real and one hundred percent happening. I leaned my shoulder on the threshold—outside looking in at all the things from my childhood that still lingered in my suite after all these years. The huge teddy bear Dad bought me one Christmas, the pink and lavender bedding with dancing ballerinas that I couldn't let go of because it was the last thing Mom bought me, and all the pictures hanging on the walls. None of it could come on this trip with me.

Tears blurred my vision as I stomped to my closet and

started pulling out tops and dresses and tossing them behind me. When I ran out of clothes to grab, I moved to the chest of drawers and emptied each one out on the floor and the bed. Anger mixed with trepidation gnawed at my insides and I didn't know how to make it go away. I wanted to scream and cry, but I knew that would change exactly nothing.

By the time Kay walked in, my room was strewn with everything I owned.

"That's it, Luce. Let it all out." She wiped my cheek.

"I chose this," I mumbled. Those three words had become my mantra. Maybe if I kept saying it aloud, they'd become the honest truth.

"I know."

"What are you doing here?" I furrowed my brows at the two suitcases by the door.

"I'm coming with you."

"You can't."

"I'm twenty-five years old, Luce. I don't need permission to go places." She rolled her luggage to the corner and turned to face me, hands on her hips, daring me to send her away. "Your dad and brother are bailing on you. I'm all you've got."

Since we were little, Kay had always had my back. I was happy she hadn't decided to stop now when I needed her the most. "We can tell him you're my bodyguard or something."

"That's exactly what I thought." She beamed at me, picking up a bra off the floor. "Tell me you're not taking this raggedy old thing with you."

"It's comfy, okay?" I snatched it from her. A genuine laugh escaped my lips, and suddenly I wasn't so alone.

"And this?" She picked up a set of pajamas with llamas all

over it. "Real sexy stuff you got here." She chuckled, shaking her head.

"I thought you were here to help." I picked up a pair of shorts that, now that I thought about it, were not that flattering on me. "I don't think it will matter what I wear. The 'butcher' doesn't sound like someone who likes to go out."

"You'll be alright, Luce." She wrapped her arm around my shoulders.

"Does it hurt?" No idea where that came from.

"Ah, you're thinking about that." She clicked her teeth. "Well, it depends on how much you want it."

"That makes no sense. Want what?"

"You know. His cock."

My ears burned and I was sure my cheeks were red. For years, I'd sat in this room and listened to Kay talk about her sex life. Kay knew I was a virgin, and she knew why. So, we mostly stayed away from talking about me. But now that I was on my way to get married, I was curious.

"Forget it. I'm not ready to talk about it." I waved my hand in dismissal. "Let's start packing."

The next day, Dad and Ronan had Red Wolves' business to attend to, so they weren't at the house when a limo came to pick us up. Not seeing them made it easier to get in the car. Though, at the last second, I did look back. I caught my trembling lip between my teeth as we pulled away from the driveway and the place that I had called home since I could remember.

We spent the next several hours in a whirlwind of traffic, getting checked in at the small airport and boarding Liam's private plane. To his credit, he had sent a nice aircraft. I hoped that the limo and all the attention to detail on the trip meant that he wasn't the ruthless monster I thought he was. Who knew—if Mom and Dad made their marriage work, maybe I could too?

"What's the hold up now?" Kay leaned over my seat to look out the plane window. "We landed hours ago. It's creeping me out. We're just sitting on the tarmac, and it's dark as fuck."

Lightning ripped across the sky and illuminated the shiny runway. Seconds later, a thunderclap shook my seat, rumbling in my chest. The rain hit us harder than before with a constant rhythm that soothed my senses a bit.

"It's only been half an hour. I'm sure we're next." I leaned forward to get a better view.

According to the pilot, we had landed in an airport outside of New York City. His tone implied this was where all the very important people in the city hangared out their private jets.

"How much longer?" Kay stopped Megan, our flight attendant.

"They're expecting a bigwig to fly in, some real estate mogul." Megan sat on the seat facing us. Kay had spent the last three hours flirting with her. We were all quite chummy by now. "You might get to see him. He'll pull in right over there." She pointed at the hanger that was brightly lit.

I sat back, quickly losing interest in the bigwig who had us waiting just so he wouldn't have to wait when he arrived.

"Well, hello." Kay switched seats to get closer to the window.

I glanced up just in time to catch a glimpse of him. He stepped down slowly as he buttoned his dark suit jacket. The man had two planes waiting, but he still took his time deplaning, one slow step after another. His tall frame towered over the three guys surrounding him. No doubt they were his bodyguards.

For some reason, I thought about what he would be like in bed. I jerked a little in my seat and turned to face Kay. But she was busy still ogling the stranger. I needed to stop thinking about sex. I didn't want to be a complete wreck on my wedding night.

"We're moving." Megan stood. "We'll have you out of here in a few minutes."

Our plane pulled into the hangar shortly after, as Megan promised. My heart beat fast as I went down the steps. It occurred to me that I probably didn't look as cool and collected as the real estate mogul did. Rain sprayed my face lightly, even though we were under the safety of the hangar. I rushed toward the door out of habit. In truth, I didn't mind the rain.

A man by the door gestured for me to enter the building. "You may wait inside while we unload your luggage. We won't be long. Your car is already here."

"Thank you." I adjusted my purse on my shoulder, looking for Kay.

She had stayed behind to chat with Megan a little more. Another roll of thunder made me do as the man suggested. I hurried inside, reading the signs as I went. For a small airport, there was a lot going on, with staff rushing back and forth. When I spotted the bathroom, I made a beeline for it. But two steps in, I ran into a wall—a very wide and muscled wall.

"Hello?" The real estate mogul offered me a wolfy grin as his gaze shifted from my face down to where my hand gripped the lapel of his suit. "You seem lost."

His voice was pure sinful honey, deep with a low baritone.

I made to inhale, but the air didn't reach my lungs. He licked his full lips and his smile fell away.

Everything about him screamed power and danger. His pupils widened, extinguishing the hazel in his irises. My body shuddered in response as fear trickled down my spine. Fear of what? It wasn't like he could hurt me in a crowded airport. But something about this stranger set all my senses on high alert. Suddenly, the lights turned bright, and his woodsy scent engulfed me completely.

Run.

My whole being screamed at me to move, to get out, but I couldn't. I was in a nightmare where my head could sense the threat, but my limbs couldn't react. Even now, my nails dug into his suit jacket.

"Well, are you?"

"What?"

"Are you lost?" he asked this time, furrowing his dark brows as if my mere existence was an annoyance, an inconvenience in his otherwise perfect life.

I was the gum stuck to the bottom of his shoe.

"No. Why would you think that?"

"No reason." He relaxed his stance, then slowly peeled my fingers from his lapel.

I winced at the sweaty spot my hand left on his crisp white button-down shirt. When he bent down, a shock of energy, raw and feral, ran down my spine and straight to my core. "Ahh." I blushed because even with the whooshing sound my pulse made in my ears, I could hear my voice, raspy and needy. What the hell was wrong with me?

"Are you always this jumpy?" With a smirk on his face, he made a big show of collecting my purse off the ground and the wallet and phone that had fallen out of it. "You dropped your purse." He pressed it to my chest.

"Thanks," I mumbled, keeping my wide eyes on him. I had this odd sensation that if I looked away, he'd pounce on me.

He glanced up, and his gaze zeroed in on something behind me. With a quick nod, he adjusted his suit coat and sauntered away from me. The second he exited the door that led to the parking lot, the room filled with air, and I could move again—as if some invisible and heavy paw had released me.

"Luce."

A hand touched my shoulder, and I screamed, turning around so fast I bumped heads with Kay.

"Owww." Kay rubbed her temple.

"I'm so sorry. That guy just put me on edge." I stepped closer to her, away from the glass doors even though he was long gone.

"What guy?"

"The billionaire who kept us waiting for almost an hour."

"Oh, man, I can't believe I missed it." She craned her neck toward the exit. "Well, our car is here, and the luggage has been loaded. You ready to go?"

"Yes, I want to be done with this day already." I motioned for her to lead the way.

As soon as we climbed in the back seat, the driver informed us the ride to Mr. Walsh's penthouse would take about forty-five minutes. I leaned against the window and settled in for the long drive. Even this close to midnight, traffic was still in full swing near the tunnel and got worse as we entered the city. I was so tired, though, I didn't stop to consider what awaited me in my new home. Instead, my brain kept going back to the stranger at the airport. His dark, luscious hair that framed his chiseled jaw and straight nose perfectly were seared in my mind's eye—and his commanding voice. I could still feel its timbre on my skin.

Only a few minutes in, and I already had a pretty consistent movie of him playing in my head. His deep, steely eyes, hazel looking, but mostly gray. But the thing that stuck with me was the recognition I saw there. Did he know me? No, of course he didn't. I'd never seen him in my life. Either way, he had definitely decided he hated me. Something about me annoyed him. Maybe that was a billionaire thing. All rich and powerful people didn't like dealing with commoners like me.

Shaking my head, I made myself focus on the buildings sweeping by us. I was in New York City to meet my future husband. That right there should be occupying all my thoughts.

"How much longer?" I met the driver's gaze in the rearview mirror.

"We're here." He pointed at the high-rise in front of us.

My heart rate spiked as the SUV went round and round the garage ramps; with every turn, it climbed one more floor, one more floor to where Liam Walsh lived. By the time we stopped in front of the elevator bay, I was nauseous and regretting every one of the decisions that got me here. I *chose* this. I repeated the mantra a few times, then climbed out as soon as two bodyguards came to meet us. They helped me onto the curb, then pushed Kay back into the vehicle.

"Luce," Kay called after me.

"She's with me. She's my bodyguard."

"We were not told you were bringing your own security,"

the older bodyguard grumbled. "Take it up with the boss. You want the lobby floor."

"Fine. I will." I gripped my purse tighter. "Kay, I will talk to Liam."

She nodded, pursing her lips. For all her efforts, I was going to have to meet Liam alone.

I entered the small elevator car and pushed the L button. The other option was a G, which told me this was Liam's private entrance. *Great.* Another rich guy who didn't like mingling with the rabble. When the doors slid opened, a woman with a stern face and hair redder than mine greeted me with a nod. "Ms. O'Brien, welcome."

"Thanks." I rubbed my arms against the cool air blowing the length of the foyer. "I'm Luce. Nice to meet you." I offered her my hand.

"I'm Mrs. Jones. This way." She gestured toward the grand staircase.

I stole a glance toward the tall windows, the white walls, and beige sofas that filled the living area. Liam's home looked like one of those penthouses on real estate magazines—pristine, shiny and very expensive. I looked for family pictures or any personal effects but didn't see any. Did he even live here?

"Where's Liam?"

"Mr. Walsh is out of town. He will see you tomorrow morning. For now, he's asked me to show you to your cage."

"My what?" I quickened my step to catch up to her, convinced I'd heard wrong.

She opened the first door to the left and ushered me inside. Yeah, Mrs. Jones meant an actual cage.

I'd never had sex before, but I knew a kink room when I saw one. This suite was exactly that—a dungeon—complete with my very own cage. What the actual fuck? I shook my head to try and process what was happening, but I couldn't make myself react.

What? I wanted to ask, but the words didn't come out. My brain was fuzzy, numb.

I didn't object when Mrs. Jones took out a small key from her apron, when she unlocked the door and gently guided me inside. Even as I saw her walk away and leave the room, I just sat there, mouth wide open, and stared at the red door.

Was I supposed to sleep here? I sat up with my legs stretched in front of me. I fit perfectly if I stayed in this exact position. My gaze flitted from my bare feet to the wide circle over my head. The two panels were secured by another padlock. By the size of the opening, I knew my neck would fit there, too. Anger pooled in the pit of my stomach. I gripped both sides of the cage and screamed, rattling it as I finally let out all my fears and rage.

What the hell did I get myself into?

No, that wasn't the right question. What the fuck did Dad get me into?

CHAPTER 5
The Celtic Cross Pendant

SANTINO

Manhattan, New York

I turned the silver ring on my finger and rubbed the wolf's head engraved on it—a family heirloom of sorts, a gift from Dad the night I had my first kill. I rapped it against the handrail. Standing at the entrance of the VIP loft, near the grand staircase, I let my gaze linger on the betting tables below me. How Rex put up with this club scene, day in and day out, was beyond me. All the people down there in their fancy garb and drinking expensive wine were exhausting to me.

This was Rex's M.O. I was good at hunting people down. He was good at keeping secrets, their secrets. He kept them all here, hooked on gambling, booze, and sex, so he could manipulate them into doing whatever the fuck he wanted. All in all, I'd say he was a good king for the Society.

I scanned the crowd below me. Of course, I wasn't expecting her to be here. Red—the woman who slammed into me at the airport. I didn't get a chance to ask her name, so I gave her one that made me think of her fiery red hair. Since the night I flew in from Chicago, I couldn't stop thinking about her.

The resignation in her eyes disarmed me. I'd punished plenty of assholes in my time. There was always a point during our interview, right before they broke and started talking, when a glint of surrender would flash in their eyes. That was always my cue to push a tad more to get exactly what I wanted.

Red had the look and the scent of someone who had already surrendered. What happened to her? She was too young to have already given up. The illogical part of me wanted to see her again. That same part wanted to show her that there were still a few things in this life worth living for. Without a doubt, that same illogical part would be the part that could destroy her. Someone as innocent as Red didn't belong in my world.

For whatever stupid reason, my pulse spiked when I spotted a redhead sitting at the bar. I leaned closer to the banister to get a better look. Her long legs and graceful fingers caught my attention. Those features were seared into my mind's eye. As if sensing my eyes on her, the woman at the bar tensed then shifted her weight to face me. With a knowing smile, she slid off her seat and ambled toward the stairwell that led up to the VIP loft. When she reached the bottom step, the bouncer glanced up at me. She wasn't Red. She wasn't the woman from the airport. Disappointment washed over me, and I shook my head no. He immediately stepped in and sent her away.

"How's your dad?" Rex appeared out of nowhere, patted me on the shoulder, then braced both his hands on the handrail, watching over his flock.

"He went home last night." I blinked a few times to bring his features into focus. "The old man is not going anywhere. If that's what you were worried about."

"I want you to unseat him already." Every move Rex made was calculated.

To him, people were at his disposal, no more than chess pieces to use as he pleased. The problem was, whether I liked it or not, I was an integral piece on his board. He wanted me to step up as Don and take my seat at the table as Don Buratti because Dad was a liability to the Society. His heart condition was the least of his health concerns. The dementia could get us all killed.

"Half the time he doesn't know what year we're in. He wants to shoot everything that moves, Al Capone style." His tone was cool and casual.

"Do you mean unseat or kill?"

"He's making it easy for you."

"Right. We're back to the marriage thing." I rested both forearms on the rail and formed a steeple with my hands. "The answer's still hell no."

When he didn't come back with the usual retort, I turned to face him again. I followed his line of sight to the woman at one of the poker tables. She wore a backless dress that offered a full view of her smooth back and a tiny bit of the curve of her waist. Next to me, Rex released a breath.

"You know, I was thinking maybe I should throw my name in the hat for the king position." Such a thing wasn't possible, but I knew his attention had shifted to Caterina Alfera, the woman who almost got him killed last year. As a reward, he had married her. "Still thinking with your dick, I see." I gave him a hard pat on the back.

"Fuck off." He adjusted his jacket, his gaze never leaving his wife.

"Your obsession for her should've killed you."

"But it didn't." He smiled in her direction. It was there only for a second. If I hadn't been studying his profile, I would've missed it. He shifted his weight, then turned to me, apparently satisfied now that Caterina was making her way toward us. "I hear my message wasn't well-received in Chicago."

"That's one way to put it." I shrugged. "I gave them their first and only warning. They seem to think they no longer answer to the Society."

"We'll have to remedy that."

"Yes, we do. How are we going to do that? You're the mastermind here. I'm just your puppet. Do make it something not diplomatic, though."

"Agreed. We're past that point with that lot."

I cocked my head to make eye contact with Caterina. I adjusted my cufflinks and flashed her my most charming smile. "Caterina, half the men in this room can't stop staring at you. You look more beautiful than I remember."

She chuckled at my cheesy flattery, shaking her head. When I made to bring her in for a hug, Rex put out his hand. "They can look all they want, as long as they keep their distance. That includes you."

I put my palms up in mock surrender—finally, some good entertainment to keep me busy. "Does she get to speak?"

"Enough." Caterina wedged herself between Rex and me and offered me her hand. "Good to see you, Santino. I called the hospital this morning. They said your dad had gone home. He gave us quite a scare."

"I don't think Rex was that worried." I shrugged.

Rex leveled me with one of his glares. For whatever reason, he cared if Caterina saw him as the monster he was. We were all monsters here. I was certain she knew that. But he liked to pretend. For her.

"Of course, he was worried." She pressed her delicate fingers on his chest.

His features softened, and he wrapped a possessive arm around her waist. "The old man wants to step down, but Santino won't meet him halfway."

"Are you telling on me now?" I furrowed my brows at him.

"I already knew." She beamed at me. "What about Donata? She's smart and beautiful."

"And would possibly kill me in my sleep. Pass." I turned my attention to the room below us, still scanning for redheads.

"This is new." She pointed at the Celtic cross pendant hanging from my neck.

"It's Irish."

"I know." She cocked her eyebrow. "We're not Irish. Where did you get it?"

"I stole it." A crime of opportunity, really. The piece of jewelry slid out of Red's purse when she dropped it. I couldn't resist taking it.

"Why?" she asked.

"I don't know. A memento, I suppose." I yanked at the silver chain and the pendant fell into my palm. I lifted it up and let it spin a few times.

"Tell me you didn't do anything stupid in Chicago, like mess with the Irish? We're on the brink of war as it is." Rex stepped closer with his usual lethal stare.

What was he going to do? Make me return it to its rightful

owner? I would love nothing more. "This has nothing to do with your war." I switched my gaze to meet Caterina's.

Here was a woman who was ready to fight for her family. The glint in her eyes was all strength and something feral—a basic instinct to protect her own. Even now, she stood next to Rex as if ready to jump in front of a bullet for him. What would make Caterina lose that desire and give up on life? What the hell happened to Red? Or who happened to her? The idea of anyone inflicting pain on her soft skin made me want to punch a wall. No fucking idea why.

"One of your victims?" Caterina's playful tone told me she thought I had slept with the owner of the pendant.

No, I hadn't slept with the woman from the airport. But Caterina's intuition wasn't that far off. Without meaning to, I had developed an obsession for the redhead with sad eyes and plump lips. I had vivid dreams of Red's slim fingers gripping my suit coat and yanking it off my shoulders. The next image quickly had her naked and brushing her long curls over my cock. I'd had plenty of time to conjure several scenarios in my head.

"Not a victim yet." I captured the pendant tightly in my grip. "I have to find her first."

PART TWO
Big Bad Wolf
WOLF DUET, BOOK ONE

CHAPTER 6
Do As You're Told

LUCE

New York City

I didn't want out of the cage. As fucked up as that sounded, it was the truth. I had spent the better part of the night kicking and screaming, begging for help, until I realized that even if someone like my best friend Kay showed up and let me out, I wouldn't have the guts to leave. Not when the livelihood of my family was at stake.

Of course, Liam Walsh wouldn't go after Dad or my brother Ronan, if I walked out on him now. But he would most certainly take back the small army he promised the Red Wolves crew in exchange for a virgin wife—me. I slammed my foot on the side panel again, and the metal rattled with a satisfying clank.

By now, I knew my five by three little jail was sturdy and wouldn't budge. But it felt good to kick and protest and pretend I had a way out. If I let my anger brew at the pit of my stomach, I wouldn't have to deal with the fear gripping my spine, or the horror that was this place.

Pressing my feet to the mat below me, I lay back and closed my eyes to shield them from the rays of light seeping through the red velvet curtains on the opposite end of the room. At some point during the night, I had managed to sleep in this position. Though that didn't last long. My bladder hurt from having to hold it all night.

Turning on my side, I tucked my knees to my chest and let my gaze roam Liam's sex dungeon. What else could this place be, with the crimson leather panels covering the walls, the metal rings on a track hanging from the ceiling, and the odd furniture dotting the space? My cage had a nice view of all those things, along with the table laden with whips, knives, handcuffs, and other objects I didn't recognize.

Tears streamed down my cheeks again. At some point in the very near future, Liam would use all those things on me. I hugged myself tighter to ease the quiver that shook my entire body. No one was coming to save me. I was alone in this. And all I could hope was that Liam had made good on his word to help my family, that by now his men had fought off the Italians and won. I would've loved to have gotten confirmation from Dad that my sacrifice had been worth it. But he was too ashamed to talk to me. Now I understood why he wasn't home yesterday morning when Liam's limo came to pick me up.

A bit of warm liquid slowly trickled down my thighs, and I balled my body tighter. I was in a pretty fucked-up situation, if holding my pee was the only way to cling to the last of my dignity. Was that what Liam was waiting for? For me to soil myself as proof that he had broken me? I was Luce O'Brien, a proud Irish woman. That would never happen. Liam had bought and paid for my body, but not my soul.

Suddenly, the door creaked open. When I opened my eyes, the first thing I saw was Mrs. Jones's pristine leather shoes. She was the one who had greeted me at the door last night and then ushered me to this room. She left me here without my luggage and without an explanation.

"You'll need to work on controlling your bladder." She made quick work of the lock. Her tone was clipped, but she wasn't angry with me. "You're expected to stay in the cage until Mr. Walsh is ready for you. He will not tolerate this level of disrespect."

What? I was supposed to hold it to show him respect? "I've been holding it all night."

"You will learn to control your bladder." She opened the side door and motioned for me to get out.

I crawled out and tried not to dwell on how that made me feel. To be on all fours, happy to make my way toward Mrs. Jones's leather shoes, like a good little pet. I couldn't let the situation get the best of me. I had bigger things to worry about. "When will I get to meet Liam? His bodyguards last night wouldn't let my friend Kay come with me. I mean, she's my bodyguard, and a friend."

Shit. I should've gotten my story straight in my head before I opened my mouth. Kay was my best friend. She understood why I had agreed to marry Liam Walsh and had volunteered to come with me, so I wouldn't be alone. When we arrived, though, Liam's men took her away. They didn't even let me explain that she was here as my own bodyguard. She wasn't really, but I was willing to lie to get her to stay with me.

"Mr. Walsh."

"What?"

"You will address him as Mr. Walsh."

"Fine. When will I get to talk to Mr. Walsh?"

"I'm not sure. He didn't say. For now, I'm here to make sure all is in order for his return."

"What the hell does that even mean?" I stepped toward her. As terrifying as this woman was in her skirt and crisp white shirt, she was shorter than me. Her small frame seemed almost frail next to mine. At five-foot-seven, I had a good four inches on her.

She lifted her hand and slapped me hard across the face. I didn't even have time to react. No one had ever hit me before. As the daughter of a kingpin in south Chicago, I was always well cared for and protected. Dad would've punished anyone who dared hurt me.

I cradled my cheek as my eyes welled with tears.

"You will watch your tone and your language. You're to be the wife of a powerful leader. You need to behave accordingly. Do you understand?"

I nodded, blinking to clear my vision.

She exhaled loudly in exasperation. "You speak when asked a direct question."

"Yes, I understand."

"Sir."

"What?" I took another second to figure it out and then answered, "Yes, I understand, Sir."

"Take off your clothes."

"What?" My hands instinctively covered my chest. "Why?"

"You're not here to ask questions. Do as you're told. Leave

56

your soiled clothes here, there's a bathroom through there." She pointed at the door to the left of the cage.

With trembling hands, I unbuttoned my shorts while I kicked off my strappy sandals. I had been so naive to dress in a silky top and bottoms for my first meeting with my future husband. My heart thumped against my ribs. I had been naked in front of other women before, but the way Mrs. Jones's looked at me was very unnerving.

I had assumed she'd turn away to give me some privacy, but she didn't. Instead, she kept her gaze zeroed in on my legs, then my pussy when I dropped my underwear.

"Quicker. I don't have all day." She pointed at my blouse. "Bra too."

I did as she asked and then rushed to the bathroom where I finally relieved myself. Could people really get used to holding their pee for hours? No way that was a thing. I was so out of my depth here. I had no clue what I was doing. What they wanted from me was way more than sex.

On the other side of the door, I heard Mrs. Jones's confident and determined footsteps tapping on the marble floors. She turned on the water in the shower. Two seconds later, she swung my door open. I supposed privacy wasn't a thing with her.

"You have five minutes. There's shampoo and body wash in there." She reached for my elbow and pulled me off the toilet.

I padded across the cold tile and got in the steamy shower stall. The fog on the glass panels helped me ignore her prying eyes, while I made quick work of the mint-scented soap. After a long day and an even longer night, getting cleaned up felt like heaven. As soon as I finished rinsing off, Mrs. Jones reached inside and shut off the water.

"Let's take a look." She pointed at the fluffy bath rug.

I stepped on it and met her gaze, pushing wet strands away from my face. She held my jaw with bony fingers and turned me left then right before she tugged on my lips to inspect my teeth. I doubted prize pigs were scrutinized this much. What would happen if I told Mrs. Jones to go to hell with her inspection? Sure, she'd slap me again, but then what? Would Walsh call off the deal with my family?

She moved onto my chest, tweaking my peaks until they got hard in protest. I winced in pain, lifting my shoulders to hide from her prying fingers. "Stand up straight, dear." She pinched both nipples at the same time and pulled me up until I was as erect as she wanted me. "Your tits are smaller than what Mr. Walsh prefers. But that can be fixed if it bothers him too much." She cupped one breast to feel its weight and then the other.

"Like implants?" I bit my lip to tamper the urge I had to smack her rough hands away. She had no right to handle me like I was some sort of new toy.

"Possibly. We'll determine that after your first child."

"I thought Mr. Walsh wanted a wife." I said through gritted teeth. My fear had now been fully replaced with anger and disgust. I hated that this woman felt she could invade my body, and on top of that, deem it not good enough.

"He requires an heir, dear. Don't make the mistake of thinking you're here for more than that."

"So more like a cow. Got it."

"Watch your tone. Mr. Walsh doesn't have my patience."

She cocked her head to the side to check my pussy. "If you lied about your virginity, now's the time to confess."

"I didn't lie." My voice quavered. Would she require proof? How would I even do that? And what if she decided I wasn't a virgin?

"That's what I'm here to check." She pointed at a small bench next to the free-standing bathtub. "Open your legs and part your pussy lips." When I didn't move, and simply stared at her with doe eyes, she slow blinked at me as if she was on the verge of losing her patience. "Go on."

My knees knocked against each other with the first step. Somehow, I managed to sit down and show her a part of me no one had ever seen before. With the same interest she showed when she examined my teeth, she looked at my entrance.

"You didn't lie. Mr. Walsh will be pleased. You can sit up." She stood, towering over me.

I got the sense she enjoyed having this kind of power over people. Dad had made sure I learned self-defense. Because of all those years of training, I could handle my own. As much as I wanted to punch her in the face, I couldn't do it. Too much was as stake. Without Liam's help, the Red Wolves didn't stand a chance against the Chicago outfit. My sensibility didn't matter right now—not when the Italian mob was so close to taking over our territory.

"What is this?" She pointed at my knee, or more specifically, at the moon-shaped scar I had there.

"Bike accident."

When I was ten, I liked to ride my bike to Kay's house because it was on a steep hill. We would spend hours hauling our bikes up, just so we could fly down. The cool wind on my face and the freedom and feel of being weightless was the biggest high. One time, I picked up too much speed. I hit the brakes hard, and my bike flipped over. When I got up, I had a gash just above my kneecap. A half smile pulled at my lips while I ran my finger over the whitish line on my skin. I was happy at home all my life. Being put in a cage, examined like a lab rat, and married off, was a sacrifice I was willing to make for my family.

"We'll apply makeup to cover it up."

"So, did I pass your inspection?"

"Tone." She pinned me with a stare. "Yes, you will do."

"Did Mr. Walsh hire you just for this?" I bit my lip and braced for another slap.

To my surprise, she answered with a sweet smile that made my skin crawl.

"No, dear. Mr. Walsh didn't hire me for you. I've been at his service for five years. My only job is to train his pets."

Her features relaxed, and I could only assume she enjoyed her work very much. The implication in her words made me wonder if maybe not all of Liam's pets were willing participants. A part of me had wanted to believe that maybe Liam Walsh, the Butcher, wasn't the horrible human being people said he was. Though the logical part of me told me he was exactly what everyone thought. And now his madame was just as bad.

"Train how?"

"We begin tomorrow. I want you to at least have the basics by the time he comes home." She had said she didn't know when he would return, but I was sure she was lying.

Her words implied she had a full regimen planned out for me. That meant, she knew exactly how much time she had with me. I supposed that didn't matter, though. If training delayed my meeting with Liam, I was okay with that. Mrs. Jones was the lesser of two evils. Because once my so-called fiancé came home, my whole life would change.

"Do I get clothes?"

She ambled toward the vanity and picked up the bundle sitting on the counter. When she returned, she slipped the bodysuit over my head and yanked it all the way to my hips. She narrowed her eyes at my pubes, as if considering something. I pursed my lips because I knew what she'd say next.

"I'll come back after lunch, and we'll do a Brazilian wax." She said as she expertly snapped the crotch buttons together between my legs.

Once I was covered up again—well sort of, the sheer fabric didn't leave much to the imagination—I unclenched my jaw, and my body relaxed a bit. To my surprise, Mrs. Jones also took the time to brush my hair and French braid it.

"What kind of training? What are the basics?" I turned to face her.

She glared at me for what seemed like hours. My chest rose and fell with every ragged breath I took. My life was in the hands of a complete stranger, whose job was to prep me for her sadist boss.

"I understand that you're the daughter of a kingpin." She took a handful of the delicate fabric pooled at my belly and tugged at it until the crotch of the bodysuit parted my pussy lips. When she released it, the wedgie stayed in place. It was itchy and uncomfortable. She met my gaze as if daring me to take it out. When I didn't move, she continued, "I also understand that you were raised to think you're special. But here, none of that matters. You are not special. Walk. We start tomorrow." She gripped my shoulder and escorted me back to the cage.

I crawled inside and waited for her to leave. She ambled around me and flipped open the top. "Sit up. Head here." She placed her palm over the hole, the one I had already figured out was for my neck.

I scooted up until I was lined up where she wanted me. Like a good little pet, I let her shut the panel around my neck.

"When I come back, I want to find you exactly like this."

Fresh tears rolled down my face. Kicking and screaming hadn't helped my case before. After an hour with Mrs. Jones, I understood that no one was coming to save me. This was my life now.

CHAPTER 7
It'll Burn Just the Same

SANTINO

"I can smell her perfume on you." I turned my back to the man standing at the front entrance of my penthouse and poured myself another whiskey.

When I came home earlier, I hadn't bothered with the lights. This time of night, the city skyline cast a shimmering glow on the marble floors, the high ornate ceilings, and the grand piano near the terrace. When he ambled toward me, he was no more than a gray shadow.

"Your security is shit." Rex unbuttoned his coat jacket.

"If you were anyone else, you'd be dead by now." I took a long swig from my tumbler.

As the sitting king of a hundred-year-old secret Enclave that managed all organized crime in the country and parts of the world, Rex Valentino was denied access to very few places. My condo was practically a fortress. Not for Rex, of course. My men let him waltz right in.

"But seriously, I can smell Caterina on you." I pointed at his dark suit.

"Then you have a pretty good idea of how much I didn't want to leave home tonight." He joined me at the bar cart and took the glass I offered him.

"Fine. I'll bite. What's the problem?"

"The fucking Irish."

"They went after Hell's Kitchen again?"

"Not yet. This—" he motioned with his hand as he tried to recall the name, "—Liam Walsh asked Rossi for a meeting. I did a bit of digging on him. They call him the Butcher. He recently rose to power as the leader of the Irish gang in Harlem."

I nodded, because the name and the details sounded vaguely familiar. Rex was the one who dealt with information, intelligence, and strategy. His business was to keep tabs on politicians, cops, influencers. In short, anyone who might be of use to the Society and the industries we managed. Keeping their dark secrets was how he got things done.

My family, on the other hand, was responsible for investments and real estate. Our firm was the most profitable front the Society owned. Partly because Rex's access made it so I didn't have to deal with red tape and silly legalities. And also, because I was good at closing deals.

I liked to keep my ear to the ground. Something as big as a rival gang changing leadership was hard to miss.

"Yeah, I've heard the name." I scratched the stubble on my cheek. "So, two weeks ago, he mounted an attack on the New York Faction and now they want to talk? Hmm. Sounds like a trap."

"Rossi thought so too. It's why he came to me. He wants to

set it off." He cocked his eyebrow. "I thought you might want to join in the fun."

"Isn't it rather early for me to take out the trash?"

I was good at running the family business, but I was also good at killing. Not because I enjoyed it, but because, sometimes, assholes made it their mission to threaten our way of life. I had been raised, same as Rex, to protect and defend the Society above all. *Fac fortia and patere—do brave things and endure.* Since the beginning, our primary goal had been to safeguard our own and all gangs across the country. If that meant taking a life, I would always be more than willing and ready to do so.

I never hesitated. And I never looked back.

"That's not what I meant." Rex chuckled softly, shaking his head. "We're not going to interfere. We're there to observe. Nothing more. I want to understand what makes Walsh tick. How he operates. And most of all, I need to understand Walsh's sudden urge to expand. Why is he willing to go to war now?"

"New leader. He has to do something big to prove himself." I shrugged. "Or maybe, he has a small dick."

"I need more information on this asshole before I decide how I'm going to handle him."

"You're using Rossi as bait?"

Chase Rossi was also a newcomer to the Society. His grandfather was shot and killed last year during a heist with the Venezuelan cartel. As the only surviving heir, Chase had to take over the New York Faction. Shortly thereafter, he helped Rex catch an FBI agent who was hell-bent on bringing down our organization. Since then, Rex had decided he trusted Rossi. He even offered him a seat at the table and a title of

Don. Good thing he'd said no because something about him didn't sit right with me.

"He volunteered. He wants this resolved as much as we do." He finished his drink and set it down on the coffee table. "We need to go now. You coming?"

"You know I am."

Assuming Rex had parked in my private garage, I headed toward the elevator door below the grand staircase and pushed the call button. When the doors slid open, I stepped in and pushed the G button.

The second Rex's driver spotted us, he jumped out of the SUV and opened the door. Sure as fuck, Rossi was in the front seat. I should've known he'd be coming with us.

"The whole gang is back together again." I climbed in the back seat and unbuttoned my suit jacket.

"Good to see you too." Rossi nodded once.

Maybe this was the thing I didn't like about him. He was too fucking nice. Too serious. Since the entire Gallo family had been wiped out, Rex had an empty seat at the table—one he had been trying to get Rossi to fill. Chase wasn't raised by the Society like the rest of us were. He didn't have a killer instinct.

"So, this is a recon mission. But tell me you brought weapons." I faced Rex.

"Of course we did. We're going in with a half-ass plan. We need all the backup we can get." Rex tapped his driver's shoulder.

The Escalade slowly rolled out of the parking spot and toward the exit. As soon as we merged with the traffic, Rossi shifted his body to meet my gaze. "Rex is right. We don't have much of a plan. Walsh wants to meet at a pub in Harlem. He claims it's neutral territory, but he's fucking lying."

"Did he say what he wanted?" I asked.

"He said something about how he doesn't want to be on bad terms with the Italians. He wants to talk about what happened in Hell's Kitchen and prove he had nothing to do with it." Rossi exchanged a meaningful look with Rex. "Meeting the Irish in person is the best move right now. I'm willing to take the risk and explain to them that war isn't an option."

Walsh fucked up big when he went after Rossi's crew and failed. But I had to admit, his next move had merit. He was right in his assumption that Rossi would want some sort of truce. Even if Walsh was lying about his involvement in the attack, Rossi was willing to hear him out. Mostly because he didn't want a war and he was desperate for information that could give him an edge. He was willing to serve himself up as bait to get what he needed.

"You have balls. I'll give you that." I braced my hand on my knee, tapping my finger while I considered our options.

"We're trying to prevent a gang war. If all he wants is money, we can give him that." Rex raked a hand through his hair.

I had no doubt he was thinking about Caterina, the love of his life, and the promise he made to her to keep the peace. Why else would he be here himself? He could've sent anyone else to gather intel. But he wanted this matter resolved, sooner rather than later.

Personally, I didn't care which way things went. Because at the end of the day, there was no way in hell Walsh's resources could match ours. Rex and I alone could squash him like a bug.

"I'd like to keep the FBI out of our business," Rossi added. "I've had enough of them to last me a lifetime."

"So if we assume Walsh wants a truce, you'll listen to him, Rex will come up with a Machiavellian plan to get him under control, and we all live happily ever after? What if Walsh just wants to kill you tonight?"

Truly, Walsh only had two choices tonight; make good with the New York Faction or declare war. I supposed Rex invited me along in case Walsh opted for the latter.

"That's a possibility. In which case, my men are ready to retaliate." Rossi's gaze darted between Rex and mine.

And then the FBI pigs would crawl out of every corner and come after us. Just fucking great. The Irish could suck my balls.

"We're here, Boss." The driver spoke as the vehicle rolled to a stop on a dark street in Harlem.

A block away, the Limerick Pub stood out with its green neon sign and banners with Irish lettering. Of all the businesses around, the bar was the only one that looked like it was open.

"Where did everybody go?" I leaned forward to get a better look. "Looks like Walsh is also expecting trouble."

"Let's get this over with." Rossi nodded toward Rex and climbed out of the car.

Within seconds, his form was no more than a dark shadow on the poorly lit and deserted street. When he entered the pub, the driver slowly pulled into the alley and killed the engine.

"I thought we were going in too." I took in a breath to slow down my pulse. The thrill of the hunt had already kicked in, and I was ready for a fight.

"We're here to observe, remember?" Rex's voice rumbled

in the car. "I'm not ready for Walsh to know who we are and what we can do."

"You're hoping his intentions are noble, aren't you?" I shook my head. "A year ago, before Caterina, you would've gone in there with guns blazing. Be careful not to lose your edge, Rex."

"I haven't lost my edge. I've gotten smarter." He pinned me with a cruel stare that would make most men shit their pants.

I wasn't most men.

"Hmm." I climbed out of the car.

Sitting still had never been my style. I wanted to see this Liam Walsh who had, in a few short days, become a thorn in my side. Why would Rex make any kind of concessions for this asshole? He wasn't worth our time.

I stayed close to the shadow of the buildings. With the line of cars parked on the street as my shield, I zeroed in on the pub and the people inside it. A man with graying hair sat in front of the window. I could only guess he was the man of the hour, since Rossi kept his attention mostly on him.

"This is all cheap theater he's putting on. But for whom? And why?"

What was Walsh up to? He set up a clandestine meeting with the leader of the New York Faction, only to put it on display for everyone to see. Was this talk to show his people he had influence with the Italians, with us? What was this asshole up to? Rossi was a sitting duck, but so was Walsh. He had to know Rossi wouldn't come alone.

"That's why we're here." Rex stepped silently next to me.

I couldn't hear what they were saying. But by the look on their faces, I could only guess they were in the process of comparing dicks.

In the next beat, the air stilled around me, and a new scent invaded my senses. Walsh's men pulled out their guns and aimed at Rossi. What the hell happened? They were just talking and now they weren't. I hated being right.

I sat on my heels and shifted my body to check behind me. Rex stepped out of the shadows and kneeled next to me. "He needs a diversion."

"I know." I removed my shoes and took off my socks. "Give me your socks."

He didn't ask why, which meant he knew exactly what I planned to do, and he agreed with it. I made quick work of the four pieces of fabric and tied them together.

"You call that a knot?" He shook his head as he unscrewed the gas cap of the nearest car.

"It'll burn just the same." I fed the makeshift line into the tank and fished a lighter from the inside pocket of my jacket.

We were mobsters. Fire had come in handy more than I cared to count. I made a point to always be prepared. If Rossi was paying attention, and I was certain he was, he'd see the sheet of flame coming at him—a perfect distraction for him to bolt out the back door.

As luck would have it, the pimped-out Civic was unlocked, which was a good thing given how Rossi was running out of time and locks weren't my thing. Inside the pub, he had his arms up in surrender, though his mouth had not stopped moving. He was still trying to talk his way out of getting shot. I crawled into the front seat and pulled on the steering wheel, all the way to the left.

"Let's push."

Between Rex and me, we hauled ass and sent it on its way. I lit the line of silk socks and made a run for it. The explosion happened faster than I had anticipated and sent me flying across the asphalt. I landed with a thud and a loud ringing in my ears. *Fuck, that hurt.* Another detonation disrupted the screams and alarms going off. Like hearing voices under water, Walsh's men yelled orders that I couldn't quite make out.

My whole body ached, and I couldn't find the strength to get up.

Tires screeching in the distance made me shift my body in time to be blinded by the SUV's headlights. A hand pulled me by the elbow and shoved me inside the Escalade. I didn't fight it, quickly scooting all the way to other door, ready to jump out if necessary.

When my vision cleared and I spotted Rex and his driver, I melted into the seat, cradling my ribs. "Where's Rossi?"

Shots pelted the bulletproof windows. Out of nowhere, Rossi landed on the hood of our ride and then climbed inside. "Let's go. Let's go," he yelled as he slammed his hand on the dashboard.

The Escalade careened out of there with two other vehicles in full pursuit.

"Our guys are just on the other side of that divide." Rossi pointed up ahead.

Sure enough, as soon as we reached the edge of Harlem, a caravan of vehicles—including a fucking school bus—blocked the street behind us and started shooting at the Irish.

"That was the stupidest fucking plan." I shook my head. "Of course the asshole wanted you dead."

"Did you get it?" Rex asked.

"Yeah." Rossi nodded and gave Rex a thumb drive. "You were right. His house is divided. He wants to prove himself to

71

his new crew. He promised them Hell's Kitchen—new clients, new business ventures."

"That's our territory," I said through gritted teeth. Walsh thinking he could come in and push us out was a direct and personal insult to me. "Is the asshole ready to go to war?"

"Yes, he is." Rossi winced in pain, holding his side with a bloody hand. "Now what?"

"Now we give him what he wants." Rex met my gaze. "The Society will take it from here."

"Time to take out the trash." I smirked. This was more my speed. I was done with recon missions.

Our organization had been created for this very reason. We were the peacekeepers—the protectors. It was up to us to keep chaos at bay, in whatever way we deemed necessary.

CHAPTER 8
Good Little Lamb

LUCE

I arched my back to ease the stress on my hips. Assuming I hadn't passed out for a whole night, I had been sitting in Liam's pet cage for two weeks. He hadn't shown his face, and that was fine by me. Mrs. Jones was the only one allowed in or out of the dungeon. She'd gotten into a routine that I was sure she'd used many times before.

My mornings were spent doing after care—shower, fresh clothes, and movement. By now, even though it hadn't been that long, I understood her system well. If I obeyed and did everything she asked, she rewarded me by answering my questions. Yesterday, I even asked her for a favor, and she'd said yes.

Today, she would let me have some of my things. Though she warned me that the clothes I had brought with me would need to be thrown out, as Liam would not approve of any of the outfits I had. I didn't care about that. I cared about my mother's necklace. And my phone.

I sat up a little straighter, and my neck hit the opening on the top panel of the cage. I'd had time to consider what this position was for. Sitting on my heels with my head sticking out of the cage could only be for one thing—a blow job. On the top, there was plenty of room for someone to straddle my little jail and feed me his cock. I'd never done that before—had never even considered what it would be like.

Squeezing my eyes shut, I tried to think of something else while I waited for my keeper to come and help me out. I pictured my childhood home in Chicago and all the happy days I shared with my family and the Red Wolves crew. When the image faded, I bit my lip to try and stop what I knew would come next. I didn't like that he kept showing up in every thought I had when I was alone—the stranger from the airport.

His gray eyes, chiseled jaw, and dark hair, had haunted my dreams since the first day. Every time I made to mentally escape from my horrid situation, he invaded my mind. Tears stung my eyes as I gave into the fantasy. What else did I have?

The door to the dungeon opened, and I relaxed with a smile. With his usual wolfy grin, he straddled my cage, while he unbuttoned his fancy suit jacket. His crisp white dress shirt still had the sweat stain I left on him the day we met.

"Were you a good girl?" He pulled on his belt and let the ends fall to the side.

I squirmed in place, pulling on the rope binding my wrists behind my back. I opened my mouth to answer him, but the words didn't come out. He ran his hand over my hair, and I squeezed my eyes tighter. I didn't want this dream to end.

The cage creaked under his weight as he moved up to nudge my lips with his cock. "Yes," I mumbled as I took his entire length. His erection hit the back of my throat as he settled into a smooth and sensual rhythm. Something moved between my legs. It was tight and achy. The same thing happened every time I thought of him. I clung to his memory because it was what made this place bearable.

"Wake up." Mrs. Jones hit the side of the cage with a strap.

She had already pulled back the heavy velvet curtains. The light streaming into the bedroom burned my pupils and made it hard to focus. I blinked several times to focus on her form. For the first time since I met her, her features appeared soft and there was a hint of a smile on her lips. Was this the happy version of Mrs. Jones?

She petted my hair. Something she'd only done once before. "I have some good news for you." Her smile widened as she pulled open the top panel of the cage.

"Good news? Is my father here to see me?" A long shot, but I had to ask.

"No, dear. Better. Mr. Walsh is finally home. He wants to meet you." She wiggled her fingers in a come-here motion. "Hurry. He doesn't have all day."

With wobbly legs, I stood and climbed out. The other times, she had made me crawl out through the side. Big day for her, I suppose. As per our routine, she escorted me to the bathroom and ran the warm water.

I blinked away tears as I turned my back to her to face the shower. The routine Mrs. Jones had set up for me had made me let down my guard. For a moment, I had forgotten why I was here. Without a doubt, tonight Walsh would have sex with me. With a bit of luck, I might get pregnant on the first try.

As much time as my keeper had spent teaching me obedience, she didn't focus at all on the actual act. I still had no idea what to expect. Sure, she made me wear a butt plug for a few hours a day, but was that sex?

"Finish up." Her voice startled me back to reality.

I rinsed the mint soap off my hair, shut off the water, and stepped into the warm towel she had ready for me. "Will he be joining me here?"

"He's busy. His world doesn't revolve around you. You will meet him in his study downstairs." She handed me a bodysuit that, like the others, left nothing to the imagination with its sheer fabric.

I pulled it over my head and tried to work the snaps at the crotch. When I couldn't get them because of my shaking fingers, she fastened them for me. Stepping back, she examined me from top to bottom.

"Sit." She gestured toward the vanity bench.

I did as she asked because, at this point, I just wanted to get this virginity thing out of the way. Like a lifeless doll, I stared at my reflection in the mirror as she combed through my hair and put it up into a French braid. She reached for the blush powder on the counter. I didn't even flinch when she pulled down the front of my leotard and brushed my nipples with the makeup. They went from light to a darker pink with sparkles. When she replaced the white fabric over them, they really stood out.

What kind of a man required this much ado just to have sex? Maybe he couldn't get it up. The second I thought of his cock, an image of my stranger's erection appeared in my mind's eye. I had no idea if I had it right or not. I pictured it to be huge with a thick head and big veins. No idea where I came up with that, but I liked it.

"I said get up." Mrs. Jones gripped my elbow and pulled me to my feet. "Let's go."

I followed behind her, barefoot and with my heart in my

throat. Would it hurt? I wanted to ask. "What about my things? I was good. Wasn't I?" I winced at the begging tone in my voice.

"Yes, you were good." She nodded, sounding pleased as she glanced down at her watch. She took another moment to consider then gestured toward the vanity table. "Go ahead."

My purse sat under it. With tears in my eyes, I rushed to it. I didn't care about the money in my wallet or the lip gloss. All I wanted was my mother's pendant and my phone. I tossed all the contents on the floor and rummaged through it. When I didn't find what I was looking for, I turned to Mrs. Jones. I had thought today would be the day I talked to my family. "Where's my phone? And my necklace?"

"Mr. Walsh decides when you speak to your family." She motioned toward the sex dungeon outside the bathroom. "You honestly think I would allow your camera in here?"

I hadn't considered that. Why on Earth would I want to post pictures of this online? Shame washed over me at the idea of someone back home finding out what I had been become— some man's plaything. "What about my necklace? It's a family heirloom. I want it back."

"I personally went through your things. There was no necklace. Perhaps you forgot it at home."

"No, I didn't. I one hundred percent know I didn't forget my mother's necklace." I raised my voice, towering over her.

"Watch your tone." She pursed her lips. "Let's go. Mr. Walsh doesn't like to be kept waiting." She escorted me down the stairs, through the sterile living room, and Liam's office across the way.

I pushed away the pain in my chest, over losing the one

thing I had that had belonged to Mom. How could I have lost it?

"Stand up straight." She said under her breath as she let the door swing open.

My jaw dropped when I got my first glimpse of the man I was to marry. I was easily half his age. He was old and gray with a scowl across his forehead. His hard features sent a cold shiver down my spine. For the first time since I arrived, I wanted to run.

This was the Butcher—a killer. It was written all over his stern face, though looking at Mrs. Jones' expression, I had to wonder if we were staring at the same person. She had a bit of a glint in her eyes as if she loved him. I wasn't surprised. Who in their right mind would sign up for her job? She had spent several days making me prim and pretty for him—she waxed me, showed me how to use a butt plug, showed me how to position my body so I would be comfortable in my cage. Liam, the dungeon, and Mrs. Jones were all too weird and fucked up —surreal.

We both stood at attention for a good five minutes before Liam decided to look up from his laptop. When he did, she stepped forward. "Mr. Walsh, this is Lucinda O'Brien." She didn't bother to introduce him to me.

His gaze settled on my glittered nipples, then roamed all the way down to my feet. My stomach clenched, and I had to swallow the bitter taste in my mouth. I didn't want him touching me. How was I going to get out of this now? He prowled around me. Like Mrs. Jones, he inspected every inch of me. I braced myself, waiting for his touch, while Mrs. Jones watched me intently. When he gripped my waist and turned me to face him, I did my best to hide my disgust.

"Is she ready?" He licked his lips.

"Yes, sir." She nodded once with an odd sense of pride. I was her good little lamb.

I could only imagine what he wanted me ready for. Following Mrs. Jones' advice, I remained silent. Maybe if I didn't move or speak, he'd get the sex over with quickly.

"I expected no less. Thank you."

Mrs. Jones' eyes watered, and she stood a little taller. I averted my gaze. Her eagerness to please was just too hard to witness. They were about the same age. I supposed Liam liked them young, and so, Mrs. Jones didn't fit the bill.

"I was hoping to get started with her tonight, but I have a business meeting. Will she behave?"

"Wait outside." Mrs. Jones turned to face me.

I nodded once and padded out of the stuffy library. My first impulse was to shut the door behind me, but when I heard their hushed voices, I decided to stay close and listen in.

"Yes, of course she's ready. I only locked the cage the first night. She didn't even try to leave the bedroom." The pride in her voice made me all kinds of angry.

I inhaled deeply to make all my emotions go away. So, the door wasn't locked? I could have walked out at any time. But what would have been the point? If I left, my family would pay the price. Liam and his men would not help us with our feud with the Italians. That alone was all the reason I needed to stay.

"What happened last night?" she asked. "I hope all went as planned?"

"It did. The Italians are a brute bunch, brainless. It didn't take much to get them to act like animals."

Last night? So, he had been in town, but not in this house?

79

He definitely didn't live here, then. No doubt this was the place where he kept all his pets, which was exactly what I was. The whole marriage thing didn't make sense though. Or maybe it did if all he wanted was children. Someone as proud as Walsh wouldn't want an illegitimate son. I wasn't his pet, more like a cow, here to breed.

"Put her in a dress. Something regal. This Rex Valentino guy is the pompous type with a beautiful wife. I want to show him he's not the only millionaire in town." He practically spat the words when he mentioned the name Rex.

"Who's he?" She used a soothing voice.

I smiled because I'd used a similar tactic to get what I wanted from Dad.

"A club owner, very high-end. He wants to do business with me. I'm willing to hear him out. He's well-connected with politicians and other rich assholes in the city."

"You'll do great."

"I hate all those assholes born with a silver spoon in their mouths. They don't know what it takes to survive. But if his business offer is solid, our crew would benefit."

Whoever this Rex was, I sent him a silent thank you. Because of him, my time with Liam would be postponed. I could only hope there were more business meetings to keep him away. Tears welled up in the corners of my eyes. I was repulsed by him. It wasn't just his looks, but his demeanor, the coldness in his eyes.

"What time will you be leaving?"

"Seven sharp. Make sure she's ready."

"As you wish." The sound of her footsteps jerked me into action.

I rushed to the bottom of the staircase and waited for her

there. When she spotted me, she looked back behind her, as if trying to figure out if I had been eavesdropping on their conversation. My heart thrashed in my ears as I fisted my hands. Would she punish me for that? I'd done everything she'd asked to avoid experiencing any of the contraptions in the dungeon. She didn't say I couldn't listen in.

"You'll be going to a masquerade ball tonight. Your job is to make Mr. Walsh look good. You will only speak when asked a direct question. Keep your eyes down. Do you understand?"

"Yes, ma'am." I sighed in relief. Maybe the party made her relax her rules tonight. Either way, I wasn't in the mood to play Walsh's pet in public.

"Come on. We don't have much time."

CHAPTER 9
Hello, Red

SANTINO

I snapped my laptop shut and sat back in my desk chair. Outside my office, my assistant Lia had already gone home. The city lights were visible in the distance, beyond the high ,windows. I glared at the breathtaking view until it became blurry and was replaced by the events of the previous week. Something happened that night, something significant, but I couldn't quite figure out what it was.

Walsh's cheap theater had a purpose. That much was clear, but what was it? The same question had been swirling around my head all day. My crew had managed to capture one of Walsh's men, but he'd been sitting in a holding cell for hours, eating our food and wasting my resources. I had proven methods to make people talk. But what good were they when I had no fucking idea what to ask him?

Lately, the Irish seemed to occupy my entire time. I had spent the better part of the morning looking for Red, the owner of the Celtic Cross pendant. All my contacts had come back empty on who she was and where she'd gone. I had met her at the airport, but apparently, she hadn't flown in that night.

I pinched the bridge of my nose and closed my eyes. Weeks had gone by since our chance encounter, but her features were still tattooed on my mind. I saw her clearly—her big sad eyes, round, plump lips, and that fiery red hair. I couldn't remember the last time I had this much trouble tracking someone down.

My phone rang and brought me back with a jolt. Good. Now wasn't the time to go down the usual path with my mystery woman. I glanced up to see if Lia would pick up, then realized she was already gone. I hit the button for line one and then the speaker phone.

"Buratti here."

"Santino, it's Rex." Rex Valentino's voice boomed in my dim lit office, and suddenly I needed a drink. He never called with good news. "Liam took the bait."

Those four little words made me sit up and pay attention. "He liked my proposal on the tax deeds venture. I knew he would."

"He liked the pitch. Now he wants details."

I chuckled, because now Liam Walsh was in for it. We had managed to lure him into our world of excess—booze, money, sex, gambling. "When?"

"Tonight, at the Crucible. We're hosting a masquerade ball, and he's agreed to join us for a private meeting. I need you there."

"Of course. I want the Irish situation handled already. I don't like puzzles."

"You and me both. I'll see you tonight at seven." He hung up.

"You're smiling. That can't be good." The silhouette of a woman appeared at my door.

All my employees were terrified of me, which was how I liked it. I wasn't here to make friends. I had a business to run. None of them would dare address me with such familiarity. But then again, Donata Salvatore wasn't my employee.

She was one of us, and technically, the next in line to be Don for the Salvatore family, one of the five original families who founded the Society Enclave, along with the Buratti, Valentino, Alfera, and Gallo. Though thanks to the FBI, the Gallo family no longer walked the Earth. Last year, they killed every single one of its members. Another reason to make sure Liam's antics didn't call attention to the FBI pigs.

"Donata, always a pleasure to see you." I let my gaze roam her beautiful features.

"Hmm. Don't lie." She sauntered toward my desk with assured steps. The woman oozed confidence and wealth.

"Okay." I rested my hands on the arm rest of my chair. "What can I do you for? You never visit."

"Your father said he needed a second medical opinion. He wouldn't make an appointment at my clinic, but he said he'd meet me here."

I chuckled. The old man would stoop so low as to trick Donata to come see me, at night and alone. What did he think would happen? That I would be overcome with desire and take her, get her pregnant and then be forced to marry her.

"I don't think the old man is coming." I grinned at her. "Can I offer you a drink?"

"Jesus fuck. Are you serious?" Shaking her head, she ambled to the bar cart and poured herself a whiskey. "First Rex, now you? What am I? A prized pig?"

A few years back, Signoria Vittoria, Donata's aunt and sitting Don, did everything she could to get Rex and Donata to marry. But what Signoria Vittoria didn't know was that Rex had already developed an obsession for Caterina Alfera. In the end, Rex won and married his Caterina. And now my own father was trying to set me up with the beautiful Donata.

"More like a very powerful woman in need of a husband." I rose to my feet and met her in the lounge area that faced the city lights.

"Hmm." She took a long swig from her glass. "Powerful, yes. In need of a husband, hell no."

"What is it with people and marriage? My old man acts like it's the answer to everything." I took the drink she offered me and sat on the sofa. "Sorry he dragged you into this. He's gotten worse in the last few months. He's obsessed with me taking a wife."

"I know." She cocked her eyebrow. "I should've known something was up when he came to visit Aunt Vittoria. That woman thinks she owns me."

"At least you don't have to take over the family business if you don't want to. It's nice to have a choice." I glared at the amber liquid in my tumbler.

"Yes, Santino, I'm very lucky." She didn't sound like she truly felt fortunate.

The thing about this mobster life was that we didn't belong to ourselves. We belonged to the Society. I had no doubt she had guessed what the old man was up to when he asked her to meet him here, in my office, late at night. But she had to do as he said regardless. We all did. The Dons ruled our lives. The stickler was, the Dons didn't have much more freedom than we did. They answered to the Enclave. Duty was their sole motivator for everything they did.

"Speaking of lucky and things we're required to do." I set my glass down on the coffee table. "I have a meeting with Rex."

"Me too." She braced her elbow on the back of the sofa and ran her long fingers through her blonde hair. "The Irish is all Rex talks about these days."

"You know what's at stake. Let's not forget the Gallos."

"Right." She closed her eyes and melted a bit more into the soft leather.

"I have to stop by my place to change into something more appropriate. Can I give you a ride home?" I offered her my hand, glad she was against marriage as much as I was. If she was the one to say no to the old man's proposal, it would save me the trouble and yet another fight with Dad.

"Yes. But only if we take the long way around. I'm not in the mood for kissing Irish ass." She blew out a breath.

"Done."

At five minutes past seven, I was showered and dressed for one of Rex's Machiavellian nights. My driver pulled into the private garage, just as my phone pinged with Rex's text.

Rex: We're starting without you. Join us when you get here. Blue room.

The VIP loft had several rooms to accommodate any, and all, needs for the Crucible guests. Mostly, Rex and all the members of the Society used the space for secret meetings. The Crucible had a whole other floor dedicated to sex and other fantasies. For tonight's affair, we were on the gambling floor.

The sweet scent of the casino greeted me as soon as the

elevator door slid open on the forty-first floor. I adjusted my tuxedo jacket and made my way through the throng, smiling at the leotard-clad men and women suspended from a long rope way over our heads. A few of them had torches and kept breathing fire toward the gamblers.

The one with the silver rhinestone mask slowly descended until her heaving chest was at eye level with me. "A drink, Mr. Buratti." She pressed the bottle of vodka against her tits as if she meant for me to drink from them.

"Not tonight." Not too long ago, I had done way more than use her body as a shot glass. Though lately, I just wasn't feeling it. "Some other time." I touched the tip of my index finger to her chin and continued my way toward the VIP loft.

Even at this early hour, most of the blackjack and craps tables were crowded with people dressed in evening gowns and masquerade masks.

I indulged in my most recent obsession and scanned the room for redheads with creamy, soft skin. One caught my eye and stopped me in my tracks. Adrenaline pumped hard through my body while I waited for Red to turn around. The anticipation died quickly in my belly when the woman faced me. Her friendly smile confirmed she wasn't my Red.

Maybe I should give Red a rest for tonight. I had more important things to deal with. The lives of many depended on our ability to get Liam Walsh under control. My dick could wait.

At the far end of the warehouse-like space, a grand staircase with red carpeting and a banister with intricate design curved up to the VIP loft. I slowed my gait when I reached the bottom of the steps and nodded once to the bouncer. He immediately reached over and removed the crimson rope to let me through.

A server met me at the top of the stairs and offered me a glass of Pappy. I took the tumbler off the tray and sipped. The main sitting lounge faced a set of tall windows that framed Central Park and the New York City skyline to perfection. Rex liked this over-the-top excess. I could take it or leave it.

I glared at the impressive view until a woman in a green velvet dress rose from one of the white leather sofas and blocked my line of sight. Her hair was braided into a loose French braid that softly brushed her bare back with every move she made. Like before, my adrenaline spiked as I waited for her to shift in my direction. I could only assume women did so because they could sense the danger. I was the predator. She was my prey.

My gaze lingered on the silvery flowers in her red hair, the shape of her long neck, and the soft glow on her shoulders. I could take two long strides and make her look at me, but I didn't want this feeling in my chest to go away just yet. I didn't want her to turn and have the wrong face.

She sipped the last of her champagne and set the flute down on the side table. In the next breath, she froze. Her gaze didn't lift up to meet mine, but I could see enough of her profile to know she was Red—same bright green eyes, plump lips, and pink cheeks. She was my mystery woman in the flesh. She slowly rose with her mouth shaped into an "o" in recognition.

The pressure around us shifted, and neither one of us could move. My body heated as if I had tiny, fire-breathing acrobats swirling in my chest. I had spent too long pining over this woman. But my life was already too chaotic to add a relationship to the mix. I had to fuck her and get her out of my system quick.

I decided on my plan, right there and then.

Apart from the server and the bartender, we were alone in the loft. But I wanted to have her all to myself. I dug into the inside pocket of my tuxedo jacket and pulled out the Celtic cross pendant. I let it hang from my fingers, meeting her gaze. Her eyes turned into big saucers as she pursed her lips. The necklace was important to her. She was pissed I took it.

And then I saw it. She was more than angry. The thing that had been missing the first time I met her at the airport. I had sensed the defeat in her gaze was out of character for her. And I was right. The fire burning in them now was intoxicating. I wanted to drink from her, possess her. In a flash, all my fantasies about her rushed to the surface and gave me all kinds of ideas.

I stuffed my hands in the pockets of my trousers and left her standing there.

Behind me, she sighed but didn't move.

I continued down the corridor to the left of the lounge area and tried the first door. The suite had a fully stocked bar, a set of leather club chairs, and an extra-large chaise lounge. In my mind, I saw her bent over one of the armrests, with her dress around her waist, and her ass on display. My cock twitched, and a feral urge consumed me.

I had no doubt in my mind she would come after what was hers. But I hated waiting. Patience wasn't exactly one of my virtues. I poured myself a drink and sat on the club chair facing the door.

By the time the whiskey touched my lips, she appeared at the threshold, still holding all kinds of contempt for me.

"Who do you think you are?" She fisted her hands, then shot a quick glance over her shoulder.

"Hello, Red."

"What?" She furrowed her brows. "Give it back."

She held her ground, instinctively knowing that keeping her distance from me was the only way to keep safe. I dangled the necklace again.

"Come and get it."

She sucked in a breath. Every second she took to make up her mind, my skin burned with a kind of desire I had never felt. For reasons unknown to me, I managed to stay put and wait for her to come to me, while I held the pendant tightly in my grip.

After what seemed like hours, she took a single step inside and shut the door behind her. The air crackled with an urgent and untamed energy. If the goosebumps across her chest were any indication, she felt it too.

She'd walked into the wolf's lair of her own accord. And with that, she sealed her fate. But if I was the predator here, and she my prey, why was she the one stalking toward me, with so much hunger in her eyes?

"Didn't your mother teach you not to talk to strangers?" I grinned at her.

CHAPTER 10
That's His Face

LUCE

What in the world was going on? The billionaire real estate mogul who made us sit on the tarmac because he didn't want to wait his turn to land was looking at me like he wanted to devour me. Maybe being trapped in a sex dungeon for so long had finally taken its toll on me because I wanted him too.

He was taller and more handsome than I remembered. I thought I had memorized his intense gray eyes, but the image I had of him in my mind didn't do justice to the impossibly gorgeous man sitting in front of me. I inhaled his scent and let it travel to every inch of my body. Since the moment I saw him out in the lounge area, a sort of humming gripped my pussy. I'd never had sex or even masturbated, but I had a feeling he could ease the hot sensation within my folds.

My marriage to Liam was inevitable. Once we were wed, I would officially become the baby making machine he'd bought. He would own my body for as long as he wanted. That could be the rest of my life. The universe had offered me a kindness.

It brought me to my mystery man from the airport, and so much more, because I was sure he wanted me too.

Liam would probably be gone for an hour. So much could happen in that span of time. I glanced back at the door. I could run, but then I would never know what he tasted like.

I shifted my body to face him. He relaxed against the club chair and spread his legs apart ever so slightly—an invitation to take him in, admire his imposing physique, and just how crazy hot he looked in a tuxedo. So many times I had fantasized about kissing his bare chest and running my hands all over him.

As if he could read my thoughts, he let out a breath that sounded like a feral groan. "You came here for the necklace. And a bit more." It wasn't a question, more like an observation. His voice sounded restrained and hoarse.

Wait. My what? Oh Jesus, my mother's necklace. How did I forget?

I glanced away for a second to break whatever trance he had put me under. "Give it back. Why did you even take it?"

"I don't know." He braced his elbow on the armrest and let the pendant fall from his grip to sway in a circle.

Putting aside all my dirty thoughts, I stepped toward him and yanked it away from him. I made to shuffle back, but my legs wouldn't move. From this distance, his woodsy scent was intoxicating. I took in another lungful, something to remember him by.

"Red." He rose to his feet until he stood towering over me.

I almost answered, "yes," but managed to bite my lip first. With a knowing smile, he lifted his hand and pulled at the end of my braid, so it would rest on my breast. "Ask me."

I shook my head. My glossy gaze locked on his.

"You shouldn't take things that don't belong to you." My voice sounded so far away.

"No, I shouldn't."

I was talking about the necklace, but his tone implied he thought I meant me. Or maybe that was all me and my imagination. I sucked on my bottom lip harder to keep from begging him to touch me and took a step back.

In the next beat, he bent down and captured the side of my mouth that wasn't trapped between my teeth. His body heat, his scent and that raw energy about him hit me all at once. For a moment, I fought back by not letting go of my lip. But then he swiped his tongue across it, and that was my undoing.

"Hmmm." I moaned. "Who are you?"

"Later." He panted, cradling my face with both hands as we both descended into a frenzy of pent-up desire. He kissed me hard and desperately, as if he had been thinking of doing exactly this for a long while.

I ran my hands up his chest and into his hair, while he worked magic with his mouth. "I can make you feel so good. Ask me." He puffed a breath in my ear then moved down to my neck to nibble on my heated skin.

"Yes." I fisted the lapels of his suit jacket and pushed it off his shoulders.

In all honesty, I had no idea what he meant to do, but I could only assume it had to do with the intense ache between my legs. When he cupped my pussy, I unraveled and melted into him—the complete surrender of someone with nothing to lose.

"Red," he whispered, pressing his forehead to mine.

For a second, I thought he was having doubts, but then he wrapped his arm around my waist, walked me back until I was flush against the back of one of the club chairs, then he turned me around. I braced my hands on the seat, just as the skirt of my dress landed around my hips and his hands found my bare ass.

A moan escaped my lips when he pressed his face to my throbbing pussy. The bit of release was enough to make me moan loudly. I didn't know it could be like this. I didn't know so much pleasure could be found in that spot. I just didn't know.

He swiped his tongue along the seam. With each pass, he increased the pressure to make my folds part for him and give him access to a place no one had ever touched before. The sensation drove me crazy with want. I wanted more of that. I wanted to get to the other side of that mounting need and finally know what I had been denied all these years.

"Yes. Hmmm." I stood on my tiptoes to give him better access.

He kneaded my butt cheeks and pressed deeper into me, lapping around my entrance. "You're dripping wet. You're going to come for me, aren't you?"

"Yes." I squeezed my eyes shut.

The heat and the humming at my core increased—like a pot of water about to break boil. He was right. It was coming. I scratched the plush leather of the cushioned seat, and then he stopped. Shifting my body, I blinked a few times to clear my vision. He was on his knees, still facing my ass, but he had his phone on his ear.

"This better be life or death," he said through gritted teeth. "Oh, fuck me." He rose and almost knocked me over into the club chair.

Even in my state of delirium, I could tell our session was

over because he had some life or death situation happening. I glanced down at my legs, and heat rushed to my cheeks in embarrassment when I spotted my underwear around my ankles. What the hell was I thinking? I didn't even know the guy.

I quickly pulled them up and fixed my skirt, taking deep breaths to come down from my cloud and back to the real world.

"I'll be right there." He dropped the phone in his pocket and donned his jacket. When he met my gaze, he flashed me a smile that made me want to drop my panties again. "Be a good girl and stay."

I blinked. My head was still reeling from what happened. I could still feel his tongue swirling in my pussy, making me feel things I never knew could be.

I blinked again. And then he was gone.

Gathering my skirt, I sat down and then bounced off. What? I couldn't wait for him. Liam would be done with his meeting any minute now. I scanned the suite for a clock, but there wasn't one. *Shit.* How long was I in here? And omigod, did I almost have sex with a guy I had just met? I clamped a hand over my mouth. I was ready to give him my virginity. Liam would've killed me and then my entire family. Our entire contract hinged on that small detail.

Shit. Shit. Shit.

I ran to the mirror behind the small bar to look at myself. My lipstick was gone. My cheeks flushed. And my eyes—they were big, like saucers, and so shiny. I looked like I had just been fucked. I inhaled deeply to calm down then started from the top—I fixed my hair, used my long braid to cover the red blotches on my neck, and then moved on to my dress, to make sure it was all back in place. I pressed a cool hand to my cheeks and made myself breathe evenly.

A few minutes later, I was ready to go out and wait for Walsh. Out in the lounge area, Caterina had returned. Earlier, when the men walked into the meeting room, she had pulled me aside and offered me a drink. Before I could finish my champagne though, her brother had come in and asked if he could have a word. Then my mystery man showed up.

"What time is it?" I asked the bartender.

"Eight-thirty, Miss. Another champagne?"

"Yes, please."

If Liam saw me drinking when he came out, I could blame my red cheeks on the wine.

"They'll be done soon. Don't worry." Caterina smiled at me.

"Oh, I know." I returned the gesture.

In that white strapless dress, she looked like a real-life angel. When we were first introduced, I was jealous of what a perfect couple her and her husband, Rex, made, like they were meant for each other. I envied the way they gravitated toward one another and how she looked at him with so much love in her eyes.

I knew crazy and passionate love would never be for me, but seeing her be so in love made me yearn for a caring partner.

"Your champagne, Miss." The bartender placed a cocktail napkin in my hand then followed with a flute.

"Thanks." I drank, looking around the room to see if my mystery man was still around, but he was gone.

When I brought the napkin to my lips, the writing on it caught my attention.

I must see you again. Tonight. You know the place.

My heart rate spiked. I crumbled the napkin and tossed it on the counter. As if he delivered clandestine messages every night, the bartender picked it up and tossed it in the trash. In a perfect world, I'd be free to meet up with a gorgeous man who set my body on fire. But my body wasn't my own anymore. I couldn't see him again.

He'd be left waiting.

"Luce." Walsh snapped his fingers in my face. "I think you've had enough to drink." He took the glass from me and set it on the counter. "We're leaving."

"Of course." I nodded. When I turned to say good-bye to Rex and Caterina, Caterina was still alone. I cleared my throat. "Is everything okay?"

"Yes. I heard enough." He gripped my upper arm and headed for the grand staircase.

"It was great meeting you." I managed to wave at Caterina.

"It was great meeting you too. Please, do come see us again." She followed us to the top of the steps.

"What happened?" I was practically running to keep up with him.

"Nothing that concerns you."

"Okay." I let him steer me through the crowd and the many gambling tables. Whenever he stopped to move people out of the way, I would look up toward the VIP loft, hoping to catch one last glimpse of my mystery man. No such luck. The night was over.

Liam didn't speak the whole ride to his house. So, when we entered his study and he pulled me into his arms and tried to kiss me, I was completely shocked. My first instinct was to shove him away. He wasn't expecting that, so he stumbled back.

"Everyone tonight kept undressing you with their eyes. But I'm the one who gets to take off your clothes." He advanced again.

"We're not married yet." I wiped the wet off my cheek and put more distance between us. Mrs. Jones had warned me that talking back would earn me a severe punishment. But I was too scared to care. Anything was better than sex with this cruel man who was twice my age. "The contract says we're to be married. I'm not giving up my virginity out of wedlock."

He didn't need to know that an hour ago, I had almost done exactly that with a beautiful stranger.

"You have my word."

"You keep saying that. But I still haven't seen any proof that you have held your end of the bargain." I gestured toward his computer. "Where are the resources you promised, the men and money?"

"You don't trust me."

"I just met you."

"I was trying to protect you. But if you think you can handle the truth. Here it is." He strode around his desk and opened his laptop. After typing and clicking for a bit, he turned the screen around. "I delivered the men. But the Italians are animals. They retaliated."

"What?" I squinted at the footage playing.

A car in flames drove straight into a pub and set the whole thing on fire. Gun shots rang everywhere as men scurried out to take cover on the street.

"I don't understand."

"Because of my help in Chicago, the Italians from Hell's

Kitchen came after my crew. I lost two men that night. You lost three. Burned alive. All of them."

"No. That can't be." I gripped both sides of the screen, trying to make out what was what in the video. The quality was so bad, it was hard to tell. "Tell me who?"

"Patrick O'Brien."

My head snapped up at him. "No, you're lying." I zeroed in on every detail on display. "He can't be gone. If Dad was dead, I would've felt something." Except, I had spent the last couple of weeks making myself numb, so I could survive Mrs. Jones and the dungeon. "I mean what was Dad doing in New York?"

"He came to meet with me the day before you arrived. There were some details of the wedding contract that I wanted finalized before you showed up."

The room swayed and made me nauseous. Dad hadn't been home the day I left Chicago. I figured he didn't want to see me out of guilt because he had agreed to sell me to Liam. But Dad had left because he had unfinished business with my future husband.

"I'm all you have left, Luce." Liam said softly, as if he cared about me, which I knew wasn't true. He needed an heir and a pet. "Your family has forsaken you. With Patrick gone, I'm all you've got. Do you understand?"

"No." I shuffled away from him.

"I'll honor our contract. You'll marry me, and in return, I will continue to help the Red Wolves in Chicago." His lustful gaze swept down to my chest. When he spoke again, his voice was barely above a whisper. "You can still be my queen. Together, you and I can have it all."

"I want to see him. Take me to see Dad. Please."

"The police haven't released the bodies yet." He closed the space between us, taking in my scent. "We both lost something tonight, Luce. But we can still get what we want. I will continue to hold my end of the deal and fight off the Italians for you." He gripped my arm.

"I need to see my brother then. Where is he? Why is he not here?" I didn't care about what Liam wanted or our ridiculous contract.

He puffed out an exasperated breath. "I tried calling him last night, but he's not answering. My men haven't seen him since they arrived in Chicago." He cocked his head and tightened his hold on me. After several beats, he let go and picked up his phone off the desk. "Call him if you want."

I yanked it away from him and quickly dialed Ronan. I waited for him to answer as tears brimmed my eyes. My heart needed to hear a familiar voice right about now.

"Do you believe me now? The situation has changed slightly. But I'm still your best bet." He ran the back of his fingers down my cheek.

I rubbed my temple. I still couldn't wrap my mind around what had happened. Dad was dead. My crew needed me now more than ever. I was all they had left. Someone had to step up and be the boss. The knot in my belly tightened painfully, and my stomach lurched.

As I sifted through the myriad of emotions going through my head, the video on Liam's laptop replayed the gruesome scene—a man pushed a car into the pub with Dad inside, and then, set it on fire. Men ran out of the way, but Dad stood his ground. Why? I didn't look away this time. I glared at the next part of the footage until he came into full view. "That's his face."

"I know." Liam paused the video on Dad's killer. "And he will pay. I promise you that."

"You know him? What's his name?"

Blood rushed to my head and all I could see was red. I squeezed my eyes shut, and tears streamed down my cheeks. Even though I'd glanced away, his features were etched on my mind. His imposing body, those eyebrows, and strong jaw were hard to forget. Mainly because they were the same ones I had been fantasizing about since I got to New York.

He couldn't be an Italian mobster—my enemy.

"Santino Buratti." Liam said the name with all the disgust and contempt I was feeling. "I met him tonight."

CHAPTER 11
I Didn't Mean to Kill Him

LUCE

Mrs. Jones added more glittered powder to my nipples then helped me into yet another white, sheer leotard. She seemed happy, excited even. Liam wanted to consummate our deal tonight. The wedding, he assured me, would happen the following Friday.

"Mr. Walsh wants an intimate ceremony. So, it will just be us and a handful of friends." She arranged my French braid, so it sat over my left breast.

A lump churned in my stomach. I had many friends and family who I would've invited to my wedding. "That's fine."

"Smile, dear. Mr. Walsh doesn't like sad faces."

"My dad was killed last night. He waited a whole day to tell me. I'm allowed to mourn." I blinked and more tears streamed down my cheeks.

Mrs. Jones plucked a tissue from its box and dabbed under my eyes. "Tonight will take your mind off of things."

Things? My father being murdered on the street wasn't just a thing. My breathing became erratic as she walked me to the full-length mirror in the bathroom to show off her work to me. I looked like a doll, empty and lifeless.

She never talked this much before, but she continued with more instructions while she tidied up around the bathroom. I stood there and watched her blurry figure move about the room and then into the dungeon. I blinked to focus, but it was no use.

A high-pitched ringing in my ear muted her words. Everything had changed. Did she not realize that? I rubbed my chest. With Dad and Ronan gone, the crew was vulnerable. They needed a boss, or they would start going at each other's throats. An internal war would leave them open to a takeover by the neighboring crews. I could see all the bloodshed on the streets. The Irish fighting their own to take control, while the Italians moved in for the final blow.

No, I couldn't stay here anymore, playing pet to Liam, hoping he would make it all better. My crew needed me more than they needed Liam's small army. I had to get back to Beverly. Dad would've wanted me to go home and be a leader.

I followed Mrs. Jones into the sex dungeon where she was busy re-arranging sex toys. When she was done, she shoved a wooden table with a dark marble top up against the wall facing my cage. In the middle of the room, spotlights shone a red hue on a contraption that looked like a torture wheel with rope and handcuffs. That was new. I supposed she had brought it in just for tonight.

"And remember, only speak when asked a direct question." She kept tinkering with different items on the table.

The whole room came into focus. My head was a jumble of theories and to-dos. I wanted to be with my crew, but I also wanted revenge.

Santino Buratti.

The name flashed in front of my eyes.

Clarity washed over me. Everything came into focus, and I knew exactly what I needed to do. I had to find Ronan and warn him about what the Italians had done in New York. He had to know the Red Wolves needed him, us. But first, Santino had to pay for what he did. He set the pub on fire with Dad in it.

He had to pay.

Hate replaced the pain in my chest.

My gaze zeroed in on the huge dildo sitting on the edge of the marble counter—the one that had been in my mouth when Mrs. Jones showed me how to do a proper blow job. Bile rose to the back of my throat. My whole body shook with anger as a plan to escape formed in my head. By the time I wrapped my fingers around the face of the fat cock, my grip was steady.

I picked it up and hit Mrs. Jones with it across her temple. Her small frame flew across the floor. Before she could get up, I hit her again on the back of the head. The second blow knocked her out, and her body went limp on the carpeted floor.

No time to second-guess myself. I dragged her body to the contraption in the middle of the room and handcuffed her to one of the rings. A ball gag came next. And just because I didn't know how good she was at this, I used some jute rope to tie her legs to opposite ends of the torture wheel.

My heart thrashed in my ears as I glanced around the dungeon. I needed real clothes. In the bathroom, I only found a red cloak—more kinky stuff to help Liam get it on. I threw it over my shoulders and darted out of the room.

By now I was sure the apartment was only used for Liam's pets. Because only defenseless women and Mrs. Jones lived here, security was minimal. Earlier today, when we left for the Crucible, I only spotted two bodyguards outside the building. And one in the garage.

I padded over to Liam's study where light streamed from under the door. He was still in there. With a shaky hand, I placed my hand on the knob. Mrs. Jones was easy to overpower, but Walsh was ruthless and bigger than me, not by much, but still. I couldn't fight him.

As much as I wanted to hurt him for what he put me through and for what he did to my family, I couldn't kill him. I wasn't a killer. I didn't even have a gun on me. Or any kind of weapon. I scanned the living room for something I could use, but the place was almost bare, except for the furniture and a few knickknacks.

I bolted for the front entrance. I opened the door just enough for me to slip through and then shut it behind me. The hallway was empty like before. I ran to the elevators and pressed the call button continuously until the doors slid open. I had ten floors to figure out how to bypass the two men downstairs. The cloak covered my face, but it was red, and it stood out, because who would wear a damn cloak in the middle of Summer.

Think, Luce.

When I reached the lobby, the doorman greeted me politely. And then it hit me, Liam wasn't expecting his pets to leave his apartment. His only concern was around his own safety. No one was here to stop me from leaving.

"Would you be needing a taxi, Miss?" he asked with zero judgment in his eyes. Though it was obvious he thought I was a call girl. I was in a see-through leotard and a red cloak. What else would he think?

"That would be great." I gathered the velvet fabric and hugged myself.

"Right away."

I wanted to kiss the man. While he made the call, I kept a close watch on the elevator. How long did I have before Walsh noticed I was gone? He had been on the phone when I stopped by his study. Maybe ten or fifteen minutes?

"Where to, Miss?"

Shit. I had assumed Liam would ask the doorman if he'd seen me. And he would no doubt tell him he put me in a taxi. I wanted to go to the airport, but I had no money. All I could do was call Kay and hope she was still in town and had a way to help me. But what if she had been in Harlem the night the Italians attacked?

My eyes watered as images of the footage Liam showed me flashed in my head. I had every detail committed to memory, including the last image I saw—Santino Buratti.

"Miss?"

"The Crucible, please."

If I didn't make it, if Liam found me before I could get home to Chicago, I wanted to at least get this one thing done. My father's murder couldn't go unpunished. Santino had to answer for what he did. And as luck would have it, I knew exactly where he'd be tonight.

A minute later, the taxi arrived. I flipped my hoodie on and let the doorman escort me to the curb. My gaze darted to each end of the street. Two men were to one side of the lobby door, but they were too busy talking and sharing a smoke. I didn't have time to see their faces and confirm they were here for Liam. I climbed in the back of the yellow cab and sat heavy in the worn and torn seat.

The driver didn't even say hello. He put on his blinker and peeled off as soon as the road was clear. Holy fuck. I got out.

At the Crucible, the taxi stopped at the main entrance. It was past midnight but the rave out on the street was still in full swing. So when I bolted and disappeared into the crowd, the driver had no way to come after me. Caterina had explained to me that the Crucible was by invitation only, but people liked to line up outside to see if they could spot any celebrities or maybe get invited in. I hoped that the bouncer at the door would remember my face. Otherwise, I'd have no way to get in.

Clutching the front of my cloak, I approached the big guy holding the red rope in place. As soon as he saw me, he nodded once. "Ms. Red."

"That's..." not my name. But I decided Santino's nickname for me was a better option. After I killed Santino, they wouldn't know who to look for. I donned my hood. "Thank you."

Once inside, I made my way to the VIP loft where, again, the bouncer was expecting me. Santino had been so sure I'd return. Why? Because I turned to putty under his ministrations or because he knew who I was? The reason didn't matter. Dad would be avenged tonight.

When I opened the door to the suite, it was as if time hadn't lapsed. As if I hadn't left with Liam and gone to his place, as if I hadn't gotten the second worse news of my life. Though when Mom died, I had no one to blame but the cancer eating away at her. Revenge wasn't possible for her.

"Jesus, are you trying to kill me?" Santino rose to his feet.

The desire burning in his eyes stopped me in my tracks. My body reacted to his scent and the sizzle in the air. I had not expected that. So, when he closed the space between us and kissed me, I simply melted. My lips molded to his. When his tongue collided with mine, a spark ignited at my core.

He pulled away first to remove his jacket. As soon as my gaze zeroed in on the gun strapped to his shoulder holster, I remembered why I had come back. *Santino was a murderer.* He deserved to be shot. I yanked at his gun and flipped the safety off.

"Don't touch me." I aimed the gun at him.

"What?" He took several steps back, shaking his head as if in a daze. "I'm confused. And honestly—" his steely gaze roamed up and down my body. "—so fucking turned on."

"You took a life." My voice trembled. "And now you're going to pay."

The accusation sobered him up. He released a breath and braced both hands on his hips. "I wasn't expecting this. First, you're ready to give up on life, and now you're here to kill."

"You killed my dad."

"In my line of work, I've killed a lot of dads, love."

"So, you admit it?" I blinked to clear my vision, gripping the handgun tighter.

"Get on with it then. Take your revenge."

He met my gaze so sure I wouldn't do it.

I pulled the trigger.

The impact flipped him over, and he fell on the chaise lounge. My heart thumped so fast and hard against my ribs, I thought I was going to throw up. I set the gun down on the floor and backed away until I reached the door. Blood stained his white dress shirt. The stench of it had never bothered me before. But then again, I had never been the one to make someone bleed. I wasn't a killer.

I turned around, fumbled with the doorknob until it finally gave and opened. My head had been so jumbled up from everything that happened tonight that I didn't consider what would happen if my half-ass plan actually worked. I aimed straight at his heart. If no one helped him, he wouldn't make it through the night.

But now what? I headed out toward the elevator bay. No one took notice of my choice of clothing. The masquerade ball was still going. All the women were dressed in corsets and long gowns. Expensive perfume lingered in the air, as I shoved my way past them. As soon as I hopped into the elevator car, I backed into a corner and sunk to my knees.

I didn't mean to kill him.

A man was bleeding upstairs, and Dad was still dead.

"Miss, are you okay?" A bouncer held the elevator door open. When I glanced up with tears in my eyes, he stepped forward to help me up. "Can I call you a cab?"

"No, I need to call someone."

"Sure." He handed me his cell phone.

I took it and called my friend Kay. She answered on the third ring. "Dude, it's past midnight. This isn't the time to be selling shit."

"Kay, it's me." I turned to face the mirrored wall to get a bit of privacy from the bouncer as he was still guarding the door and watching me intently. "It's Luce."

"Omigod, Luce. Where are you? I've been trying to get to you, but no one knows where Walsh took you."

"I don't have time to explain. Are you still in the city? Can you come get me?"

"Yes. I am. I've been staying in a hotel. Where are you?"

"I'll drop you a pin."

"Okay. Stay there. I'm leaving now."

"Thank you." I wept into the mobile after she ended the call. Then I remembered I was still in the elevator and the bouncer was still watching me like I was some wounded bird he was afraid to touch. "Thanks. I have a ride now." I gave him his device.

"No problem. You'll be alright?"

"Yes." I fisted my cloak shut and ambled toward the lobby.

The bright lights from the massive chandelier hanging from the ceiling hurt my eyes. I felt exposed in the huge space with its white marble floors and tall windows. My best bet was to wait outside where it was dark and crowded.

I hurried past the bouncer and made a left toward the line of people waiting to be invited in. After a few minutes, my pulse came down to a normal beat. I hugged my body and scoured the mob once more. A yelp to my right caught my attention. When I turned, I spotted one of Liam's bodyguards.

They found me.

I bolted farther into the sea of bodies. Everyone was wasted and easily moved when I shoved them to one side or the other. At the end of the street, I came into an alleyway. It was dark and empty. But on other end, there was light and cars moving freely. This was my only chance to lose them. I could get to a safe place and call Kay again.

Because I was out of choices, I took off running without looking back. Halfway down, a door swung opened, and a man came out—maybe a server going out for a smoke. I didn't care or slow down to find out. I pressed on, urging my legs to go faster. But my bare feet could only handle so much.

"Stop her." The voice echoed between the two buildings.

In the next breath, a man yanked me by the waist and pinned me to the asphalt. A pair of Italian leather shoes came into my line of sight, and I glanced up. "No."

CHAPTER 12
What Am I Going to Do with You?

SANTINO

"You tried to kill me." I glared at Red's beautiful face, while the same words kept bouncing around my head—she actually did it. She pulled the fucking trigger. She shot me.

"You're alive." Her eyes watered.

And I swore I saw relief in them.

Earlier, my men rushed into the suite as I was waking up after hitting my head on the granite counter. Luckily, tonight I had chosen to wear my high-tech, bulletproof shirt on account that we had a meeting with an asshole trying to get us killed.

"Sir." My right-hand man, Joey, tapped my shoulder. "Tommy says she called someone before she walked out. I got the number."

I gripped Red's elbow and propped her on her feet. She immediately clutched the front of her cloak closed. Before this night was over, I had to find out what that getup was about. A part of me—the part controlled one hundred percent by my dick—wanted to believe that she wore that leotard for

112

me. I still couldn't get the sight of her pink nipples out of my head.

"Sir." Joey offered me his phone. "Tommy says she seemed to be running away from someone."

"That would be me and my wrath." I pointed at the stitches on my temple. After my men found me, I let one of them take a minute to stop the bleeding and patch me up, while Joey searched the club for Red. The potential broken ribs would need to wait until morning.

I glanced at the screen. He had the call ready for me. Tapping on send and then the speaker phone, I met Red's green gaze. The fear in her eyes told me she cared about the person on the other end of the line. For some odd reason, that made my blood boil, which only made my throbbing headache worse.

"Luce. Where the hell are you?"

"Hell sounds about right." I kept my attention on Red. "Who is this?"

"Who is this? Who the fuck are you?" She panted as if she were running. "I swear, if you touch my girlfriend, I will cut up your balls and feed them to your dog."

"That sounds painful."

"I got you, asshole." She ended the call.

While her threat didn't intimidate me, we did have to get a move on. We were exposed out here in the alleyway. Even if we were surrounded by my people, we couldn't stay out here—especially when someone was coming for Luce.

"How long?" I asked Joey.

"He's here." He stepped onto the asphalt to wave at my driver who was hauling ass from the other end of the street.

The black SUV stopped in front of us. I ushered Luce

inside and climbed in behind her. When she tried to scoot all the way to the other side, I yanked at her arm and made her nestle on my chest. My arm hurt like a motherfucker, but it was strong enough to cage her in.

Joey shut the door and walked around to the passenger side. "Go, they found us."

As soon as he said the words, bullets assaulted the back window. I shifted my body to look at the shooters and spotted five men. So, one woman and five men were here to rescue Luce from me.

"Who is she to you?" When she didn't answer, I squeezed her tighter. I meant for the effort to crush and hurt her, but fuck her body felt too good next to mine. "Red, you will answer my question. Or this situation will turn incredibly bad for you."

"She's my bodyguard."

I turned away from her to hide a smile. Bodyguard, not girlfriend. The way the woman said her name had me thinking she might be an actual girlfriend, the kind with benefits. "How about a boyfriend?"

"A fiancé." She shoved at my chest to get away from me.

I released my grip on her because the pain was killing me and because her answer threw me off. "What?"

"That's right. He's looking for me. When he finds me, he going to make you pay." She wiped her face. "He's very powerful and rich."

"Is he also a killer?"

"Yes."

"Hmm."

I didn't think that part was true. But the fiancé bit sounded real. She was taken? Then why would she agree to let me eat her pussy if she had a man waiting for her. I almost wished she hadn't said yes. Because now, her tiny moans and her perfect ass were all I could think about.

The SUV pulled into my private garage and came to a full stop in front of the small lobby. When Joey opened the door for me, I gripped Luce's elbow and dragged her with me. No way I was letting her out of my sight. I took long strides to the elevator, ignoring Luce's complaints about walking barefoot.

On the way up to the penthouse, I glanced down at her feet. Sure enough, her feet were covered in cuts and bruises. What the fuck happened to her tonight? She was fine when I first saw her in the VIP loft. Slowly, she wandered inside. I let her take the place in as I shut and locked the door behind me.

I inhaled, smiling at the back of her head.

"Is this your place?" She hugged her body as she ambled toward the floor-to-ceiling windows with a skylit view of Manhattan. "Am I your prisoner now?"

"Yes, you are." I gestured toward the grand staircase. "If you try to leave, my men have orders to shoot you on sight."

She squeezed her eyes shut. After a few breaths, she braced a slender hand on the banister and headed up the steps. My whole body screamed for me to take her to my suite and bury myself deep inside her until my desire for her was spent. I needed to get her out of my system. But first, I needed to find out who she really was and who this fiancé of hers was.

I made a mistake before, when I let my dick do all the thinking. Getting a taste of her sweet pussy had been an utter mistake too. But she was here now. I had all the time in the world to figure her out and then have my fill of her. A week or two in my bed should do the trick. And then her so-called fiancé could have her back.

Acid pooled in the pit of my stomach. We'd have to see about the last part of my plan.

"No lair?" She turned to face me when I swung open the door to my bedroom. "I figured you'd have a torture wheel and cages for all the women you kidnap."

"No lair." I rather enjoyed her spunk. Better than the girl with dead eyes I met at the airport last month. "Seems you have experience with that sort of thing though." I pulled at the string holding the cloak together, then yanked the whole thing off her shoulders. "Not that I'm complaining. But what's with this getup? Are you a pet, love?"

She gasped at the BDSM term, and her nipples tightened into a mouth-watering bud. Were she and her fiancé into that kind of thing? I've dabbled in the lifestyle, but even that became dull after a few years. When you can have anything you want, everything becomes mundane and not enough after a while.

Luce was the first one to awaken something in me. It had been a long time since anyone had made me feel alive.

"What am I going to do with you, Luce?"

Her chin jutted upward as she stood there, proud and unyielding, something that made me want to fuck her into submission. But I had to stop thinking with my dick. The woman shot me. I had to focus on that bit and figure out why. She couldn't leave until I was certain she wouldn't come after me again and finish the job.

Being the next in line to take over the family business made me a target within the organization. The Society was an old Enclave, and our by-laws were set in stone. But if the loss of the Gallo family taught us anything, it was that anyone could be replaced.

"If you let me go now, I'll ask my fiancé to spare your life." She crossed her arms over her chest, doing her best to cover up her luscious tits.

"So kind of you." I kept my gaze on hers because I needed to stay on track. "Does this fiancé of yours have a name?"

"You don't need to know that." She shot daggers at me with those big, green eyes. "All you need to know is that he's coming for you. He won't stop until I'm home."

I surveyed her features. She almost choked on the word home. Why? I was intrigued by her—intrigued and so turned on. Seeing her pussy through that sheer fabric was putting all kinds of ideas in my head. I was dying to hear her little moans again while I buried my face in her folds.

I prowled toward her. Her cheeks turned a pretty pink as she straggled back. With our gazes locked, we kept going until her back was pressed against the cool window. I cradled the side of her face and wedged my knee between her thighs while I tried to find the truth in her eyes.

"Hmm." She puffed and panted, as her body melted into mine. "Don't. Don't touch me."

"Why not? You obviously want me to. I can see it" My cock steeled inside my trousers. "I can feel it too."

"Because I hate you."

"I see that too," I said through gritted teeth. Why did it bother me? A lot of people hated me. That was part of my job description. "Tell me, Luce. Does a nice girl like you understand the difference between torture and punishment?"

"What?"

"Simple question. Answer, yes or no?"

"What does it matter? The end result is the same. Pain."

"You're absolutely right." I lowered my hand to her pointy nipples and pinched them hard.

"Ahh." She arched her back. "So that's it, you brought me here to torture me because I tried to kill you?"

"No, I brought you here to punish you." I bent down until my lips brushed the shell of her ear. "Torture is inflicting pain to achieve a goal. The recipient may or may not understand why. But you understand why you're here. Don't you?"

"I shot you."

"Correct. So, here's the real difference between the two. You will accept my punishments because you know you deserve them." I smirked at her. "I'm not letting you go, until I'm convinced you won't try to kill me again."

"My fiancé will cut your balls and feed them to your dog."

"Yeah, your friend mentioned that."

Every time she said the word fiancé, my insides twisted into a tight knot. I cupped her swollen pussy. When her juices covered my fingers, I cocked my head to study her reaction. She watched me with hooded eyes for so long, I thought she would beg me to take her next. But instead, she glanced away. She was fighting her attraction to me. As much as I enjoyed the chase, I wasn't about to take something she had already decided not to give me.

Licking my fingers, I stepped away from her. "I didn't kill your dad."

She bolted to the other end of the suite, where her cloak laid on the floor, and threw it around her shoulders, gripping the ends tightly to her chest. Her gaze darted between the door and me as if trying to decide if my men would follow my orders and shoot her on sight.

"I have proof. I saw you."

"That's interesting." I racked my brain for the details of the last time I had to kill someone.

The thing about killing is that it was impossible to forget. Over time, I had learned to lock the memories away and keep the darkness at bay. But their faces, their eyes, as the realization that they were dying sunk in, were tattooed on my mind, etched in my soul. I didn't enjoy taking a life. It was a necessary evil to stay alive.

"Does he have red hair like yours?" I would remember that color hair.

"Yes. He was injured too. It wasn't fair." Her voice cracked. She seemed so alone, standing there with her bruised feet and dirty cloak.

"Like I said, I've killed a lot of people in my time. But no one with that description."

"You lie." She furrowed her brows, still shooting daggers at me but with less conviction than before.

"I have no reason to. I'm not the killer you're looking for. So that brings us back to my original question. What am I going to do with you, Luce?"

She pursed her lips, her whole body rising and falling with every breath she took. In the next beat, she darted for the door. My legs jerked into a run. But with my ribs bruised and my head still hurting, she got away from me fast. I chased her the length of the hallway and down the stairs. I didn't catch up to her until she was almost at the front entrance. I wrapped my arm around her waist and pressed her hard against my chest. Her soft skin felt so good.

"Santino," she whispered, and time slowed down.

I brought her closer to me, nuzzling my face in her neck. "Say it again. Say my name."

"No." She kicked and punched to get away from me.

With every move, I held her tighter. But she was strong, and I was convalescing. Her fighting brought me to my knees. I set her down on the cold marble floor and braced my body to hers, caging her legs between mine as I gripped both of her wrists over her head.

"You know my name. But you have no idea who I am, do you?" I bent down so our noses were touching.

"You're with the New York Faction." She struggled. "I didn't know that before when I saw you at the Crucible the first time. But now I do. You're with the greedy Italians. That makes you my enemy."

"You got that half-right." I took in her scent and let it fill me. Her smell alone made me feel alive.

"My fiancé will come for me."

"No one is coming for you." I raised my voice, which made her squeeze her eyes shut. "Look at me." I cupped her jaw and made her face me. "Here's what we're going to do. I'm going to prove to you that I didn't murder your father. But only because I need you to accept your punishment for trying to kill me."

And because I couldn't stand seeing the hate in her eyes. I needed her to know the truth and surrender to me.

My heart thumped hard against my ribs, shooting pain up my spine—a reminder of Luce's bullet that almost pierced through me.

"You can't keep me here." She glared at me.

"I can keep you here for as long as I wish."

CHAPTER 13
You'll Live

LUCE

Santino Buratti had the ability to suck all the oxygen out of the room. He was like a blinding light in the middle of a dark forest. My body craved him in a way I never knew was possible. Even now, as he pinned me to the floor, claiming me as his prisoner, the only question in my mind was—what did he look like under that tuxedo?

His heated gaze hypnotized me, and I couldn't look away from his handsome face. I wanted to run my fingers along his thick eyebrows and full lips. But Santino was my enemy. Whatever I wanted from him didn't matter. I had to stay focused and figure out a way to escape and get back to Chicago. My brother was in danger. Whoever killed Dad would surely go after him next.

I squirmed under Santino's weight. His hard muscles pressed against every inch of my skin, and it made every nerve ending feel alive. A puff of hot breath brushed my cheek—and with it, his erection stiffened even more. He was rock solid, stoking the aching need between my legs.

"Why should I believe you?"

"Which part?" His nose lowered to the side of my mouth as his gaze roamed my breasts. "That you're my prisoner now or that I had nothing to do with your father's murder?"

"I saw you. There's footage of you."

"Good." He let go of my wrists, stood, then pulled me up like I weighed nothing. "I was afraid we'd have to start from scratch. You can show me the evidence later."

Gripping my elbow, he ushered me up the grand staircase for the second time tonight. When I winced in pain from the cut on my foot, he bent over and swooped me into his arms in a fluid motion. In my fantasies about him, I never thought to include this part where he carried me away. Maybe because I was certain there was no escaping Liam, I did my best to ignore Santino's woodsy scent and the warmth of his body against mine.

"Where are you taking me?" As much as I didn't want to engage with him, talking helped me keep my mind off all the bad ideas in my head.

"I believe that the punishment should fit the crime."

"What does that mean?" I squirmed in his arms to get away from him, but he held me firmly to his chest.

He caged me in like that the rest of the way, then set me on the marble tile once we entered the en-suite bathroom. I stood there, eyes wide, as he removed his tuxedo jacket, the cufflinks and then started on the studs of his dress shirt. With a wince, he peeled the fabric off, revealing a chiseled chest and abs. The V-muscle above the waist of his pants tightened as he bent down to assess the damage.

Several minutes went by before I remembered I probably should not be staring. Santino was a stranger. A few hours ago, he was no more than a memory, a fantasy to pass the time in Liam's dungeon.

He cocked his brow and met my gaze. "What do you think?"

Perfect. He was perfect. I glanced down at the bulge in his pants for a beat before I answered. "You'll live."

"Right." He chuckled. "I meant do you think my ribs are broken?"

Santino was my father's murderer. But as a nurse, I had sworn an oath to do no harm. I hadn't meant to shoot him. I was so angry and hurt before; I wasn't thinking clearly. Revenge never brought anyone back from the dead. I would know.

"Well?" He stepped closer and brushed his index finger along the sutures on his temple. "You've been eyeing my stitches like you don't approve of them."

"It's a shoddy job."

"Do you have medical training?"

"That's why there was so much blood. You split your head open."

"You left me for dead."

"I was in a hurry." I tentatively reached for his left side.

When he put his arms down, I ran my fingers along the bruised area, feeling for anything that was out of place—a bone, pooled blood, a bullet. His breath came out in puffs as my hands roamed his soft skin. He was in a lot of pain. But instead of going to the hospital, he decided to come after me, just so he could get his revenge on me.

"So that's a yes. You're a doctor." His tone was low and gentle as if he didn't want to scare me away.

"A trained nurse." I hadn't meant to say that. The less he knew about me, the better. "I shot you point blank. Where did it go?" I lifted my face to look him in the eyes, which was a total mistake. He was beautiful, mesmerizing. Every time our gazes locked, I fell into some sort of trance.

"Bulletproof tuxedo." He bent down to pick up his coat jacket. "The fabric is high-tech, weaved to stop bullets. It absorbed some of the shock, but not enough. It still knocked me out."

"Do you always wear bulletproof clothes to parties?"

"I was meeting with a potential customer, one I don't particularly trust. The suit was standard protocol." He turned his back on me and sauntered toward the bathtub.

"What are you doing?" I gasped when he toed-off his shoes then dropped his trousers along with his underwear.

Somehow, he looked taller now that he was fully nude. I stood there, ogling him while he ran the hot water. Within seconds, the room filled with steam and a lavender scent.

"Your punishment." He stepped into the tub and sat down, bracing his arms on the lip of the tub. Closing his eyes, he let his head fall back. "You will assist me with my bath. And anything else I need while I recover from the severe bruising you gave me."

Anything else? What exactly was anything else?

When I didn't move, he exhaled. "If you run off again, my men will shoot you the minute you set foot outside the penthouse."

I scanned the room quickly, going through my options. The only way out was to play his stupid game. I had escaped one cage and walked right into another one. Meanwhile, my brother Ronan was in danger. Did he know about Dad? I had to assume he didn't. Otherwise, he would've come for me. He would've given me the news himself.

"Now, Red."

His deep voice jolted me back to reality. With a sigh, I ambled toward him and picked up the washcloth. I dipped it in the soapy water, then gently scrubbed his front, starting at his neck. I'd never seen a naked man in my life. Not in person anyway. And not one that looked like Santino. Sitting here with his arms out and legs wide, he oozed confidence and testosterone.

Every time I dipped the small towel in the water, the bubbles would clear out of the way. My heart thumped in my throat with anticipation because, underneath the suds, I could see the outline of his huge erection. Was that even normal? He was way bigger than I had imagined.

"Hmm." He gripped my wrist. "Not so hard, Red. It hurts."

"Then why don't you do it yourself?" I yanked my arm away, but he pulled me toward him. With our noses touching, I had to brace my free hand on him so I wouldn't fall in the water.

"Because I want you to do it." His gaze dropped to his thick thigh, where my fingers were gripping his bulging quads.

It was a miracle I hadn't landed on his cock.

"You can scrub my back now." He propped me up and then sat forward.

I'd been so distracted by his striking body, I hadn't realized what he was doing. He was showing off. He was making me see all of him. And I had fallen for it. My palms itched to touch the muscled planes along his wide shoulders. Everything about Santino was a huge turn-on. Why?

"You're a brute." I made quick work with the washcloth to clean his back, and then, tossed it at him.

When I made to leave, he snaked his arm around my waist and tugged me toward him. My butt lingered on the edge of the tub for a beat before I fell over backward. I landed on top of him as water sloshed over the sides.

"You don't leave until I say so." His lips pressed to my ear. "Do you understand? Your body and soul belong to me now."

"You can't keep me here. I have to go home."

"Why?" He wrapped both arms around me. "To get back to your fiancé?"

I had hoped the mention of a future husband would put Santino off. But he didn't care. He didn't care that I belonged to someone else. Because regardless of what happened tonight, one thing was for certain, I belonged to Liam—in his mind anyway. He would never stop looking for me. Back at the Crucible, he almost caught me. His men showed up just as Santino shoved me into his SUV and whisked me away. If it hadn't been for Santino, I'd be back in the cage, waiting for my wedding day.

The punishment for leaving Liam would be severe. But I couldn't stay with him. I never agreed to being his pet.

"Answer me."

"Yes. I know he's out there looking for me right now."

His cock pressed between my legs, and my whole body ignited.

"Does he make you feel like this?" He cupped my breasts and pulled at my nipple over the sheer fabric of my leotard.

"Yes." I arched my back to meet his hand.

"I don't believe you." He moved down to my pussy. "Earlier, you came to me because you wanted this. The desire in your eyes was hard to miss. I don't think you've ever been touched. Not properly anyway."

He drew circles around my aching clit. The sensation intensified until it almost hurt. But I didn't want him to stop. I wanted to know what would happen next, what it was all building up to. I had never climaxed. For some reason beyond comprehension, I wanted it now. I didn't want to wait anymore. I wanted to know what it was like. Just this once. I needed to feel alive.

A moan escaped my lips as his ministrations extended deeper into my folds, closer to my entrance. "Santino." I reached down and pulled off the snaps at the crotch to give him access.

"I know, love."

He captured my mouth with a demanding kiss. I sat on his lap in a contorted angle with my face up to meet his and the rest of my body under his control.

"You want to come."

It wasn't a question, but I nodded anyway, gripping the edge of the tub. I was so close. Blood swooshed in my ears while my heart pounded hard against my chest. Omigod, I never knew it could be like this.

"But not yet." He stopped and stood, lifting me up with him. "You left the Crucible after I asked you to stay put, that's one. Then you came back and shot me, that's two. Left me for dead." He stepped out of the tub onto the bath rug, then reached for me and scooped me up into his arms. "That's three."

"What?" I got it. He was numerating all the things I'd done tonight. But why?

"You tried to escape after I explained why you were here. That's four." He carried me to the four-poster bed and set me down on the edge. "Bend over."

"Excuse me?"

"I'm in a lot of pain right now. I'm going to make sure you feel it too." He removed my wet cloak then guided me to face the mattress, so my ass was up in the air and on display for him. "Count."

My clit was still throbbing from when he touched me there. When he smacked my right butt cheek, the vibration shot straight into my pussy, like hot tendrils lapping every spot that felt good.

"I said count."

"One." I squeezed my legs together.

He spanked my left side. Ribbons of desire spiraled from my core and up into my chest, while heat continued to pool around my clit. I needed relief.

"Red."

"Two."

The next two blows came one after the other. "Three. Four. Argh." I collapsed on the bed. My ass was on fire, but no more than my aching bud. Fisting the duvet, I glanced over my shoulder while Santino towered over me with his chest rising and falling and his erection on full display.

He positioned himself behind me and cupped my soaked and needy pussy. Slowly, he rubbed the length of it, spreading my juices all over my swollen folds.

"Come for me." He gripped my French braid and whispered in my ear, "Now, Red."

He increased the tempo, kneading and pulling. The front of his chest rubbed against my back and added to our connection. His cock wasn't inside me and yet, it was like we were one. I lifted my ass to give him access.

Something hot and untamed sprouted deep inside me. I closed my eyes and pictured it chasing me through the woods, like a wild beast, panting and thrashing through the trees. A good girl would be afraid. But I wanted it. I wanted it to find me, and finally release me. With a guttural moan, he rubbed me faster, until my orgasm ripped through me. The thumping of my heart moved up into my throat, and for a moment, the room went dark and quiet.

My voice sounded far away—the words incoherent. My body went limp as he wrenched out every ounce of pleasure from me. When he removed his hand, I bit my lip to keep myself from begging for more. Though the damage was already done. I wanted more, so much more.

Through the ringing in my ears, a door slammed shut. I flipped on my back to find the suite empty. Santino was gone. Even though I had climaxed, my pussy still burned with desire, with want for him. I wanted to feel his cock inside me.

Wait? What?

I jumped off the bed. I couldn't do that. What the hell was wrong with me? I shoved a hand in my disheveled hair. My braid was all but undone and dripping water. Why in the world did I let him do this to me? The Italians back home were literally killing us one by one. They were *his* people. That made Santino my enemy. If this was his idea of punishment, I knew I wouldn't survive. I had to get out of here.

In the huge closet next to the bathroom, I found a drawer full of white undershirts. I removed what was left of my leotard and donned a clean top. Before I walked out, I stopped to inspect all the expensive shoes and suits that hung neatly under a shelf that ran the length of the wall. Spotlights shone brightly on a collection of watches that sat on top of the chest of drawers. I inhaled and took in the familiar woodsy scent.

Was this Santino's bedroom?

I placed a hand over my mouth. No idea why I felt that being in his suite was way worse than sleeping in a sex dungeon.

Get out now.

My body screamed at me, so I listened. I darted to the door and swung it open. The hallway was empty. In fact, the whole penthouse felt empty. If Santino left, this could be my only chance to escape. I made my way down the staircase and headed straight for the front entrance.

As soon as I opened it, two guards turned to face me. They didn't say anything—no threats or warnings—they simply stared and waited for me to put two and two together.

It was as Santino had said. I was his prisoner until he decided otherwise.

CHAPTER 14
We're All Mobsters Here

SANTINO

Marie huffed and puffed around the dining room as she delivered the breakfast I'd ordered—eggs, bacon, fruit salad, pastries, waffles, sausages. I didn't know what Luce ate in the morning, so I got a bit of everything. No doubt by now Marie had noticed the woman sleeping in my bed. By the deep furrows on her forehead, I had to assume she wasn't too happy about it.

"Go ahead and ask." I sipped from my black coffee.

"How long will she be staying?"

"A while."

"Fine." She set a cheese platter and French bread in front of me. "Anything else, sir?"

"Yes, she's going to need clothes."

"I'm sorry?" She lifted her head to glare at me properly.

I cocked my brow and stared back, until she conceded and lowered her head. Marie had been with me for a few years now. Her job was to come in twice a day to tidy up and cook for me, nothing more.

"I meant, what's her size?"

I glanced down at my palm and remembered how perfectly her tits fit in my hands. The one image quickly turned into a movie of Luce in my head: her pretty pussy, that heart-shaped ass, her abandoned moans when she came.

"Never mind." She shook her head. "I'll figure it out."

"Make it a priority." I gestured toward the door. Luce and I needed privacy. "Before you leave, let Luce know breakfast is ready."

"Of course." She pursed her lips as she headed out the door. Presumably to fetch Luce.

My cock stiffened in my trousers, which was the main reason why I hadn't slept in my own suite last night. Until I figured out who Luce really was, I had to keep my distance. She intrigued me and my Spidey senses told me she was in some sort of trouble. Admittedly, she was also all kinds of trouble.

"I'm not hungry." She stood at the double doors with her arms over her chest.

The just-been-fucked hair was a good look on her. I was glad she'd thought to change out of that see-through leotard. Though the white undershirt was just as sexy on her. Her bright green eyes shot the usual daggers at me, and fuck me, if I hadn't been looking forward to seeing them again—seeing her in the light of day, just to make sure she was real.

"Sit down, Red."

The edge in my voice startled her. She inhaled and trod lightly toward me as her gaze zeroed in on the food. She was most definitely hungry. I picked up her plate and started her off with eggs and bacon. When she sat, her eyes watered as she brought a forkful of eggs to her mouth.

"When was the last time you ate?"

"Dinner." She sipped her coffee.

"Last night?"

"The night before."

I gripped the armrest. Why did I get the feeling her so-called fiancé had something to do with that? He sounded like a real asshole. Mostly because I wanted him to be, which reminded me that today I had plans to figure out exactly why she was dressed like a pet last night when she came to shoot me.

"You're a nurse. Where do you work?"

"That's none of your business."

The fire in her eyes made me want her even more. "I'm going to find out one way or another. You might as well tell me?"

"I don't have to tell you anything." She bit into a piece of bacon, then licked her shiny lips.

She wasn't eating because I had ordered her to. She obviously had a mind to escape. For that, she needed her strength. A hunger strike wouldn't serve her at all, so she swallowed her pride and ate. She was sexy and smart, and all I could think about was eating her pussy again.

"Sooner or later, you'll talk."

"You're wrong. My fiancé will find me and take me away from here sooner than you think." She drank her water and then grabbed a piece of waffle.

Her knight in shining armor was really getting on my nerves. Was she thinking about him last night when she came on my hand? Like a virus, the idea invaded my mind, and before I thought things through, I gripped Luce by the elbow and walked her back upstairs to my suite.

"You keep talking about this asshole like he's your whole life. But does he have a name?" I shouldered off my suit jacket. "Because I don't recall you screaming his name when you came last night. You were begging for me." I unbuttoned my dress shirt and let it hang open.

"What are you doing?" She shuffled back.

"Getting the answers I want."

In the lounging area near the window, I had left a box with the Crucible emblem on it. A standard issue package for anyone who agreed to visit the orgy floor of the nightclub. When I took it last night, I had envisioned a very different outcome with Luce. I never would've guessed I'd end up making use of these tools to get her to talk.

"Are you serious?" Her eyes widened as she followed my movements from the coffee table back to the bed.

Yet again, another thing that didn't add up with her. She wasn't appalled by the contents of the box. In fact, I would venture to say she recognized the items inside. I started with the jute rope. She didn't even flinch when I tied one of her wrists. "You've done this before?"

"Bite me." She pursed her lip.

"Later." I wanted to kiss her, but that would sidetrack my plans.

So instead, I tied both her wrists to the headboard. She kneeled awkwardly on the pillows as she tried to figure out how to best keep from falling forward. When she coiled herself against the corners, I reached for her ankles and pulled her down onto her back.

"You think this is going to make me want to talk to you?"

She kicked her legs to free herself from my grip, and in the process, flashed me that pretty pussy of hers.

"Maybe not." I reached into the box and picked up the vibrator with the biggest top.

The light buzz froze her in place. Her lips parted, and I could almost see all the scenarios playing in her mind's eye. "That's your plan? Make me come until I answer all your questions?"

A wide grin pulled at my lips as her cheeks turned a bright pink while she labored to catch her breath. I bet she was wet too. I braced a hand inside her thigh and applied the slightest pressure with the dildo. Her hips bucked off the bed—not away from me, toward me.

"What's his name?"

"Bite me."

Taking my time, I braced a knee on the mattress and inched toward her. Her breath hitched when she realized where I was headed. I buried my face in her pussy and moved the vibrator to her ass.

She rewarded me with a sweet moan that sounded something like my name. I nibbled the inside of her thigh as I worked my way toward her clit.

"Mr. Buratti?" Marie's voice filtered through the door.

"You gotta be fucking kidding me." I growled. "I'm in the middle of something very important."

"You have a visitor, sir." The annoyance in her tone was hard to miss. "It's Don Valentino."

"Fuck my life." I tossed the vibrator on the bed and stood to fix my shirt.

Luce brought her legs together, panting into her shoulder. She'd been so close to coming. If the daggers she was shooting my way were any indication, her pent-up desire had turned to pure frustration. I knew the feeling well.

"Be a good girl, Red, and stay put."

The last time I said that to her, she took off without a trace. But not today. She was mine now. And she wasn't going anywhere.

"What?" She yanked at the ropes. "You can't leave me here."

"This won't take long." I took in the sight of her with her bare ass and long legs sprawled on my duvet. Then, with my balls aching like hell, I left the room.

Rex better have a real good reason for interrupting my day.

I strode out of the room and met Marie halfway down the stairs. "Where is he?"

"In the library."

"You rarely leave your ivory tower." I strolled inside and shut the door behind me. "What happened?"

"I went by your office, and you weren't there." Rex sat behind my desk.

In the past year or so, we had managed to rekindle our childhood friendship. But this almighty act of his would never sit right with me. "I had a personal matter to tend to this morning. You're in my seat."

"I know." He typed fast on the iPad in front of him. "Remember how last night we couldn't figure out why Liam was so pissed after he saw you?"

"Maybe he didn't like my handsome face." I shrugged.

Who the fuck cared about Liam Walsh right now? I had Luce waiting for me upstairs.

"Well, it turns out, he recognized you." He turned the screen around to show me a scene I knew well. "Our guys checked the street that morning and again later that night. They assured me there were no cameras, hidden or otherwise."

I glared at the feed of me shoving a line into the gas tank, pushing the car toward the Irish pub, and then lighting it up. "This won't hold in court."

"I'm not worried about the police. Walsh now thinks you're with the New York Faction."

"He's not wrong. I mean they answer to us, to the Society."

"That's not the point." Rex rubbed his forehead. "What's with you today? Do you not see what's going on here? Our element of surprise is gone. That ten-million-dollar carrot we were dangling in front of him means nothing now. He knows it was all just smoke and mirrors to keep him occupied and away from Hell's Kitchen."

"Can't we just shoot the guy and be done with it?" I licked Luce's taste off my lips.

"Has that worked in the past? I'd like to think we have learned something in these last one hundred years. I wanted this dispute over territory resolved without any more bloodshed."

"Right." I perched myself on the edge of my desk, still glaring at the scene playing on repeat. "You promised the sweet Caterina we'd have peace."

Rex narrowed his eyes at me. Shaking his head, he stood and walked around, so we were face to face. "Why the lack of interest all of a sudden? Wait, I recognize that glossy look in your eyes. You have a woman waiting for you upstairs."

"Exactly. And I'd like to get back to what we were doing before you so rudely interrupted us." I stopped the video on the iPad and shut down the app. When I did a pair of familiar eyes stared back at me.

"You know what? You go back to your personal matter. I'll figure this out on my own." He grabbed his iPad.

"Wait. Who was the woman in the picture?"

"Who?" He glanced down at his device. "Oh, her. Luce O'Brien. She's Walsh's fiancé." He released a breath. "I did some digging on her to see if she would be a good asset for us but came back empty. She's one of them. She would never lift a finger to help us."

He rambled on about how he had his hacker dig up information on her. He'd hoped for a dirty secret but got nothing. She was clean and about to be married. Bit by bit, the realization of who Luce was washed over me like a bucket of ice water.

Now her words made so much sense. Now I understood why she wasn't scared when she found out I was with the Italian mafia, why she called me her enemy, and more importantly, why she thought I had killed her father. At first, I'd assumed her father had had a run-in with one of our guys. Maybe he owed money or some other bullshit. I didn't deal with day-to-day operations.

"Luce O'Brien," I repeated the name. "He's twice her age."

"She seemed fine with it."

"What? You met her in person?"

"Yes, last night when you were running late. She came to the meeting with Walsh. You didn't see her when you walked in?"

"No, I didn't." I did way more than set my eyes on her. *Fuck me.* So, Liam Walsh was Luce's knight in shining armor? What the hell did she see in him? "The old man did good."

"Yeah, he's very proud of her." He stuffed his hands in the

pockets of his trousers. "He said it was an arranged marriage. Even went out of his way to say she was pure."

"Pure? Like a virgin?" I rolled my eyes. "He's obviously overcompensating for something."

"He is. There has to be a way to use that against him."

"I was talking about his dick, Rex."

"He's insecure about something. We need to figure out what that is and use it to our advantage."

"Yeah, he's insecure about his small dick."

"What the fuck is going on with you? First you can't be bothered with Walsh, and now you're obsessed with how well endowed he is."

Rex wasn't wrong in that. Why the hell did I care if Walsh was Luce's future husband? Why did I feel like punching a wall with his face in front of it at the mere thought of his hands all over her perky tits? Why did she have to be his? *Well, too bad.* She was with me now. Fuck Walsh. I wasn't going to let her go.

A smile tugged at my lips. Was the old man boasting? Or was he telling the truth? Luce was a virgin? No wonder she acted as if she'd never been touched before because she hadn't. And to think that I almost sent it all to hell last night and fucked her brains out. She pretty much begged me to after I made her come. I thought of her waiting for me upstairs, tied to my bed, with nothing on but my undershirt.

Oh Luce. You should've told me who you were when you had the chance.

What was I going to do with her now, my little virgin?

"I have to go. I wanted to warn you in person. Walsh knows who you are. He might come after you." Rex swung the door open and then stood very still as if he'd come face to face with some wild animal. "What the fucking fuck, Santino?"

"Right." I walked past him and placed myself between him and Luce. "Luce, this is Rex. Rex, you remember Luce?" I pressed my lips to the shell of her ear. "If Marie helped you get out, she will answer to me."

"She didn't." Her gaze darted between Rex and me as she connected the dots.

That's right, sweetheart. We're all mobsters here.

"He kidnapped me," Luce blurted out as soon as she got over the shock of seeing Rex.

"She shot me first." I crossed my arms over my chest and winced. "Almost broke my ribs in the process."

"Santino." Rex's tone was laced with warning. "Whatever you're thinking, no."

"Too late for that." I stood tall, glowering at him. King or not, Rex wasn't leaving here with Luce. She was mine. "She's not leaving."

"Why? Because she tried to kill you?" He pinched the bridge of his nose. "When your dad and I asked you to find a wife, we didn't mean this."

"What? No. I have no intention of marrying her. But I can't let her go. She might come back and finish the job."

"Jesus fuck. Listen to yourself. Who's thinking with his dick now?" He raked a hand through his hair, eyeing Luce with interest.

"You couldn't resist throwing that word back in my face, huh?" I shook my head. Not too long ago, I had said the same thing to him when he put his own life on the line to save Caterina's.

"We're at the brink of war with the Irish and you thought it would be a good idea to kidnap the boss's wife?"

"Fiancée," I corrected.

"No harm done." Luce stepped in front of me, pushing me out of the way like I was some willful child. "If you could just give me a ride home, I'll make sure my family rewards you for your kindness."

Rex actually nodded at Luce's nonsense.

"I don't think so." I gripped her upper arm possessively. Rex had to understand I wasn't fucking around here. "She's not leaving. She shot me. She deserves to be punished for it."

"Listen to yourself, Santino. This is just a convoluted scheme you came up with to get what you want from her." Rex prowled toward me. "If you want to get laid, come to the club. Plenty of women there would jump at the opportunity to fulfill the need."

"She stays."

"I don't have time for this. You know very well what's at stake here. Send her back. If you don't, you'll have to deal with me." He raised his voice.

Behind me, Luce whimpered like a scared mouse. I brought her closer to me to show her that as long as she was with me, she'd be safe—from Rex, Walsh, or anyone else.

"Thanks for stopping by." I gestured toward the door.

"Ten days, Santino."

CHAPTER 15
The Enemy of My Enemy

LUCE

"Irish mob? You're fucking Irish mob?" Santino slammed the door as soon as Rex left.

I wanted to run after him and get a guarantee that he would make good on his ultimatum to Santino. I had to go home to my brother and my crew. The longer I stayed in New York, the more I realized how much danger my Red Wolves were in. Liam had angered the Italian mafia in New York and Chicago. Even with all the men at his disposal, he couldn't fight two gang wars at once.

"The client you didn't trust, the one you met with last night, that was Liam?" My head was still reeling from everything Rex had said. Somehow, as powerful, and as filthy rich as Santino was, Rex had some sort of control over him. "Rex is a mobster too?"

"Yes." He glared at me. "Answer my question."

"Yes."

"Are you an assassin for the Irish? Did Walsh send you to

kill me?" He prowled toward me. His chest rose and fell so slow, like he was holding his breath in between exhales.

I shuffled back on instinct. Last night, after I shot him, he was annoyed, angry—but this, this was something new—he had murder in his eyes.

"Red." His tone was laced with warning.

As much as I didn't want to tell him about me, I didn't know how far he'd go to make me talk. He was a killer. I had no doubt he would hurt me to get what he wanted. I opted for a half-truth because I wasn't ready to tell Santino, or anyone else for that matter, what Liam turned me into.

"No, he had nothing to do with it. I came here on my own."

"Don't defend him. That will get you nowhere with me." He stepped toward me.

I put more distance between us, even after I hit the bottom step of the grand staircase. The cold floor on my feet reminded me that I wasn't home, that even if the suite upstairs felt like a refuge, it wasn't. I had nowhere to run.

With shaky legs, I climbed the stairs slowly, keeping my gaze locked onto his. I imagined being in a forest, dimly lit by the moonlight, with a wild animal chasing after me. If I ran, his instinct would kick in. So, I moved as if I were climbing through mud.

"Is Walsh the fiancé you'd been waiting for all day?" He gripped the banister and started his ascent.

From my vantage point, his wide shoulders took up most of the space. While I tried to come up with a response, I missed a step and fell on my ass. What could I say to make him go back to the version of him from last night, when punishment in the form of orgasms was all he wanted? "What do you want from me?"

"The Goddamn truth. First time I met you, you seemed lost. You intrigued me. I wanted to know what happened to you. But then when I saw you again, you had changed. You looked at me like I was your last meal. Except the whole time, you've been Walsh's pet."

I opened my mouth to deny it.

"Don't lie."

The threat in his words sent a shock of adrenaline through me. "We're engaged to be married."

"Did he fuck you?"

"What?" I pulled myself up. "That's none of your business."

"You keep saying that." A wicked smirk pulled at his lips. "Has that old man been in that little cunt of yours?"

"Fuck off." I swung around to run away from him but slammed against the hallway wall.

He had me cornered. This entire time he had been leading me back to his suite. He could go to hell. With a quick glance toward his door and then the small space between him and the top of the stairs, I bolted toward the front door.

His arm snaked around my waist as he lifted me up. I kicked and screamed while he carried me back to his bedroom and dropped me on the bed. The pieces of rope on the duvet rubbed against my bare ass, and my pussy throbbed in anticipation.

Last night had been a foolish mistake because now I knew what could be, how it felt to orgasm, and how good Santino was at it. He braced a knee on the edge of the mattress. His dress shirt was still open, and his hard pecs and abs were on full display. I scooted away from him, but he grabbed my ankle and pulled me back, so I was caged between his thighs.

My knee jerk reaction was to shove him away. Another mistake. His hot skin under my touch sent tiny flutters of desire to my core. If he looked now, he'd see how swollen and wet with need he'd made me.

"Jesus, Red." He held both my wrists over my head with one hand, while his other rested on my neck. "I'm trying to understand our situation." The strain in his voice, but mostly the big bulge in his pants, told me he was at his limit too.

"No."

"No, what?" He pressed his body to mine.

"We didn't have..." I peered into his dark eyes. They softened a little, which made his handsome features stand out. The man was beautiful. It was so hard to look away and break the spell. "We didn't do it."

"Sex? You didn't have sex?"

That one word put all kinds of images in my head—most of them came from our time in the bathtub and then this bed.

"No sex." Those two words were my most intimate confession.

"Hmm." He touched his nose to mine. "Last night was your first orgasm?"

For some reason, I was embarrassed to tell him he was the first one to make me come. Telling him Liam and I were not intimate was one thing, but admitting I was a virgin, and beyond that, I had never touched myself, that he was the first and only one to make me come was too much.

I didn't want him to have that over me, or for us to have that kind of indelible connection. Of course that was already a thing between us, something I would carry with me for the rest of my life, but he didn't need to know that.

"Red." His fingers drifted from my neck, over my hard nipple, my stomach, and then, settled on my mound. "Answer me, yes or no." He drew circles around my clit, slathering it with my own juices.

"Ahh." I let my head fall back.

Greedy, I was greedy and selfish and wanton. In this moment, I didn't care about anything. I wanted to experience that same explosion from last night all over again. I thought that if I came once that would be enough, that I would be able to move on and get back on track with what I came to New York City to do. Though right now, I couldn't remember what that was.

"Well?" He stopped.

The absence of his hand gave me vertigo, like standing on the edge of a steep ravine. It hurt. "Well, what?" Then I recalled his question. If I answered, I was sure he would help me find the release I was aching for. The logical part of me told me I should demand he let me go. But the greedy part of me, the bigger part of me that wanted to feel alive again, won over. "Yes, it was."

He slid his fingers into my folds until he reached my entrance.

Oh, the sensation spread to every inch of my body.

"Are you a virgin, then?"

"Yes." I panted a breath. "It hurts."

"I know." He pressed his lips to the shell of my ear. "I can make it all better."

I nodded, and he rewarded me with long, rough strokes along my pussy. In the next beat, his weight lifted off me, and my wrists were free. The agony I felt struck me deep in my chest. I didn't want him to leave me like this. He towered over me, and his dark gaze shifted to the spot between my legs.

"We didn't finish before, did we?" He bent down and pulled gently on a strand of my hair, letting the curl wrap around his palm. Then he shifted his attention to my right breast to pinch my nipple through the soft fabric of the under-shirt—his undershirt. "I didn't finish eating your little cunt. And now that I know the truth, I want it even more. To hell with all of them."

He picked me up by the waist and set me high up so my mound would be in his face and then his mouth latched onto it. By the time his tongue broke past my folds and found my clit, I was ready to explode.

I fisted his soft hair, and we fell into a familiar rhythm that shouldn't be. We weren't lovers or even friends. He tongued my entrance, cupping my ass and rubbing my clit all at once until I came. This time, it was hard and raw—uninhibited. The waves of pleasure shot through me like wisps of fire that burned through everything it touched until there was nothing left.

"I'm right here, Red," he whispered on my neck, as if I had called for him.

Did I?

He lay there on top of me with one leg between my thighs. His whole body trembled as if he could barely contain his need for me. Slowly, I slid my hand over his muscled shoulder and then into his hair. When his breathing returned to normal, he lifted his head to look at me.

"Why are you marrying him?" His deep voice touched

something I didn't recognize inside my chest. It threw the beating of my heart out of sync, and it hurt.

"I love him."

"You're a terrible liar." He swiped his thumbed over my too sensitive bud. "So let me re-phrase. What were the terms of your contract?"

I gasped because I didn't think he would know. "How do you know about that?"

"Rex told me." He shifted off me to lie on his side next to me.

Even though I was free to move, I didn't even try. My body wouldn't have obeyed anyway. So, I glanced away from him, and let the usual shame wash over me. Yeah, I sold my body to the devil in exchange for help—help that came too late.

"Walsh boasted about it during our meeting. Of course, that was before I got there. I was busy and showed up late." He flashed a charming smile when I turned to face him.

He had been late to the meeting because of me. When he got to the VIP loft of the Crucible, I was the only one there. And then I made him even more late.

"He will come for me, you know."

"I know. If I were him, I would turn this entire city upside down to find you." He ran his index finger over my bottom lip.

The scent of my arousal on his fingers put a thought in my head. I blurted it out before I had the sense to keep it to myself. "Are you going to fuck me?"

"I haven't decided." He chuckled. "I had plans for you. But am I willing to start a war to get what I want?" He ghosted his lips over mine. "That's the ten-million-dollar question, isn't it? Because I do want you. I want to bury my cock so deep inside you, you'll never think about anyone else but me."

His words should have been appalling to my ears. I should be insulted that he had zero respect for my engagement to another man. I shouldn't be so turned on by him. He sat up and started buttoning his shirt. Instinctively, my hand reached out to stop him, but I caught myself and rolled away from him instead. "You can't keep me here."

Slowly, he rose to his feet. Impressive, imposing—even those words were too trifling to describe him. His feral energy was all-consuming. I was trapped, a wounded animal who'd fallen prey to a predator.

He cupped the side of my neck, pressing slightly on my throat with his thumb. "You don't know me, Red. You have no idea what I'm capable of. If I haven't fucked your brains out its because I'm not the type who thinks with his dick."

Before I could protest, he bent down and captured my mouth with his. His kiss was an extension of him, savage, raw, and hypnotizing. I had the thought of pushing him away as I opened to welcome his tongue and its wicked thrusts.

He mimicked the same movements he had done to my folds and the entrance to my hole. I squeezed my legs together to ease the heat building in my pussy. I wanted to scream because I knew he wouldn't offer me relief this time.

When he pulled away, he sucked in his bottom lip as if getting one final taste. His gaze skimmed down from my face to my bare feet in one languid sweep. Then, he turned around and left.

I sat on his bed, lost, and so aroused.

At some point later that day, Marie came back with several bags of clothes, toiletries, and a tray with a bagel sandwich and fruit. I ate it all. I wasn't going to starve myself just to piss him off.

As much as I hated to accept the clothes Marie brought, because it all came from him, I decided to swallow my pride, shower, and put on a decent shift dress.

I sat near the window and watched the sun go down. When the stars shone brightly in the sky and the buildings came alive with twinkling lights, I decided to go out onto the terrace. The cool air and soft piano music that played somewhere below me reminded me of home. I stopped to listen to the sad tune, something about it was erotic and so alive. I sat on the lounge chair and thought of Dad, Ronan, and what I had to do next.

Santino was Liam's enemy.

The enemy of my enemy is my friend.

Was that true? If I asked, would Santino, the Italian mobster, help me save my crew from the Chicago Outfit? Why would he go against his own people to help the Irish though? No, Santino would never do anything that didn't serve him. He had no reason to rid us of the Italians back home.

Regardless of how my body reacted to his touch, Santino was still one of *them*. He only knew how to take, with little regard to the people around him. Santino wasn't the answer. Sooner or later, Santino was going to let his guard down. I needed to be ready when that happened and use the opportunity to escape.

CHAPTER 16
Fishy As Fuck

SANTINO

I glared at Luce's photo on Rex's iPad. She was dressed in the same white gown she wore to the Crucible Masquerade, which posed an interesting question. Rex had eyes and ears all over the city. How was this the only picture he had of her? Was it because she was recently engaged? Or because Walsh was that good at keeping her hidden?

My gaze moved down from her stunning face to the globes grazing the top of her dress. A bit of that pink glitter dusted her clavicle. I sat back to ease the pressure in my pants because I knew that powder was all over her perfectly round nipples and her pretty cunt.

Since Rex's visit three days ago, I'd been trying to figure out Luce's role in Walsh's plan to take over Hell's Kitchen. That she was an assassin for him, sent to kill me, made sense to me. The part I couldn't get behind was why Luce would agree to marry that old man, who obviously had some kinky tastes. I snapped the iPad shut. A lump churned in my stomach every time I thought of Luce as his pet. I wasn't an idiot; she was dressed in that leotard for him. Everything about how she was dressed and prepped screamed submissive. But I knew she was anything but.

That was the part that intrigued me about her. The fire in her eyes and her eventual surrender had become a drug to me. I hadn't even fucked her yet and I couldn't stop thinking about her.

"Mr. Buratti?" My assistant Lia stepped sideways into my line of sight. "Er, your next appointment is here." She gestured toward her desk outside my office, where one of Rex's guys stood waiting.

"Let him in."

Finally, I was going to get some answers.

"Don Buratti." He put out his hand, then took it back and did a quick bow.

"Don Buratti is my father. Sit."

"Of course." He swallowed, placing his laptop on my desk. "I have the information you requested."

"How did you get this feed? You told us that day we didn't have to worry about cameras."

If someone had sent it to Rex to intimidate us, I couldn't well trust its contents. In the aftermath of the assault, we were so concerned with getting out alive, we didn't bother to look back to see what kind of devastation we left behind. At least, I didn't. But now that the proverbial dust had settled and Walsh knew we were Italian mob, the time for shifting our tactics had come. I needed to know everything that happened that night.

"There were no cameras in the vicinity, sir. This was shot with a phone on the scene." He sat closer to the edge of his seat. "That is, Walsh's system is sophisticated, but not enough that I can't beat it. Erm, my theory is that someone came in after you arrived and recorded what you did. The video will hold in court."

"I don't give a shit about that."

We had enough cops, lawyers, and judges on our payroll. I could shoot someone on national tv and get away with it.

"I want to know why this footage exists. I don't like that Walsh thinks he has something to hold over my head."

"I think that's what happened. He had someone hide and wait to capture what you did."

"He didn't know what I was going to do. Hell, I didn't know." I pointed at his screen, which was playing the scene over and over. "This was a spur of the moment kind of thing. We needed a diversion. That aside, how did you come by it?"

"Don Valentino asked me to hack their system and gather all the information I could. I ran into the video as part of the database sweep. I wasn't looking for it. We got lucky."

"Hmm. There's no such thing as luck." I sat back on my chair. "What else? Do you have the names of the deceased?"

After Rex kindly informed me that Luce was engaged to Walsh, it didn't take me long to put two and two together. If I added her responses, as short as they were, I had a pretty good idea of what happened to Luce's Dad. The old man made a deal with his buddy, Walsh. He sold off his daughter. I knew that much, though I had no idea what Walsh offered in return.

Luce landed in New York a little over two weeks ago, which means so did her dad. That timing added up. When Luce accused me of killing him, she hadn't mentioned if he'd died in the city or Chicago. But if she assumed it was me, he was obviously killed here.

"Oh fuck. Now it makes sense. Damn it," I said mostly to myself.

"Sir."

"She saw this video."

"Who?"

"Never mind. Was there an O'Brien on the list?"

"Yes, sir. Two." He turned his laptop around to show me the list, which consisted of five names.

Jesus Christ. How did Rex manage to keep that major incident under wraps?

"No descriptions or birthdays?" I was looking for someone old enough to be Luce's dad.

"No, but erm."

"Out with it."

"We have access to the morgue. We could take a look."

"You're good." I chuckled. "What's your name?"

"John, sir."

"Okay, John. We're going now. You can fill me in on the way there." I stood and called for Lia, who immediately rushed into my office. "Get my car."

"Right away."

By the time we made it downstairs, my driver Leo was waiting for us. I climbed in the back seat while John, the hacker, gave him instructions on where to go and how to gain entrance to a private garage connected to the building.

When the SUV peeled off the curb, John shifted in the passenger seat to face me. "The woman with Walsh, we've only seen her a handful of times after we set up surveillance on Walsh's place in the city.

"He has more than one place?"

"Yes, sir. He spends most of his time in the Hamptons. But

he visits his apartment in the city almost daily. That's where we spotted the woman. She left with him once to attend the party at the Crucible."

"That's when you snapped her picture?"

"Correct. Her face was hidden most of the time, but we managed to get it. Anyway, the second time she left, she was in her cloak again and alone. We haven't seen her since. We lost her trail that night."

Of course they did. Luce left with me that night. So, Walsh had kept her tucked away since she arrived. No wonder I couldn't find her. After two weeks of looking for her, I had started to think that maybe I had imagined meeting her at the airport. The Celtic cross pendant was the only proof I had that she existed. Now I had way more than that. I shifted in my seat when my cock stiffened.

"Don Valentino wanted us to keep an eye on her. He thought she might be a way to get to Walsh."

"I wouldn't count on that." If I had any say in it, Luce was never going back to that asshole. "What else do you have?"

"He's made deals with the Bratva. Sex trafficking. Turns out the brothel we dismantled a few years back was his brain-child. But that was before, when he was a soldier. Now he's the boss."

"New money." I glanced out the window. "I knew he was overcompensating for something."

"His crew is divided. Some think he killed the old boss to take over."

"That's usually how that works, isn't it?"

"Yeah." He swallowed again.

This guy needed to get his shit together. He seemed afraid of his own shadow.

"He has big plans for expansion."

"We know that. He wants Hell's Kitchen."

"Sir." My driver interrupted. "We're here."

"Right. Let's get this over with." As much carnage as I'd seen in my lifetime, dead bodies didn't sit well with me. Too much of a reminder of all my sins.

As soon as the SUV pulled up to a side door inside the garage, a woman in a white coat appeared to meet us. "Welcome, Mr. Buratti. I'm Sofia." She offered me her hand with a huge grin on her face.

"Show us the way, Sofia." I smiled at her.

Her eyes widened as she licked her lips. "Right through here." She gestured for us to go inside, into a long corridor.

The stench of ammonia assaulted my nostrils. In my world, dead people and bleach always went hand in hand. I stayed alert, keeping my gaze on the doors on either side. The hospital beds along the dirty white walls made me nervous—the bulge could be a body, or it could be guns. I turned to face Leo, cocking an eyebrow that said, I didn't like this. Question everything, trust no one, that was how we stayed alive.

"She's with us," he responded.

"Don Valentino makes sure my family and I are comfortable. I'm here for whatever you need, Mr. Buratti." Her gaze dropped to my chest then back to my face.

My life was so much simpler when I didn't have a certain redhead clouding my mind. "I need to see the two O'Briens."

"Right." She pointed to the door at the far end. "Here we are."

The putrid smell intensified once we were inside huddled around the two metal tables. The first O'Brien was a man about my age, late twenties—too young to be Luce's dad and too old to be her twin brother. For some reason, I expected someone pretty.

When she revealed the next body, my chest tightened. This had to be her dad—old man in his early sixties, red hair, oval face. Even with his grayish skin, I could see the resemblance.

"I thought he died in the explosion. No burns." I pointed at his torso.

"Shotgun wound." She outlined the area below the autopsy sutures. "Three bullets in the belly."

"Well, that's good news." I patted John's back. "The old man didn't die at the Irish Pub we blew up."

"Oh, I'm sure of that." Sofia picked up a clipboard. "He was killed a couple of weeks before that day. Roughly, it's hard to pinpoint an exact day and time."

"Then why was he on the list?"

John stepped in. This was his area of expertise. "He was found in the wreckage, sir. Both the hospital list and Walsh's data confirmed this."

"Hmm. Well, I'm no detective. But this is fishy as fuck."

"Agreed, sir."

"It's been days since the altercation at the pub. Why are they still here?" I was thinking of Luce and how lost and confused she seemed the day she came to shoot me.

"There's an ongoing investigation." Sofia pulled the sheet over Luce's dad. "All five bodies are on lockdown until the authorities release them."

"You mean, until Rex decides that keeping them here no longer serves our purposes?"

"Exactly." Sofia nodded twice. "The cops haven't even come by. You're the first to visit and ask questions."

"Imagine that."

"I'll let you know if anything changes. You know, if the investigation gets going."

"Do that." I patted her upper arm. "You've been a great help."

"So, what did I know so far?" I asked when John fell in step next to me.

"Walsh wants to expand into Hell's Kitchen." John checked his iPad.

"He tried and failed. But then he called for a meeting with the New York Faction. We showed up, he pulled a gun on one of our own, and we, rightly so, retaliated with fire. Now there's evidence that I was responsible for the explosion—and a dead body that doesn't belong on the scene."

A body that happened to be the father of his fiancée.

"Correct, sir."

On the ride back, I decided to go straight home. I still had work to do, but nothing I couldn't finish at the penthouse. Not to mention, I wanted to see her. In truth, I wanted to do way more than that. I'd stayed away from her for the past three days because I wanted to follow my own advice and stop thinking with my dick.

The result was that instead of gaining clarity and focus on what I had to do, I had spent nights and a good part of my days thinking about her, her glittery tits, and that little moan of surprise she did every time she came on my hand.

Though I had to admit that today wasn't a complete bust. Even if I still had no clue who killed Luce's dad. I, at least, could prove to her that it wasn't me. Someone murdered her dad and tried to pin it on me. That someone had to be Walsh. But why would he want to off his future father-in-law? Especially if they had an agreement between them.

He had to know that the Chicago crew would come after him—Irish or not. Hell, he would have to know that Luce would come after him. If she lived with him, she would have no problem slitting his throat while he slept. I had no doubt about that. Luce wasn't the murderous type. But I remembered the look in her eyes when she came after me. Her family was everything to her. That was something I understood well. But did Walsh?

Thinking of Walsh dead in his own bed put a smile on my face. I opened the door to the penthouse and felt a sense of relief. Partly, because she was here. And also, because I had good news. Well, good for me anyway.

Suddenly, the foyer and the cathedral ceilings didn't feel small and suffocating. The natural light filtering through the tall windows put a whimsical glow in the living room, especially over the grand piano. The music helped me think. I sauntered toward it while I removed my suit coat and rolled up my sleeves. Sitting on the bench with the view of the city in front of me, I began to play a tune I'd had dancing in my head lately—or rather, since I met Red.

I pictured her now tied up in my bed, wearing nothing but my undershirt.

The information I had gathered in the past few days hadn't exactly led me to a conclusion that would appease Rex. To keep the peace with the Irish, he wanted me to send Luce back to Walsh, which I would not be doing. Not now and certainly not in another seven days. That fucker killed Luce's dad. I had no proof, but all I had do was keep digging. And then I would make him pay for putting Luce through that kind of grief.

For now, I had to make sure I wasn't running into an ambush and Luce wasn't on Walsh's side. *Fuck.* She couldn't be. That would make no sense at all. I snapped the piano cover shut with both hands. Why couldn't she give me the answers I needed? Why lie to me?

The bench scraped the marble floor as I shot to my feet. I didn't like puzzles. Tonight, she'd have to give me what I wanted.

CHAPTER 17
Don't Jump

LUCE

Earlier today, after I'd gone through Santino's entire suite, bathroom, and closet, looking for something that might help me escape, I ventured out into the rest of the penthouse. Marie wasn't home to stop me, and neither was he. For good measure, I checked the front door. Yeah, his guards were still there. My plan when I came downstairs had been to look for a way out, but somehow, I ended up in his library instead.

He had a lot of books. Some were textbooks on financial investments, fiction—the murder kind, and poetry. The one with a series of poems called my attention because Mom had that same edition. She'd let me read it before bedtime. Dad would always complain that I was too young for that kind of reading.

I ambled along the wall, running my fingers over the spines of the books, while I surveyed all the knickknacks and framed photos on the built-in bookcases. I stared at the one with

Santino and a woman that could be his mom. He looked so handsome when he smiled. Good thing he didn't do that often.

On his desk, I found a bunch of papers that meant nothing to me. When I pulled open the top drawer though, my blood boiled instantly. I thought I had lost my mother's Celtic cross pendant the night he kissed me at the Crucible—the thief. I fixed the delicate chain around my neck and fixed the clasp shut. In the same drawer, I found a ring with a black stone setting that had the profile of a wolf carved on it. Did he steal that too?

I read the engraving on the inside of the band. *Fac Fortia et Patere*. No idea what that meant. For a beat, I considered taking it just to spite him—not because I wanted a memento. Shaking my head, I tossed it back in and shut the drawer. This wasn't helping me. I needed to find a way out.

I made my way to the window arch beyond his desk. The middle of it had a door that opened onto a terrace. My heart raced in anticipation. This could be it. I peered down with the wind blowing hard on my face. We were forty some floors up, climbing down wasn't an option. But what if I could walk across to the apartment next door? I rushed back inside and grabbed one of the club chairs.

Then I froze. The piano music that had lulled me to sleep for the past three nights was playing in the living room. I wasn't alone anymore. I darted to the library entrance and opened the door just enough so I could peek through it, but all I could see was the grand staircase. I wedged my body forward a little more, and then, I saw him. Santino at the grand piano fully lost in the piece he was playing.

I stood there and watched for a whole minute. His presence was so magnetic, my body craved to be near him. Damn him. I closed the door and darted back to the terrace with the chair in tow. With trembling limbs, I climbed to the top of the wall.

The ground was so far down, it made me nauseous. Between the gushing wind and the cacophony of cars honking and tires screeching below, I felt dizzy. I leaned on the cement wall and ordered my legs to inch over to the other side.

"Red, don't jump."

I glanced over my shoulder. Would Santino give chase if I walked across the ledge to the next window? Maybe he was afraid of heights and wouldn't come after me. He was too fast though. Before I could make up my mind, he spun me around and pulled me down by the waist. I crashed into his hard chest as he carried me back inside.

He put me down but didn't let go. His heart drummed fast against my cheek. If I didn't know any better, I'd say he was worried I'd fall over. "What the hell were you thinking?" He spoke after several minutes.

His scent made me dazed with want. I pushed him away, but he held me tightly. "I was thinking that I needed to get away from you."

"There's nothing out there."

"I was hoping your neighbor would want to help me."

"Jesus, Red. This is the penthouse. I have no neighbors." He gripped my shoulders. "Sit down. We need to talk."

I stared at him with my mouth slightly open. This wasn't like me. Dad always said I was the prudent one, the one who thought things through, the one with her head on her shoulders. My brother Ronan was the wild card. I was the good daughter.

"I see you've been going through my things." He pointed to my necklace.

"You stole it from me."

"You dropped it when I kissed you." He reached for my face and swiped his thumb over my lips. "I was holding it for you."

I pulled away and did my best to ignore the effect his touch had on me.

"I saw your dad."

"What?" I shot to my feet. "Where?"

He blinked and took in a breath. "The morgue. I told you I was going to find out who killed him. I needed to see him."

My hands were so cold, I couldn't feel them. Tears streamed down my cheeks. Dad in the morgue made his death more real. Since I hadn't seen his body, a tiny part of me hoped Liam had lied to play a sick joke on me. I knew that was impossible. But the hope was still there, nonetheless. Now it was gone completely.

"I didn't kill him. And I can prove it."

"He died in an explosion you ignited." I glared at him with all the hate I could muster. "I saw you in the video. He was there in the window. And you plowed through it with a blazing car."

"Wait. What?" He furrowed his brows. "What do you mean you saw him there?"

"Liam showed me the surveillance feed. Dad was there. You were there. Then the explosion happened." I hit him in the chest. "You did that. You killed him."

How could he stand there and tell me he wasn't guilty when he was the one who started the fire? How could he cause so much devastation and then act like nothing happened? As if he were innocent. I hugged myself and swallowed the bitter taste in the back of my throat. Thinking about Dad and the fire, the screams, and all the shooting in the video made me feel sick. It all hurt too much.

"Your dad died from a gunshot wound. Two weeks before the explosion at the pub." He reached for the laptop on his desk and pulled up a document on the screen. "This is the autopsy."

"How did you get a hold of that? Liam couldn't even get me to see Dad."

"I'm not your average mobster."

I wiped my eyes, taking a long breath in. This was important. For the first time since I found out Dad was dead, I finally had some answers. I pulled the device toward me and sat on Santino's leather chair. My heart broke into a million pieces as I read the document. Most of it wasn't relevant, but one thing was very clear. The autopsy put Dad's time of death around the time I came to New York.

The irony wasn't lost on me. I was Santino's alibi. "And the video I saw?"

"My guess? It was tampered with. I can show you the original. It's been authenticated. I'm told it would hold in court." He leaned on the edge of the desk next to me with his legs stretched out in front of him. "I get the sense Walsh wanted you to think I did it."

"Why?" I blinked away my tears to focus on his face. "He doesn't know I know you—I mean," I stumbled on the phrase "know you" because Santino and I were way past merely being acquaintances.

"I didn't think about that." He shrugged. "I don't know how, but I know he's involved. He has to be."

If Dad didn't die in some gang war commotion, something bigger was at play here. I had to get back to my family. Without Dad, the crew would need a new leader. I bit my lower lip with my gaze fixed on his muscular thigh. Before I could overthink it, I placed my hand on it.

"Santino."

He exhaled loudly, reaching for my fingers.

"I need to go home. Even if I don't know who did this to Dad, this new information proves something bad is coming for my crew. I need to warn my brother. If he knew about Dad, he would've come looking for me and he hasn't. Please."

He tightened his hold on me. "No. You're not leaving this place."

"Why not?" I pulled away from him. "I believe you. You didn't kill Dad. So now we're good."

"No, we're not good. There's still the minor detail of your punishment. You know, for trying to kill me."

"People's lives are in danger."

"Don't care." He crossed his arms over his chest. "You're staying until I say otherwise."

Heat rose to my cheeks in anger. I hated that he had so much power and control over me.

"Liam will come for me, sooner than you think. And when he does, he's going to make you pay for keeping me here." I pushed him out of the way and strode past him toward the door.

Two steps in, he grabbed me by the waist and swung me around. My butt hit the edge of the desk as he braced both arms on either side of my hips to cage me in. Hot puffs of breath brushed my face as his voice boomed all around me.

"You're still betting on that old man? Even when he's obviously knee deep in the shit surrounding your dad's death? How can you be so naive?"

"He's my fiancé."

"Right. The knight in shining armor. Tell me, how much do virgin brides go for these days?"

I slapped him across the cheek. "You don't get to judge me."

"I'm not judging you. I'm trying to make you see the truth." He propped me up on the desk and wedged himself between my legs.

Our gazes locked. I panted a breath that matched his own. The intense look in his eyes softened and he lowered his head.

"There's a bigger picture here." He nuzzled my neck. "I thought I had a good grasp of it when I walked in, but you have a way to knock me off my center. Don't push my buttons, Red. You're not going to like what you get."

His body heat engulfed me like a cocoon. I melted into him, aching with desire all over again. He flipped me on my stomach and pressed his lips to the shell of my ear. "That's five." Five transgressions meant five spankings. I didn't bother to count which ones he was referring to. His sinful and warm tone traveled all the way to my core. It ignited a spark that was now familiar and so addictive to me.

Days had gone by since the first time he punished me. And I realized with horror that I wanted it again. I was being greedy, I knew that, because my desire for him helped no one's cause but my own selfish one.

"Do you understand why?" he whispered with his lips against my cheek.

I nodded.

He lifted my skirt and pulled down my drenched underwear, letting them fall around my ankles. "What was your deal with him?"

My whole body shook with anticipation. I needed the release only he could give me.

"That's six. Answer." He smacked me hard, letting his fingers linger near my throbbing pussy.

He had made a bunch of assumptions about my arrangement with Liam that were mostly right. But he wanted to humiliate me. He wanted me to say it aloud. "No."

"That's seven. Count." His palm met my ass twice more.

I mumbled a quick count to three, squeezing my legs together. My core was on fire now, my folds swollen from the vibrations that lingered there after each swat of his hand. He delivered three more blows, and then one more that landed mostly on my sex. I counted for him...four, five, six, seven. Holding out was only getting me more of his sweet torture, but no relief.

"Protection," I blurted out.

"What else?" He fisted the fabric of my dress on my lower back. "For you, I would've paid way more than that."

"Resources. Men, money to fight off the Chicago Outfit." I squeezed my eyes shut. I had sold my body and soul to the devil to save my family.

"What a noble cause." He stroked the length of my pussy with languid circular motions, spreading my juices all over, including my back entrance. He slid a finger there smoothly and easily. "I can tell you were a good pet for him."

"Please." I bit my lip to swallow my words. I hadn't meant to beg him. I was so close. I had no idea I could come like this, but it was happening. All the times Mrs. Jones made me wear a butt plug, I never felt anything. It was mostly awkward and

uncomfortable. I always assumed she did it to make me compli-
ant, to prove to me that she was in control. Now I realized, she
was prepping me for this. And omigod, it felt so good.

"Did he fuck you in the ass?" He pulled out a bit then
went inside again, slow and gentle.

"No."

"But he was going to? And you were ready for him."

"I think so. Yes." I couldn't hold it anymore, and he knew
that the slightest stimulation would make me come. What
more did he want from me? Why was he not finishing it?

"What else did he do?"

"Nothing."

He removed his hand from my ass. Tears of frustration
streamed down my face. I spun around and glared at him.

"Tell me." He pressed his body to me.

His trousers rubbed against my clit. This time I climaxed a
little, but not enough, not even close.

"I spent all my days in his sex dungeon, sleeping in a five
by three cage. He had a woman take care of me. She bathed me
and fed me when I was good." I released a breath. Saying it
aloud freed me from the days I'd spent in Liam's house. And
all the anger I felt toward Dad for putting me in that position.

"You agreed to that?" He cradled my head against his
chest.

"I didn't know what I was saying yes to." I glanced up
at him.

"And now? Do you know now?"

"I do."

He held my gaze for the longest time, then bent down to
capture my lips with his. His finger found my back entrance
again. He thrust his tongue in my mouth with harsh and steady

movements, similar to what his single finger was doing to my butthole.

His thumb rubbed my clit. And that was my undoing. Stars exploded behind my eyelids as an all-consuming orgasm ripped through my body, burning through every pore and every thought in my mind. I was floating as if the sensation was too much for my body to endure or for my brain to fully understand. How was this possible? How was it possible to feel like this? The room went dark, and I collapsed against his bare chest—spent and satiated.

"You can't keep doing this to me." I labored to catch my breath. My lungs hurt from the lack of oxygen. My heart drummed at an out of control and syncopated rhythm that was painful.

"You tried to kill me, Red. This is your punishment." He panted as he held me tighter.

I wasn't his captive.

Santino had made me a prisoner of my own depraved desires.

CHAPTER 18
Starting a War

SANTINO

"I can help you."

"What?" She lifted her gaze up to meet mine, leaving her hand on my chest just over my heart.

"Your Walsh problem. I can make him go away."

"You mean kill him?" She slid down the edge of my desk. With wobbly legs, she tried to step away from me, but she hadn't fully recovered from her orgasm, so she used me to steady herself. "You can't go around shooting people. Trust me, I know this. It won't bring Dad back."

Her soft touch all over me made it difficult to focus. My cock was so hard; it pulsated with frustrated desire. If I took her virginity now, Walsh would use it as an excuse to start a gang war with us. The problem was, I didn't see myself giving Luce up any time soon. But if she left him of her own accord... that would be a different deal.

"If only you'd figured that out before you shot me." I bent down to scoop her into my arms.

"If only." She let me carry her upstairs, and even took the opportunity to brush her lips on my pecs.

In my suite, I laid her down on the bed and went into the bathroom to wash up and get a wet towel for her. When I returned, she was still in some sort of sedated state. I got no complaints when I started cleaning her pussy and her thighs.

"Are you falling asleep?" I sat next to her and brushed a lock of hair off her face.

She shook her head no. "So much for saving myself."

So that was the thing that had her subdued. She was afraid of what Walsh would do if he found out she had sex with me. "In the most archaic sense, you're still a virgin."

"He's going to know either way." She brought her knees up into her chest. "You know that I was with you. That you..." Her words trailed off as her cheeks turned red.

Her shame shouldn't turn me on, but it did. "That I made you come?"

"Yeah, that."

"Why are you still thinking about going back to him?"

"Because we have a contract. My whole family, my crew, they'll suffer the consequences if I don't fulfill it. He could kill them all. It would be so easy too. All he has to do is let the Italians do his dirty work."

Last month, Rex had asked me to fly to Chicago and deliver a message to the crew there. But when I got there, no one seemed to know what I was talking about. They didn't take kindly to my presence there. The boss was sure I was there to undermine his authority.

He assured me his men had not mounted any kind of attack on the Irish. Back then, I had no reason to think they'd lie to me. I figured Rex had gotten bad information. But now I wasn't so sure.

I believed every word Luce said about the contract, her time with Walsh, and the threat her crew was under. So, what was really going on here? If the Chicago Outfit made a fool of me, they were about to find out the full extent of the Society's reach and power. I would make sure of it.

"Keeping Italians in line is sort of my area of expertise." I ran my thumb over her lips.

"I don't need your help. I need you to let me go. My brother is in danger. I know it."

"So, your brother is in trouble, but you're not? How does that work?"

"Whoever killed Dad—"

"Walsh."

"We don't know it was him." She glared at me.

The effects of her most recent climax were fully spent now. Her green eyes had that fire in them again. And that made me want to claim her, possess her.

"My gut tells me that whoever killed Dad might go after my brother. Especially, if that person is going to great lengths to plant Dad's body in a crime scene." She was mostly talking to herself now as if all the details of her father's death were finally making sense to her.

"If someone is coming for him, they're coming for you too, Red. What makes you think it wasn't Walsh?"

"He has nothing to gain from it. No revenge motives either. He was his future father-in-law."

Future father-in-law.

I didn't like the sound of that, but I supposed she was right. Walsh had no reason to retaliate. At least, he didn't then. Not to mention, his crew in Harlem was four times the size of Luce's gang. He had more territory, more men, more money. Killing a boss to take over his men seemed like too much work for very little pay. The Red Wolves were peanuts for him.

From what we knew of Walsh, he was new money looking to make a big splash. In a way, that made him a visionary, the kind to think outside the box. He even had the foresight to buy himself the most beautiful virgin bride.

"Either way, it's not safe for you out there. You're staying here."

"I'm confused." She sat farther up so she could press her back against the headboard. "Are you my jailer or my protector?"

"Both." I smirked at her.

"No." She glanced down at her hands, furrowing her brows. When she spoke again, it was mostly to herself. "Liam is my best bet. If I apologize, he'll understand. He has to."

For whatever reason, her words painted a very vivid image of her and Liam Walsh together—in a church getting married, his hands all over her, and the two of them fucking. I squeezed my eyes shut to chase the avalanche of images away. The idea of them together made me see red.

I cupped her face, digging my fingers into the nape of her neck. "He's no bet at all. Let alone the best."

"I have no other choice. If I marry him, he'll protect us."

Our gazes locked. The air in the room crackled with a raw charge. "You want him to be something he's not. He's not coming for you. I'm all you've got." I pressed my palm over the seam of her pussy.

"Santino." She rolled her head to the side, gripped my wrist, and pulled it toward her.

"Do you want me to stop?"

She bit her lower lip. Her body trembled as her arousal covered my fingers. I drew circles around her clit. With every pass, her little cunt plumped up with lust. I waited for her to beg me for it again. When her answer didn't come, I leaned in and freed her lip with my teeth, sucking on it gently until she let go.

I claimed her mouth with a desperate kiss and swallowed her moans. "Come on. Say it." I rubbed my erection against the side of her thigh. "I'm hungry for you."

She reached for my trousers and gasped in surprise. The first night she was here, she saw me naked. While I was in the bathtub, she spent a great deal of time stealing glances at my cock. I unbuckled my belt, and then, made quick work of my trousers, pulling them down until they were off, and I sprung out at full mast.

Her eyes widened, and she licked her lips. "I've never seen one before."

"Take it."

She lifted her eyes up at me. "Why?"

"Because you want to." I smirked.

She puffed out a breath. Her chest pressed against her top with every inhale. The seconds it took her to make up her mind felt like hours. But when she finally gripped me tight, I lost my damn mind. She felt so good. And in that moment, she sealed her fate.

Her index finger and thumb barely wrapped all the way around. With greedy eyes, she explored my length, the throbbing vein on the inside, and the shiny tip covered in pre-cum. The muscle below my navel tightened painfully. I wanted her so badly; I could barely keep myself in check.

Adrenaline infused with pent-up desire shot up my spine and chest. I didn't think it would be possible, but I got even harder. My mounting need had reached a boiling point. She felt it too because, in that moment, she squeezed me tighter and glanced up at me.

"You drive me crazy, Red."

"I know the feeling." She swiped the droplet off the tip of my cock and brought it to her tongue to taste it. Closing her eyes, she leaned toward me. "I want more."

"I will fuck that mouth of yours. But right now, I need to be inside you." I removed her dress and climbed into bed with her.

Her instincts took over and she let go, moving a leg along my side to welcome me in. "Hmm. What are you doing?" she whispered in my ear, fisting my hair.

"Starting a war." I braced a hand on the side of her face, while I used the other to rub my shaft on her pussy until it was coated in her juices. "Let's see how good of a pet you are."

"Does it hurt?"

"Only for a moment. I promise." I lined up against her back entrance and slid inside her hole.

She arched and lifted her tits up. While she got used to my size and the new sensation in her ass, I played with her breasts, kneading and knocking them together. When I lapped and sucked on her nipples, she rewarded me with one of her sweet moans.

"Santino." She ran her hands all over me, pulling me in.

"I'm here." I kissed her hard.

Her heated body relaxed on the mattress. She was ready. I began to move in and out of her, while I toyed with her swollen bud.

Soon, I would also claim her pretty cunt too, fill her up with my cum. But first, I wanted to show her that whatever her fiancé thought he'd bought wasn't real. It wasn't real because she was still technically a virgin, but she was mine in every way possible.

"You feel so fucking good." I increased the pace, going deeper into her perfect ass with each merciless thrust.

A few more strokes and she unraveled all over again, calling my name. Her climax was my undoing. My cocked throbbed in tandem with my heartbeat, as I pounded my seed into her. "Argh." I pumped hard against her butt cheeks until every wave of pleasure was spent.

No idea how it'd happened. But I was completely and utterly addicted to the way she came, the way she gave herself completely to the moment, her voice when she begged. Every time she seemed surprised that her body could feel this much euphoria.

In truth, so was I.

I had never orgasmed like this—it was raw, feral, and all-consuming—and it stoked the flames of my obsession for her.

"Red." I collapsed on top of her.

"Is it always like this?" She blew out a breath.

"No."

Five minutes later, I moved first. I strode to the en-suite bathroom to clean up and grab another wet hand towel for her. This time, I ran it under hot water. Her eyes fluttered open when I began to wipe her pussy with long strokes.

"Does it ever come down?" She smiled at my new erection.

"Not lately."

"Don't leave." She glanced up at me with imploring eyes. "I don't want to be alone tonight."

"Even if I wanted to, I don't think I could." I climbed in and scooped her into my arms the way I'd been wanting to do since our lips first touched.

Her body fit mine perfectly. I held her close while I ran my fingers up and down the smooth skin on her hip and thigh. When her breathing slowed down, I spoke again to keep her from falling asleep. I wasn't ready for this night to end.

"Did you find it?"

"Find what?" She made to face me, but I kept her in place.

"Whatever you were looking for in my closet and my library."

"Oh." Her nipples pebbled in my hand. "I don't know. I suppose I wanted to know more about you."

"Like what?"

"Do you have parents, friends?" She shook her head. "I mean, someone like you, you must have a lot of women."

"Yes, to the parents and friends. No, to the latter." I chuckled.

"What are your parents like?"

I exhaled.

"What do you want me to say, Red? I'm not your average guy. Understand this—we're not in some romantic fairy tale. The world I was born into is cruel and relentless. All I can do is play the game and hope to stay alive."

She wiggled out from under me, sat up, and shifted her body to face me. Her just-been-fucked hair fell past her full breasts in wild waves. I wanted her again. My gaze locked in on her pink nipples until her voice smothered my lust.

"You don't think I understand that? Why do you think I agreed to this ridiculous contract with Liam? Because of some romantic notion about marriage and babies? It was a business transaction that was supposed to help my family."

"So, you understand who and what I am. Good. Don't ask about my parents."

Where the hell was this going? Luce had a way to disarm me. My first mistake was bringing her here. The second, was not sending her back the minute I found out who she was and the kind of trouble she brought with her. But now that I'd had a taste of her, I didn't see a way out. I craved her day and night. But every minute she stayed here, she put all of us in danger.

"Forget I asked." She rolled her eyes. "I mean, they're mafia. That gives me a pretty good idea of what they're like."

"Mom was shot and killed in front of me when I was fourteen."

"Oh."

"She was my first lesson. In my world, love makes you weak. My love for her made her a target. Her love for me, got her killed."

No idea why I was telling her this. I have never said those words out loud. What happened to Mom was a part of my life I kept buried in the deepest part of my dark soul.

"What do you mean?"

"The shots that day were meant for me, but she shielded me with her body."

"I'm so sorry." She cupped my cheek. "Little kids shouldn't have to go through that."

"I survived. And learned something important in the process."

Everyone left, sooner or later, whether they wanted to or not.

"Zero attachments." She nodded as if she truly understood me now. Did she?

"Right. And you?" I took her fingers and brought them to my lips. "Have you learned your lesson?"

"What is that?" Confusion registered in her green eyes.

"Your love for your family puts a bullseye on your back. But where are they now?"

Tears stained her cheeks. "Don't be cruel. They do love me. They will find me. I know they will." She scooted to her side of the bed, jumped off and headed for the door.

My pulse quickened. Earlier tonight, when I thought she was going to jump off the terrace, old memories rushed to my mind—Mom falling to the ground with her dress, stained red. She was standing in front of me. When the shots rang, it seemed like she fell for a very long time before her head hit the sidewalk with a loud crack. Seeing Luce on the ledge about to fall a long way down killed me.

I threw the covers off and got to her before she stepped outside the suite. Wrapping my arms around her, I nuzzled her neck. "You're not leaving. The sooner you get that through your head, the better off you'll be."

"I hate you."

"I prefer it that way." I cupped her bare pussy as I caged her against the wall. My cock steeled. The moment I wedged it between her legs, she moaned and let her head fall back. I paused for a breath, and then plunged into her ass again.

We were both prisoners here.

CHAPTER 19
I Need to Say Good-Bye

LUCE

Asking about his parents had been a stupid thing to do. But in the throes of two cosmic orgasms, I felt close to him. My imagination got away from me and saw a lover in him—my lover.

I was glad he set me straight. Whatever romantic notions got into my head earlier, were gone. I saw him for what he was, a ruthless mobster incapable of love. Though I understood why. He had lost so much when he was little. His one pure love was taken away from him. And he thought it was his fault.

After Mom died, I clung to Dad and Ronan a lot more. I was so afraid of losing them. In the end, of course, I lost Dad anyway. No matter how hard I tried to protect him, he was gone. Santino was right in that. Our world was chaos and pain. All we could hope for was to stay alive for as long as we could.

Santino stirred next to me in his bed and turned on his side with his back to me. Even as relaxed as he was in his sleep, the muscles on his wide shoulders and arms bulged up in a myriad of valleys and planes. My hand itched to soothe the scratches I'd left there. I hadn't realized I'd done that. But they were fresh, so they were definitely my marks.

My gaze traveled down his impressive body, down to his hips and shapely butt. I'd seen the tattoo on his thigh, but not long enough to notice what it was. It was the profile of a wolf, like the one I had seen on his family crest and the ring in his library. I got the sense his family had been around for many generations.

As if he could sense my scrutiny of his physique, he rolled onto his back. He slept in the nude, so the first thing that caught my attention was his semi-erect cock. His size was impressive. I was surprised I'd been able to take all of him. In all the times I had fantasized about him while I was caged in Liam's sex dungeon, I always pictured him big and thick. My imagination needed a lot of work. None of it did him justice.

After our first attempt at conversation, I decided to let it rest and not make him angry or push his buttons. The good behavior earned me several rounds of sex and mind-blowing orgasms. We slept some in between sessions, but mostly I got to experience all of him.

Twice I woke up with his slick cock in my butthole. He rode me hard with my face on the pillow until we both orgasmed. He was fucking me in the ass exclusively. I couldn't tell if it was to punish me or because of some noble intention to leave my virginity untouched.

The man was insatiable, same as me. I had kept that side of me tamed for so long, now that Santino had unleashed my sexual desires, I couldn't control them. Even now as sore as I was, I wanted to feel him again, to come and feel like I was part of something bigger than me. I pinched my own nipples to ease its aching need.

"If you don't stop looking at me like I'm your last meal, I'll have to claim that pretty pussy of yours before it's time." He kept his eyes shut as a smirk pulled at his lips.

"You're a brute." I turned away from him.

"Go to sleep." He spooned me from behind with his erection pressed between us. He reached around and fondled my breasts in a soothing rhythm until I fell asleep.

The next morning, I woke up in an empty bed to the sound of utensils clanking on china. I flipped over and found Santino sitting on the terrace with a feast in front of him. Wet strands of hair brushed his forehead. He was already showered and dressed in his dark suit.

"Breakfast in bed." He gestured for me to join him. "Well, sort of."

I ignored him and sauntered to the bathroom with the sheet wrapped around me. Last night, it had been so easy to give into him, but now in the light of day, I felt ashamed. I relieved myself then brushed my teeth and finger-combed my hair. But when I went to get dressed, my new clothes were gone. I stomped back to the suite and stopped in front of him.

He kept his attention on whatever he was reading on his iPad. When I didn't move, he slowly lifted his head. "I get horny when you look at me like that."

"My clothes are gone."

"They're in the next room."

"Am I moving there?"

"No." He stopped with his cup of coffee halfway to his mouth. "Until I feel like your urge to jump off the building has faded, you don't get to wear clothes."

"That's just ridiculous." I held the sheet tighter to my chest.

"Sit down and eat your breakfast, Red." He returned his attention to his screen.

I obeyed him, but only because I was starving. A night of crazy sex would do that to anyone. The bacon was like nothing I'd ever had. It was meaty and sweet. In between bites, I stole a few glances in his direction. He was like a magnet. The attraction I had toward him was impossible to resist. When I finished the piece of meat between my fingers, I licked the bit of grease off them.

Across the table, Santino huffed and puffed.

"What?" I snapped at him. The gleam in his eyes put all kinds of ideas in my head. They were mostly repeats of what he did to me last night. His knowing smirk washed away the lingering heat that had built between my legs. My days were easier when he went to his office in the morning. "Don't you have work to do?"

"I do." He grinned at me. "Seems to me you're making plans."

He looked so freaking handsome when he relaxed and smiled. It wasn't fair. I focused on my plate of eggs and tried not to think about all the things he'd done to me in the past several hours.

"I'm staying to make sure you stay put. I'll be in the library if you need anything." His tone implied he'd be up for a round or two of sex.

At least, that was what I heard.

"I don't need your help." I bit into a piece of juicy honeydew.

"Red." Santino leaned forward, keeping his gaze on my

wet lips. "You're doing that on purpose. Was last night not enough? God, I hope not. I have so much I want to do to that pretty ass of yours."

What? Did he think I was flirting? I wasn't. Though my throbbing clit was begging for more of him, more of whatever else he wanted to do to me. "I'm not."

He was such a jerk. He was putting ideas in my head, not the other way around.

I zeroed in on my plate instead and focused on what I had to do. Ronan was my priority, but since I was stuck here under Santino's thumb, maybe I could find other ways to get my family out of the trouble they were in. Santino had offered to help.

"Does your offer still stand?" I met his gaze.

"What do you want, Red?"

"I need to find out what happened to Dad." More than anything I wanted to see Dad. Even though I knew it would break me, I had to see him for myself, and understand that he was truly gone. "You said you went to the morgue yesterday."

"I did. But what you're thinking is a bad idea."

"Why?"

"You don't want that image in your head."

"I do." Tears welled in my eyes. "Because I keep expecting him to walk through that door, even though I know it's impossible. In my mind, he's still alive."

He glared at me for several beats, as if trying to read my thoughts. Something I was convinced he could do. Or maybe, I was terrible at hiding how he made me feel. Releasing a breath, he stood and walked around the table. He reached for the sheet, covering my nude body, and pulled until I rose to my feet. When I did, he let it fall to the floor.

His intense gaze on my body made me blush. Heat rushed through me, but I stayed on track. "One of your bodyguards can drive me there."

"I'm not letting you out my sight." He cupped my breast, rolling my nipple before he bent down to kiss me.

I had a fleeting thought to push him away, but then his tongue found mine, and I caved to his ministrations. "Please," I whispered on his lips.

"I'll have Marie bring you clothes."

An hour later, I sat in the back seat of Santino's SUV with my heart thumping steadily in my throat. From the time I'd asked Santino for this favor, to the time he was able to get me in to see Dad, not even an hour had gone by. All he had to do was place a call. The morgue director and the police were more than happy to oblige.

"You look beautiful." Santino reached for my hand from the other side of the seat.

Being this far from him gave me an odd sensation, like I had forgotten something. The second his fingers brushed mine, I was grounded. "Marie has good taste."

"She didn't get that for you. I did. I called a boutique nearby. I figured you needed something black."

"Thanks." I glanced down at the expensive fabric that felt like butter against my skin. No doubt it cost thousands of dollars. "I'd never own anything like this."

"It's from the same designer that made the dress you wore to the masquerade party." He pointed at my pant suit.

"I meant before." Before when my life was so much simpler.

"We're here." The driver announced with a quick glance toward the back seat.

As soon as he did, the SUV rolled to a stop in front of a beat-up door in a dingy garage. Where the hell were we? "Is this the morgue?"

"Yeah, government building. Not exactly the Four Seasons." He winked at me.

Wait, what? Did Santino Buratti make a joke and then wink at me? I probably looked like a real mess right about now. So much so, the ruthless mobster was feeling sorry for me.

He climbed out and then strode around while his driver opened the door for me. "You ready?"

I nodded.

Santino knocked on the door and a beautiful woman in a white coat came out to greet us. "Welcome back, Mr. Buratti." She ogled him from head to toe with a big smile on her face.

"I'm Doctor Ferro." She said to me. "This way."

The doctor was stunning. Why did that bother me? So what if she was friendly with Santino. Someone like him, with his appetite, I bet he slept with every woman that crossed his path.

"Luce?" Santino gestured for me to go ahead with a knowing grin.

I didn't know why it surprised me that he knew my real name. Maybe because he never called me Luce before.

The woman led us down the corridor that reminded me of my days of nursing school. I inhaled deeply to calm my nerves. We walked for what felt like hours, but eventually, we arrived at the room that had black letters on the door that read: MORGUE.

I'd been to many rooms like this one, seen bodies, prepped them. But this was different. Tears streamed down my cheeks before Doctor Ferro pulled Dad out of the cooler.

The whole time Santino stayed by my side, holding my hand tightly.

When she finally revealed his face, my heart broke all over again. It was Dad. I leaned against Santino's body, and he wrapped his arm around me. "We can go now." He pressed his lips to the top of my head.

"No. I need to say good-bye." I steeled myself then turned around.

The doctor stepped back with her eyes full of pity for me. "I'm sorry." She offered her condolences now that she knew the body on the table was family. "I'll give you two a minute."

"Wait." I called after her. "Where are his belongings?"

"Um." She met Santino's gaze. "There's an on-going investigation, I can't release those to you."

"Can she see them, at least?" Santino stepped closer to her. "The autopsy results too."

"Of course." She sucked in a breath and then left.

I stood next to Dad's head, placing my hand on his shoulder where the sheet still covered him. His skin didn't show burns. Santino was telling the truth.

Tell Mom I love her.

I wanted to believe they were together now. And that he had found peace.

Don't worry about us, Dad. I will make sure the crew is fine.

With a trembling hand, I peeled the sheet down to his belly to see the bullet wounds. Again, it was exactly as Santino had said.

"Here you go, dear." She handed me a clear plastic bag and a clipboard.

I scanned the results quickly and confirmed approximate

time of death, which was calculated about two weeks before the explosion, or at least the date on the footage Liam showed me. Of course that didn't tell me anything other than Santino couldn't have killed him.

With a sigh, I moved on to his personal effects and immediately recognized his favorite jacket. In a smaller sack, I found his belt, a wallet, and sunglasses. "What happened to his ring?" I lifted my head to find Doctor Ferro standing next to Santino.

"That's all he had with him when he was brought in."

"Are you sure? Because he never took his ring off. It had a Celtic cross on it." I placed a hand over my pendant. Mom and Dad had matching jewelry pieces.

"I'm sorry. I processed the bodies myself. I'm very thorough. Whatever he had on him is in that bag."

"We understand." Santino rubbed her upper arm twice, then reached for my hand. "Time to go, love."

I opened my mouth to ask for five more minutes. But what was the point? Dad was gone. I nodded and let Santino usher me out of the morgue and down the long hallway. The whole way, he kept his attention on me as if he were afraid I would fall apart or explode. The latter had already happened the day Liam broke the news—I had literally gone on a shooting rampage.

"I want to know who did this to Dad."

"I'm working on that. I promise you. I will find whoever did this to him." He wrapped his arm around me and brought my head to rest on his chest.

CHAPTER 20
A Phone and a Plan

LUCE

"Obviously, the Italians did this." I shoved him away.

Who else would gain from Dad's death? With Dad gone, the Red Wolves crew was ripe for the picking. The Chicago Outfit had been trying to encroach on our territory. It was small but with a strategic location. Once the Italians took over, it would be a matter of time before the other Irish mobs fell under their control. They wanted everything.

"If they did, they will answer to us."

"What are you going to do? You're with the New York Faction. They don't have to listen to you. No more than we have to answer to Liam Walsh." I wiped my cheeks with the back of my hand.

All the pain from seeing Dad on a steel slab, lifeless, had very quickly turned into anger. Once again, the Italians were responsible for all the bad that happened in our family. Why couldn't they just go away and leave us alone? The urge to start shooting again took hold of me.

"I told you. I'm not your typical mobster. And I do have a say in what the Chicago Outfit does." He put up his hands as he talked in a soothing tone. "You're hurting. Let's go home. I can see you want revenge. But that's not going to help, Red. We need a plan that doesn't involve burning everything to the ground. If you knew me a little more, you'd know that's something I'd never suggest, which should tell how carefully we need to tread here."

He continued, but I couldn't listen anymore. Now that we were outside of his suite, I could think clearly. Santino wasn't my friend. Even now, when he seemed to want to help me, he was still only thinking of his men. He was so quick to blame Dad's murder on Liam, the Irishman who promised to rid us of our Italian problem. And sure, Liam was the Butcher for a reason, but he had no reason to go after Dad. Santino, on the other hand, he had already caused an explosion that ended in lives lost.

A rush of adrenaline washed over me, and suddenly I knew what I needed to do.

Run.

I started to back away. I didn't know the city, but if I could find a place to hide long enough to call my friend, Kay, I could get away from Santino and go home to Chicago.

"Red." Santino's voice was full of warning.

Luck was on my side too because his SUV was nowhere to be seen. When we had gone in to the morgue, he'd instructed his driver to wait for us. Maybe a parking attendant asked him to find a real parking spot. Whatever the reason, Santino was alone. I spun around and bolted toward the garage exit ramp.

Halfway to the blinding light beyond the garage structure, I stopped in my tracks. In a cacophony of screeching tires that echoed against the walls, Santino barking orders, and other men yelling in my direction, a black Sedan jumped the curb on the street and headed straight toward me at full speed. For several breaths, I stood there, like a deer in headlights, futilely willing my legs to move. Though neither direction looked like it would get me out of harm's way.

I blinked, and then the wind got knocked out of me. A man had grabbed me by the waist, threw me over his shoulder, and rushed toward the black sedan that was now idling next to me. I kicked and punched his back, but he seemed unaffected by it. He opened the car door and shoved me in the back seat. The man in front of the window turned to face me. He was one of Liam's bodyguards, O'Malley. *Liam found me.* My legs and hands trembled so badly I couldn't even sit up to try and climb out on the other side.

I had been gone for almost a week. Was Liam mad at me for running away? All I could hope now was that he would understand why I had to leave? I was crazy with grief and anger. Maybe if I told him I shot Santino, his punishment would be less severe.

The guy who grabbed me jumped in next to me, then froze with a dead grip on my upper arm. Santino had reached into the driver's side and pulled O'Malley out of the car. Santino pinned him to the wall and clobbered him relentlessly.

Seeing Santino all covered in blood towering over O'Malley, who was now unconscious, had a sobering effect on me. I began to kick and hit any part of the man holding me down. One minute he was on top of me trying to tie me down, and the next, he was flying out backward as Santino yanked him by the ankles.

I had all of thirty seconds to decide what to do—go back to

Liam or Santino. Both wanted to punish me. And both had promised to help me. In truth, I had no reason to believe either one. I climbed out of the car and stared at Santino's back as he fought against a trained bodyguard. He was formidable, and somehow looked taller, more lethal. In that moment, I realized there was only one person I could trust—Kay.

Before I could take off again, Santino's driver grabbed me by the waist and dragged me back toward the building. "It's not safe out here, miss."

Santino's SUV was still not in sight, but his men were. They had come in just time to help him fight off Liam's body-guards. I counted at least five of them on the ground, bleeding profusely and knocked out. No shots were fired, so I had to assume they were all still alive. Santino's driver half-carried me, half-yanked me inside and shoved me against someone else before he returned to the fight outside.

The old man gripped my upper arm, while he stared at the long corridor, as if trying to decide where to leave me. The morgue freezer where they kept Dad was just around the corner.

"What are you doing?" I tried to break free.

With the commotion still going on, I had a good chance of making it out alone.

"Here." He tried the first door on the left, but it was locked. Holding on to my arm as if his life depended on it, he checked the next one. "This will work." He pushed me inside the bathroom, and quickly checked the three stalls before he turned to me. "Stay here until Santino or I come for you. You leave with no one else. Do you understand?"

I nodded.

"Good." He raked a hand through his hair. "Pray he gets out of this one alive."

Pray? As in this was my fault and if Santino died, they would retaliate against me? "I had nothing to do with any of that." I pointed toward the entrance.

"If you hadn't ran out, they wouldn't have gotten the drop on him. His head is not in the game because of you. That's a very dangerous thing for someone like him." His blue eyes bore into mine. The wrinkles across his forehead deepened as he glared at me. For a second, I thought he was going to strike me down. It was written all over his face. He wanted me gone. "Just fucking stay and don't make a sound."

With that, he stepped away from me. He scanned the room again, but for the most part, he kept his attention on me. What did he think? That I was going to stab him the minute he turned his back on me? In his defense, I did shoot his boss, but still.

As soon as the sound of his footsteps faded, I ran to the door and swung it open. Sure enough, two other guys were standing guard. Since they didn't try to grab me, I had to assume they were with Santino.

Was the old man right? Was Santino in danger? I was sure they had the situation under control. Didn't they? I didn't want Santino to die.

"Omigod, Luce."

I spun around in time for Kay to squeeze me into a bear hug.

"How are you here?" I gripped her arms to make sure she was real. "Wait. The ambush, that was you?"

"What? No. No." She shot a glance around the room, then

pulled me toward the back. When she spoke again, her voice was barely above a whisper. "I followed you."

"Here? How?"

"I've been watching your building, waiting for you to come out. It's been days, Luce. Are you okay? At first, I thought Liam picked you up at the Crucible. I chased after the SUV. I figured it would be easier to help you escape than to fight off a bunch of muscle. Then, I realized the building wasn't Liam's."

"How did you know I was going to end up in this room?"

"I didn't. When Liam's men showed up, I came in here to hide." She stopped to inhale, then continued, "Jesus, my heart jumped into my throat when I heard your voice out in the hallway. I went out the window and waited to see what the old man would do next. I thought..." she trailed off. "You know. That he brought you here to shoot you."

So, I didn't imagine it. Santino's bodyguard wanted to kill me.

"Don't worry. I wasn't going to let it get that far." She showed me her handgun then stuffed it in the back of her pants. "Now, we can go home. Luce, Ronan needs you."

"What happened?"

"Short version. After your dad died in the pub fire, Ronan disappeared. And, of course, the crew is now really struggling. Liam's small army came home last night."

For days, I'd been wondering how Ronan, and everyone else, had been getting on. I'd hoped my brother would step up and be the leader the crew needed. With Ronan, I never knew what to expect. Liam, on the other hand, did exactly what I thought he'd do. He took away the resources we needed to fight the Italians.

"How bad is it?"

"The Italians moved in, mostly drugs. For now." She furrowed her brows, reaching for my hand. "Come home, Luce. You're the only who can talk sense into Ronan. He's always only listened to you. Dad has been trying to keep everyone together. But half the crew is scared out of their wits. The other half is seeing this as an opportunity to take over the gang."

"If that happens, I won't have a home to go to."

Heat rushed to my cheeks in both shame and anger. I could've been home days ago. If Santino hadn't taken me, I could've gone home with Kay that night. Or at the very least, I could've pled with Liam not to abandon my family.

"No." She shot a glance over her shoulder.

The window she'd climbed out of before led to some sort of courtyard. My pulse picked up. We had a real shot at getting out of here. "Let's go. Where's your car?"

"In the garage." She waved her hand in the general direction where the Irish and the Italians were going at it.

"There are two of Santino's guards in the hallway."

"Who the hell is that?" She cocked her head, surveying my face. "Did he hurt you?"

I forced even breaths and acted like my heart wasn't drumming fast and hard in my chest—as if the mere mention of Santino had no effect on me. Though all I wanted to do was run out there and make sure he was okay.

"No. He's with the New York Faction. Um, how about the window? Forget the car."

"You left her alone?" Santino's angry voice echoed outside the door.

He was alive. If he came back for me, it had to be because he bested Liam's men. A part of me was relieved that I wouldn't have to deal with Liam's wrath. But while I would be okay, that meant I couldn't go with Kay. I was back to square one.

"Go." I shoved Kay toward the window. "You can't let him see you."

"What does he want with you, Luce? No, I'm not leaving you again. Look at you, you're trembling." She glared in the direction of Santino's voice. "Come with me."

"It's too late now. I don't know what he'll do to you if he finds you here with me. Please, Kay. Leave. We'll try again soon." I took her hands in mine. "I promise. This isn't over."

"Okay. I know where he's keeping you." She rummaged through the pockets of her jacket. "Here, take my burner. I have a few of them. I'll text you. And we can make a real plan. Honestly, I didn't think I'd be able to talk to you today. Otherwise, I would've come up with at least a proper exit route. That was so stupid of me."

"Thank you." I hugged her. "Thank you for coming for me."

"That's what I'm here for, Luce." She sniffled, then stuffed her phone in my bra. "Don't let anyone see that."

I plastered on a smile and nodded. She didn't need to know that my bra was the least safe place to hide something. Santino had access to that and so much more. I stood there and watched her jump up to catch the edge of the window then lift herself up and out. My heart sank when she disappeared into the courtyard. I was on my own again, but not alone.

The door clicked opened, and Santino barged in. I turned around and gasped. His hair was plastered with soot and blood, same as his fancy suit, and he had a nasty gash over his eyebrow. More than that, he looked beyond furious.

When he prowled forward, I shuffled backward. "Don't come any closer."

"Why?" He furrowed his brows. In a flash, he pulled his gun from inside his jacket suit and pointed it above my head. "Who was here with you?"

"No one."

He rushed to the window. I held my breath, hoping Kay had not changed her mind about leaving me behind and that she was far enough away that he wouldn't see her. Releasing a loud breath, he holstered his weapon and leaned against the wall.

"You're safe." The fury in his eyes faded some, but the edge in his voice and the blasting heat from his body was still there. "It's over."

Except, it wasn't. It wouldn't be over until I went home. My chest tightened at the idea of never seeing him again. But this thing between us didn't have a future. How could it possibly go on when his people wanted me dead, when Liam wanted him dead?

The Italian mobster and I were never supposed to have happened. He derailed me from my duties, took me away from the people that needed me.

"Yes, it's over." I echoed his words.

What we had was a mistake, a beautiful and unforgettable mistake, that had to end soon. Thanks to Kay, her friendship, and her tenacity, I was back on track. I had a way out.

I had a phone and a plan to leave Santino Buratti for good.

CHAPTER 21
Kill Her

SANTINO

The physical pain was a good thing—the throbbing of my temple, the cuts on my hand, the searing ache in my ribs—kept my mind off the fact that I came so close to losing her.

Luce.

Her name flashed in my head along with all the other piece meal information of what happened in the garage. She was safe now. Finally, in the SUV and on the way to the penthouse, where she should've stayed today. Why did I agree to do this for her? If I were Liam, I would have a team around the clock watching the morgue. I knew he knew I had been to see Luce's dad. I also knew that if we returned, Liam would make a move.

The fact that I ignored all that just to give her what she needed pissed me off. To top it all off, she used that time to try and escape. I fisted my hand. I counted at least ten transgressions—all of which she would have to answer to once we were home.

"Santino." Her small voice made my cock stand at attention. Fuck me.

"Not now."

"I need to go home."

"No." I glared at her with the full blast of everything I was feeling.

She exhaled and inhaled, like breathing out of sync, then scooted away from me. The SUV stopped in front of the elevator bay. Now that we were here, I could take my eyes off her. I climbed out and headed for the private lobby to my building. I didn't bother checking to see if she would follow. My men had orders not to let her leave.

In the penthouse, I went straight to the bar and poured myself a Pappy. The door shut quietly. The small sound and her sigh filled the room with fresh air. I took a long breath in and let the tension leave my body. If she tried to leave me again, she would have to get through six different guards and me.

I sat on the piano bench and set my drink on the floor. My bloody knuckles were out of place braced against the black and white keys and the shiny luster of the grand piano. I played the same tune that had been plaguing my mind since I met Red. Knowing she stood by the door listening to me, compelled me to pour my soul into my composition. I had no title for it, and I probably never would.

She sniffled behind me. The length of the room was too far for us—for me. She sighed again and slowly moved away from the door.

"Stay."

"Santino."

I snapped the piano cover closed and stood, making the

bench scrape across the marble floor. Her eyes widened in surprise, but she stood her ground. I stalked over to her. The buzzing energy below my navel took hold of me until I could think of nothing else but kissing her. In two strides, I closed the space between us and claimed her mouth.

Wedging her hands between us, she pushed me away. "Your ever-changing mood is giving me whiplash."

"I was worried. When that asshole grabbed you..." I fisted my hair, then turned around to fetch my whiskey.

"I wasn't in any mortal danger. Liam doesn't want to kill me." She glanced down at her hands.

No, of course he didn't want to kill her. No, he wanted something much more sinister. He wanted to marry her and make her have his children.

"What did you think he was going to do?" She braced her hand on the banister.

"Take you away." I knocked back my drink and stalked toward her. "I couldn't let him do that."

"Because I tried to kill you." She rolled her eyes at me.

"Correct." I reached for her face, but she stepped away, hugging her chest.

"Your head needs tending." She smiled at me. "Let me help you. Do you have a medical kit?"

"Hmmm. Are you sure you don't just want to finish the job?"

Her smile disarmed me. I wanted to fuck her into oblivion, and make her forget about the outside world. "Bathroom." I gestured toward the door under the staircase and went to fix myself another drink.

When she returned, I had already stripped down to my boxers. The cuts and scrapes on my torso were minor, but the cut over my eyebrow was going to need stitches. I sat on the sofa and let my head relax against the backrest.

"Oh." She exhaled. "Um, okay. I guess we can do it here." She set the tote bag on the coffee table, then turned to assess the damage. "We'll start here."

Her fingers brushed against my temple, and the pain eased up a bit. My cock was a different matter. "Do what you will."

She gathered her tools and set them on the side table. Bracing her knee on the cushion, she leaned forward to clean the wound. "Thank you." She blurted out as she punctured my skin.

"Hmmm." The prick of the needle took me by surprise. "For what?"

"Saving me. Even though I didn't need saving."

I waited until she finished to wrap my arms around her waist. Desire unfurled at my core when she didn't reject me again. As usual, her eyes fluttered closed, and she sighed. That was more like it, more like my Red. I cupped her tits over the fabric of her silk blouse. She'd removed the jacket when she went to the powder room, which left her in a sheer top that hugged her to perfection.

Walsh didn't deserve her. She was so soft and so delicate.

"Santino." She tunneled her fingers through my hair when I freed her nipples and sucked on them, going back and forth several rounds.

What a mess I'd caused. This thing with Luce was supposed to be a weekend pastime. I was supposed to get my fill of her and then send her back to her fiancé. But the more I fucked her perfect ass, the more I wanted all of her. I buried my thumb in her wet folds. Her desire drove me to the very edge of madness.

Only a mad man would do what I did. I had no doubt Liam had been looking for her all this time. He knew she had run away, but he didn't know she was with me. That ended today. By now the men who got away were probably telling him how they saw me with her, and how I gave them hell when they tried to take her away from me.

I brought her closer, standing between my thighs, then bent down to kiss her pussy. She arched her back and didn't protest when I let her panties and pants drop to the floor. I removed her top too. I wanted to see her and memorize every plane on her body.

"You're so fucking beautiful," I whispered, blowing a hot puff of breath on her wet cunt. I glanced up to meet her gaze, then plunged my tongue and lapped on her clit.

"Hmm." She pressed her hips forward, silently asking me for relief.

Cupping her ass, I sucked and nibbled until she screamed my name, until her juices spilled, and she came hard on my mouth.

"You shouldn't overexert yourself." She panted a breath while her palm hovered over the side of my face. "Your sutures."

"You're the expert." I smirked and lay down, using one of the sofa cushions to prop my head up. "Take it."

Her eyes widened and lit up with a hint of greed in them. I could spend the rest of my life with her looking at me like that, like I was something to eat—a last meal. She could've told me to go to hell. But instead, she straddled my thighs and ran her hands over my abdomen, chest, and shoulders. When she had her fill, she gripped my shaft.

"How does it fit?" She scooted up so her pussy lips were

lined up against my erection. The tip easily reached past her navel.

"Magic." I gave her a wolfy grin.

She laughed, and I got even harder. I bucked my hips and rubbed my cock all over her.

Her lusty gaze swept up and down it, as if she was trying to decide what to do next. I was hoping she'd suck me off. I'd been dying to fuck that mouth. "Take what you need, love."

Her cheeks turned a pretty pink and she leaned forward to rub her pussy up and down my cock.

"Oh fuck, that works too." I let my head sink back into the pillow, while I gripped her butt cheeks to guide her.

"Omigod." She lifted her head as surprise registered in her eyes.

She kept at it. With every pass she made, my balls tightened and pushed me closer to the edge. When I couldn't hold it anymore, I gripped both her arms to hold her steady. She came again and that was my final undoing. I saw fucking stars as I shot up into her belly and her tits. When a droplet landed on her lower lip, she swiped it with her tongue.

"Do you like that?"

"I don't know." She licked her lips again as if to get another taste.

I cradled the nape of her neck and crushed my mouth into hers. I devoured her with a kiss. "He doesn't deserve you," I whispered in between breaths.

"You don't understand. Our livelihoods are in his hands. My entire crew, families, children, they all depend on him." She braced her hands on my shoulders and lifted herself off the sofa.

I sat up as she picked up her clothes and padded back to

the bathroom. All this back and forth with her was making me dizzy.

Getting involved with her situation was a bad idea that almost got me killed today. I had been so unhinged when she started to walk away from me in the garage, I hadn't seen the asshole who snuck up behind me. Luckily, Dad showed up when he did.

Though that wasn't exactly luck.

Rex had told him about Luce and the whole ordeal with Walsh. The old man came after me when my security detail informed him I was going to the morgue to see the Irishmen who'd died in the fire. Dad getting up in my business pissed me off like nothing in this world could.

"The fuck is going on, Santino?" Dad barged into my penthouse.

"Speak of the devil and he shall appear." I wasn't in the mood for the old man's fatherly act.

Slowly, because it hurt like a mother, I grabbed my trousers off the floor and rose to my feet. "Now what?" I donned them but didn't bother with the shirt. When I turned to face him, my heart rate spiked. I inhaled to calm the fuck down. "Another intervention?" I glared at Dad and the small army he'd brought with him.

"I didn't want to believe it when Rex told me about the Irish girl. My son couldn't be that gullible." His neck turned bright red. He was about to blow a gasket. "Find her." He waved a hand toward his second-in-command.

I jerked to attention but didn't move because the asshole went straight upstairs. If Dad believed I cared about what happened to Luce, he would make sure I never saw her again.

That meant Luce at the bottom of the Hudson River. I fisted my hands then released him to relax my stance.

"You look like you need a drink." I sauntered over to the bar and poured two Pappys.

I sipped from mine, just as the powder room light went off under the door. Luce better have the sense not to try anything with Dad. While Rex was hell-bent on peace, Dad didn't give a shit. All he cared about was his succession. If she was smart, she'd stay hidden.

"I need you to stop fucking around. First you refuse to marry and now you're fraternizing with the Irish? She's Liam's wife for fuck's sake." He threw his hands up.

The two little words made my stomach twist into a painful knot. "Fiancée," I corrected him.

"Same fucking difference. Where is she, Santino? You had your fill." He pointed at my half-naked body. "I'm taking her back."

As soon as he said the magic words, Luce popped out of the powder room. *Fuck me.* I gritted my teeth. "Red. You don't want to get in bed with the devil."

Her gaze shifted from me to Dad and both her eyebrows went up in surprise. "Um." She turned her attention back to me.

"This is my father, Don Buratti." I glanced upward then waved a hand toward her, though all I wanted to do was throw her over my shoulder and run away. "Luce O'Brien. She's a guest here."

"Enough." Dad nodded at the man standing beside him. "Bring her to me."

"No." I darted toward her, but Dad's men were well-coordinated. Three of them rushed me and forced me to my knees, while the other two grabbed Luce by the arm and walked her until she was a foot away from him. "You can't do that. She's mine." I slowly released a breath, then corrected. "She's mine until her debt is paid."

"Oh, I see. Your dick comes first. Is that it? You're willing to watch us burn to the ground just for a piece of ass." He pointed at Luce with so much disdain.

I had made a huge mistake. The old man now knew exactly how I felt about Luce. I glared at him. My body trembled with fury and desperation while I waited for Dad's final order. After my reaction, he had to know that if he hurt Luce, he would lose me forever.

After what felt like hours, Dad finally spoke. "I didn't get a good look at you before in the garage." He picked up one of her red locks and looked her up and down.

"You're the one who dragged me to the bathroom to hide me." Luce shifted her body to face me, silently asking why the hell Dad would do such a thing.

He had? Dad was the one who'd left her alone in the bathroom? No wonder my guys tripped over their words trying to explain. He could've given her to Walsh's crew. That would've been an easy way for him to get rid of her. No, what the old man wanted was to teach me a lesson.

He wanted to have something to hold over my head so I would do whatever he wanted. He wanted to break me. And he wasn't above using an innocent woman to get the job done.

"Kill her."

CHAPTER 22
Not Now, Not Ever

LUCE

"What?" I shuffled away from Don Buratti. My gaze shifted between him and the barrel of the gun pointing at me.

I was so confused. Obviously, Santino's dad didn't want me here. How had he put it before? *His head is not in the game. That's a very dangerous thing for someone like him.* Even Kay had noticed his murderous tone when he dragged me into the bathroom back at the morgue. The old man wanted me dead. So why save me from Liam? Why not let him take me away? Just so he could shoot me himself, or rather, his bodyguard could, in front of Santino?

In the corner of my eye, Santino punched the guy holding him and kicked the other to break free. In two long strides, he closed the space between us and stood facing his dad, while posing as my human shield.

I leaned on his back, glad for the comfort his warm skin provided. He reached around and offered me his arm for additional support. I took it. In all my twenty-four years, I had never had to face a gun. Dad and my crew kept me in a bubble, away from all danger. But that was before I left home.

"This is not how you get on my good side, old man." Santino's words dripped with warning and all kinds of threats. Was he threatening his own dad on my behalf?

"We protect our own."

"I know. You taught me that. That's exactly what I'm doing." The muscles on his back tensed.

On the outside, he looked calm and collected. But his whole body buzzed with the anger brewing just underneath his skin. Santino wasn't the type of man who tolerated being told what to do.

"Is that so?" Don Buratti's gaze shifted from Santino's face to mine. His features softened. He wasn't exactly friendly, but he didn't have murder in his eyes anymore. "Put the gun down." He uttered the words while still staring at me.

I inched closer to Santino. Don Buratti scared the crap out of me. He had that same predatory energy that Santino had, imposing and threatening. Of course, now that I knew a different side of Santino, he wasn't as frightening. His Dad though? I just wanted the floor to open beneath me and swallow me whole.

"She's my responsibility."

"Yes, she is." After a few more beats, he finally shifted his attention back to Santino. "You may be willing to burn your own house down for her, but I'm not. So, fix it. Do you understand?"

I hated it when men talked about me like I wasn't in the room. "I'm no one's responsibility. I'm going home." I made to get away from Santino, but he grabbed me by the arm.

"Red, no."

"Why not?" I made the mistake of looking at his handsome face. The pain I saw registered in his eyes broke me.

"Dad, I will call you in the morning." He gestured toward the door while he kept a firm grip on me.

"Rex was right about you." Don Buratti nodded at his men. When they all left, he pointed a finger at Santino. The deep furrows along his forehead showed how furious he was with Santino's actions. But underneath all that, his eyes showed pride.

Yeah, Don Buratti should be proud of his son. Santino was the most beautiful man I had ever met, but he also had a brilliant mind. He was everything—strong, resilient, feral, and a force to be reckoned with. No wonder my body couldn't get enough of him.

I couldn't get enough of him.

Because if I were being honest with myself, I had to admit that my body, mind, and soul craved him like a drug. My thirst for him was like nothing I'd ever experienced before.

"When I urged you to take on a wife, I didn't mean this." He glared at him.

"That's not what this is about. I haven't changed my mind about that. I am *never* getting married." Santino tightened his hold on me.

"Don't give me that bullshit. I recognize that look on your face. And no, you will not be getting married. Not to her. That's for sure." Don Buratti pinched the bridge of his nose, blinking slowly, the way extremely tired people do—not just physically tired, but tired of life. "The little wolf from Chicago isn't for you, Santino. There are a million other women out there for you. All the pussy you could ever want. But NOT this one."

"I've heard enough, Dad."

"Walsh wants his bride back. Think long and hard about your next move." With that last warning, the old man gave me a curt nod then left.

"Great. I'll add Don Buratti to the list of people who want to see me dead." I yanked my arm away from Santino.

"He will not hurt you. I promise." He braced his hands on his hips. "He was right about one thing though. I need to fix this."

"That's easy." I inhaled, because as much as I knew what we had to do, I realized I didn't want to leave him. The thought of not seeing him again made my stomach churn. "Let me go. I don't need your help."

"The fuck you don't." His jaw clenched.

What did he want from me? His entire family, or at least the men he was willing to listen to, had ordered him to release me. "What is this about? Some sort of pride thing with you? You fucked me, so now no one else can have me? That's insane, Santino. Even for you."

"Is that what you want?" He slow-blinked, like he was in pain.

No, I didn't want to leave, but what choice did I have? People needed me. More specifically, they needed Liam's army. "Yes. I've told you that many times."

A blotch of red covered his neck and part of his face. Pursing his lips, he stalked toward me and threw me over his shoulder. I wiggled to get away from him, but he was so much stronger than me. No matter how hard I fought him, it didn't make a difference. He kicked his bedroom door open and dropped me on the bed.

He prowled around the bed as he unzipped his pants. His

big cock broke free, while he stood there towering over me. "You want to spend the rest of your life in a bed with an old man who doesn't care about you?" He wrapped his hand around my ankles and pulled me toward the edge of the bed. "You want his dick inside you, day and night, touching you, kissing you?" His hand cupped my pussy while his other one roamed my belly, my breasts, and my face.

I had no choice. Liam wasn't who I wanted. But I couldn't leave my family behind to run away with a mafia prince who didn't even want me—or rather, who only wanted my body.

"Don't do that. Please." With every touch, my resolve crumbled a little more.

The selfish part of me, the one addicted to Santino Buratti, took hold of me every time he looked at me like I was the only one who could save him.

He relieved me of my pants and underwear and pressed his erection against my pussy, rubbing my own juices all over me. His dark, intense gaze met mine. I blinked away tears because I knew what he was thinking. If he took my virginity, the one thing Liam cared about, Liam would never take me back. He would also come after Santino and his entire family.

My body trembled with need and trepidation. What would I do then? I braced my hand on his shoulder, kneading the strained muscles there. I wanted Santino to be all my firsts. But his dad was right, I wasn't for him. And he wasn't mine.

He needed to marry a nice Italian girl, one worthy of a prince, the next in line to take on the Buratti reins. No wonder the old man wanted to shoot me. I was in the way, making Santino stray away from his duties.

He pressed his forehead against mine. "I want you in the worst way possible. It hurts to want you this much."

"Release me." I ran my finger over his eyebrows and his full lips. Flutters bounced around my chest and then moved down to my core, stoking the fire there between my legs. "It's time."

"No. I can fix this." He captured my mouth with his in a searing kiss and plunged into my back entrance.

I clung to him as he rode me hard. Santino was the most infuriating and obstinate man I'd ever met. "I hate you."

"No, you don't." He thrust deeper as he took my fingers and rubbed them on my clit.

I held my breath, but it did nothing to stop the avalanche sweeping through me. Ribbons of desire sprang from my pussy in waves, one after the other. I came harder than any of the other times we'd been together. When his own orgasm was spent, he collapsed on top of me, panting into my ear.

"You can't leave. Not now, not ever."

"So stubborn." I snaked my arms around his neck and let the drumming of his chest lull me to sleep.

When I woke up, the night sky was lit with stars and piano music filled the room. With a smile, I shifted my weight to the left of me expecting to see Santino next to me, but he was gone. I picked up my silky camisole and underwear on the way out and followed the sad tune—the same lullaby from all the nights I'd spent here.

At the bottom of the stairs, I stopped in my tracks to admire the scene in front me. A shirtless Santino at the piano, with the moonlight spilling into the living room, was a memory that I knew would stay with me for the rest of my life.

He turned to face me but didn't stop playing. The gleam in his eyes made him look younger as he asked, "Do you like it?"

Looking around the cathedral ceilings, the tall windows

with the city of New York as the backdrop, I finally understood what this place meant for Santino. This wasn't my prison. This gilded cage was his.

"You play beautifully." I leaned a hip on the side of the piano and watched his long, graceful fingers float up and down the keys.

"Don't sound so surprised." His smile brightened the room. Or maybe the clouds had shifted and let more of the moonlight filter in. "I'm not the brute you think."

"I'm beginning to see that." I glanced down at my fingers. "Your father is right. I don't belong here."

"Don't start. Please." He let his hands fall away.

"I want to know what he wants from you. He seemed very determined."

"He wants a successor. He wants me to take his seat at the table."

"And you don't want to?" I reached for the side of his face. He caught my wrist and kissed the inside of it. I understood his situation well. Even if the Red Wolves' crew didn't compare to the New York faction in size and wealth, I knew what it meant to be responsible for others. "Dad wanted me to take over for him too."

"A woman leading the crew?" He pulled me onto his lap, and gently pushed my hair away from my face. "How was he going to manage that? Don't you have a twin brother?"

"I do. But he's too much of a wild card. Dad had no doubt he would start a war on his first day." I brought my legs in, reveling in how good we fit together. "He thought that if I married the right man, the crew would follow me. My husband and I could lead them. He was, of course, assuming I'd have influence on said husband."

Santino's grip tightened around my waist. "What is it with you and marriage?"

"It's my duty. I know it sounds archaic, but a little sacrifice never hurt anyone. I can do this."

"You shouldn't have to." He buried his face in the nook of my neck and shoulder. "You're not some pawn in a wicked game of chess."

"Our world is cruel. You said so yourself. All I can do is play the game. And this is it. Selling my virginity was the only way I could have a say in anything related to the Red Wolves."

Granted, Liam hadn't been the ideal choice. Yeah, he had the means to help my crew. But he would never let me lead or influence him in anyway. He was only interested in my ability to bear children.

I bet on the wrong guy and now I had to live with it. But if my sacrifice helped my brother, Ronan, bring our family together, then it would have been worth it. Dad didn't want Ronan in charge, but he wasn't here anymore. Kay was right. If Ronan had me and her dad guiding him, he could be a good boss.

"You didn't answer my question. Do you not want to be the next Don?"

"I do. I've been groomed for it my whole life. I just don't appreciate all the hoops Dad wants me to jump through like I'm some puppy." He let out a breath and ran his teeth along the cord of my neck. "You smell so good."

"Why do we always end up here?"

"What's that? You mean sex?" A sexy smirk pulled at his lips as he rolled and played with my aching nipple.

"Yeah, that." Heat rushed to my cheeks. Because I wasn't

215

any better. I wanted him all the time. "We should really stop and think about what your dad said."

"I already know what my next move is going to be."

"Tell me."

"We're staying here. They can't tell us what to do."

Maybe they couldn't tell him what to do. But even if I lost hold of my sanity every time he touched me, I still had a very clear vision of what was the right thing to do. I needed to let Santino go. I had to leave here and find Ronan before it was too late—before our crew became so broken it couldn't be healed back together.

Santino pushed the piano bench back and scooped me into his arms. He kissed me gently as if we had all the time in the world. Though we didn't.

Tomorrow, I would call Kay from the burner phone she gave me, so we could come up with a real plan to escape Santino's penthouse. Our task was a tall order, to say the least, since this place was a fortress. But between the two of us, we would figure something out. We had to.

I bit my trembling lip and threw my arms around Santino.

We still had tonight.

CHAPTER 23
Run Little Wolf

LUCE

"You're reading it wrong." Santino put down his iPad and mug of coffee. When he sat back, he flashed me a sexy grin.

Earlier this morning, I'd been in his library looking through his poetry collection, which was quite extensive. I read a few stanzas for him before he escorted me to the dining room for breakfast. He was dressed in his usual dark suit. I tried not to think about what I had to do today and focused on our last few hours together instead.

After last night, I stopped asking him to let me go. He took that to mean that I had finally come to my senses and forgotten all about my family. Obviously, he didn't know me at all if he thought I could change my mind so easily. Though, I could get used to his blinding smile, and that easy way about him he'd had since we woke up.

"It's iambic. It reads like a heartbeat." He reached over and took the book from me. Meeting my gaze, he made that sound out loud. "Da-dum, da-dum, da-dum."

My pulse slowed down to the rhythm on his lips. If the imposing and threatening version of Santino was hard to resist, this calm and patient side of him was putting ideas in my head that I knew couldn't be. I couldn't be in love with him. He was an impossible choice.

He began to read the passage where I'd left off with his sensual and deep voice. *"But then I was young—and it took ten years..."*

Poetry for breakfast. What if my life was this? What if I let him steal me away? Then I wouldn't be me. I would be the woman who let her family die. That wasn't me. I was the woman who fought back.

I grabbed the book out of his hand and closed it shut. "Don't you have work to do?"

"I do." He chuckled. "I've been gone for too many days." He brushed the back of his fingers on my cheek. "I'll only be gone a few hours. Try not to get killed in that time."

"You know me." I shrugged. "I can't make any promises."

"That's the problem with you. I don't really know you." He cradled my face and pulled me toward him until I was sitting on his lap.

I melted into his good-bye kiss, running my hands over his chest and shoulders. Maybe I didn't need to leave today. One more day. The words flashed in my mind as he plunged his tongue inside my mouth. Everything he did, the way he held me, or looked at me, it all came from the same place. He believed I belonged to him. Being in his arms like this, I believed it too.

"Red." He released a breath, pulling a lock of my hair. "I should go before I turn you over on this table and spend the rest of the day fucking you raw. To hell with everyone else."

"You should go." I nodded as he held my face in his hands, and kept his heated gaze fixed on me.

"Be a good girl." He pressed his mouth to mine again, then propped me up so he could stand.

With another one of his panty-melting smiles, he left.

I stood in the middle of the dining room until I heard the front door close. He was gone. I had a few hours to come up with a plan and find a way out. My feet remained rooted in place and refused to listen to reason.

"Luce, get your phone," I muttered, looking down at my bedroom slippers.

In the next breath, I managed to put one foot in front of the other and make my way to the powder room under the stairwell, where I had left Kay's burner last night. It was an old school thing with no applications on it, so I couldn't text her. But even if I could, I didn't want to use her real number.

I went through the recent calls and sighed when I saw a number she had called yesterday. The timestamp read eleven in the morning, which was right about the time all hell had broken loose at the morgue. I hit re-dial and waited while my heart thrummed hard in my chest.

"Omigod, Luce." Kay answered after the first ring. "Are you okay?"

"I am. And you?"

"Yeah, yeah, don't worry about me." She exhaled loudly into the speaker. "I'm camped out near your building. Can you get to me?"

"No." I shook my head, even though she couldn't see me. "Santino has guards standing outside the door."

"So, what's the plan? Can we poison them?" Kay always had the ability to make me laugh.

"I doubt they'd take any kind of drink from me." I laughed. "But I've been thinking about calling someone else for help."

"I hope you don't mean Liam. He's so angry with you. He told Dad that you humiliated him."

"No, not him. We'll deal with Liam after I'm free." I stuffed my hand in my hair while I considered my crazy plan. "Santino's dad is a Don. He's like a big deal here and he wants me gone."

"Hmm. You think he'll help you? Let's call him."

"Yeah, I got the sense he wanted me off the map. If I promise to never come back, he might help me get through Santino's bodyguards."

Kay didn't need to know that Don Buratti wanted me dead. The only reason he hadn't done it last night was because Santino asked him not to. Technically, Santino threatened to burn his dad's house to the ground if he or anyone hurt me. Flutters built up in my belly again. And I wished I had one more day with him.

"Luce?" Kay called for me. "Did I lose you?"

"No, I'm here."

"So can we call him?"

"Of course not. He doesn't seem the type that would come running because someone asked him to."

"Right. So how do we find him? It's not like you can slide into his DMs."

"No idea." I paced the length of the living room a few times.

The front door closed again, and I turned around, expecting to see Santino—my heart beating fast as I held the device to my ear. A small gasp escaped my lips the moment I saw Don Buratti by the entrance, alone.

"Kay. Let me call you back." I hung up, ignoring the slew of questions she fired at me. "He's not home."

"I know." He stalked toward me.

"Are you here to kill me?" I squeezed my phone to stop the tremble in my hands.

"No." He laughed.

A sinister sound that made my skin crawl.

"That would make you a martyr. Santino would never forgive me." He unbuttoned his suit jacket and stuffed his hands in his trousers.

I'd seen Santino do a similar move. Of course, on him, it was crazy hot. When his dad did it, it made me want to run and hide under the bed.

"What are you planning to do with me?"

"What you said." He pointed at my phone. "If you promise to never come back, I'll get you out of here."

I swallowed. For some stupid reason, tears stung my eyes. This was exactly what I wanted. I wanted to leave. And now here was my chance. I wiped my cheek and stood a little straighter. "I promise."

"Tell your friend to meet you in the back of the building."

"And the guards?" I hit dial again.

"I already sent them away. They won't be back for another ten minutes. You need to leave now."

"Luce, what the hell is happening? Don't hang up on me again."

"Meet me in the back of the building. Right now." I ended the call and met Don Buratti's blue gaze. "Thank you."

"I'm doing this for my son."

"Right. Because God forbid he gets mixed up with an Irish girl."

"Do you have any idea who he is?" He scoffed. "Who he will be once he replaces me? He's inheriting a legacy that's over a hundred years old. So no, an Irish girl would not do." He strode to the door and opened it.

I thought about running upstairs to get a pair of shoes, but I didn't think the angry mobster holding the door for me would take kindly to that. I'd come full circle—leaving the same way I'd come in. Don Buratti followed me into the hallway and gestured toward the elevators.

Santino, don't hate me.

I said the words over and over. Though I knew the repetition wouldn't help. As soon as he found out I was gone, he would be mad at me. Even if he had no reason to, he would see my escape as a betrayal.

The longer we stayed together, the more our families would suffer the consequences. Because of me and the time I spent with Santino, I had no doubt Liam would come after Santino to make him pay for making a fool out of him. I was sure he had a similar punishment lined up for me—but one problem at a time.

Twenty feet before we reached the end of the hallway, the elevator dinged, and the doors slid open. Don Buratti gripped my upper arm and shoved me against the wall. "Take the stairs."

The impact left me dizzy. By the time I figured out what was going on, the shooting had already started. Why were they shooting at Santino's dad? I held my head with both hands and tried to focus on the figure standing there with the smoking gun.

No.

Liam's bodyguard, O'Malley, glared at the old man, looking proud of himself for shooting an Italian. "If you fight me, I have orders to shoot you. Let's go." He waved his fingers at me.

I pressed my body to the wall as I glanced up and down the hallway. The only way out was through him. In the next breath, the stairwell door opened, and two men started shooting at O'Malley. I recognized them from the garage. They were with Don Buratti.

While they dealt with O'Malley, I rushed to Santino's dad. He was covered in blood and not moving. "Who should I call?"

"No one. They know what to do." His eyes fluttered closed as he pointed at the guys beating the crap out of O'Malley. He opened them again and winced as if the small effort pained him. "Leave before you get my son killed." He inhaled and slapped my hand off him. "Run, little wolf, and never come back."

I nodded and headed for the stairwell. On the way down, I checked every floor to see if the elevator was there. I didn't have time to stand there and wait. Five levels later, I got lucky. I ran out into the hallway and bolted toward the elevator car. It dinged again, and I knew my window was closing. I ran faster and made it just in time to wedge myself through. I hit the call button for the garage several times, hoping that would get me moving faster.

With a slight jolt, I finally began my descent.

I called Kay again. "Change of plans. Can you get to the garage? I'm on my way down."

"Yeah, sure. Let me swing around."

I didn't hang up this time. I clung to the burner phone as if it were my lifeline. I suppose it was. Kay was my last hope. "They shot him, Kay. Liam's guy shot a Don."

"Oh fuck. You don't want to be anywhere near that. Okay. I'm here. But I can't get in. Entrance is for residents only."

The doors slid open again. The adrenaline kicked in when the smell of burned fuel and hot asphalt greeted me in the garage. I glanced left and right. Both ends had an exit.

"I see you." Kay honked the horn.

The loud noise made me look to the right and I immediately spotted Kay's happy face. I rushed toward her. My legs dragged like they were made of tin, but I trudged on. Any minute now, one of Liam's men or Santino's could find me and I would go back to square one.

"Come on," Kay yelled at me.

I found the strength to run faster and made it to her Prius. "Go." I put my head between my legs to catch my breath.

The car bumped forward. Then I felt Kay's hand on my back. "When this is over, I'm going to give you the tightest hug."

I laughed and wept into my hands. Twenty some minutes later, we reached the tunnel. We had really done it. I was free. My chest tightened as Don Buratti's words swirled in my head. "Never come back." That was the right thing to do. So why did it hurt so much to leave Santino? To know that I couldn't see him again or feel his hands on me, his lips.

"What's the plan, Luce?"

"We're going home."

"To Chicago?"

"Yeah, we can't spend the night here. Let's drive until we need to stop for gas."

"Okay." She released a breath and gave me her iPhone. "Plug it in. Let's get out of this hellhole."

"Yeah." I beamed at her. "Does your dad know we're coming?"

"No, not yet. I didn't even think to call him. He'll be happy to see you though. Once we have everyone together, we can talk about what to do next."

"Well, first, we need to make amends with Liam. We don't want him as our enemy." I cleared my mind and tried not to dwell on what his punishment would be. In the two weeks he kept me in his dungeon, he spent a great deal of time and effort trying to break me and turn me into his pet. What would he do now? "Do you think your dad would be willing to talk to him and negotiate something?"

"Of course, Luce. We'll work something out. Okay?"

I nodded.

I spent the next hour telling Kay everything—what Liam did to me, how I came to be with Santino, and how I was sure I had fallen for him.

"That's heavy, Luce." She glanced at her rear-view mirror and furrowed her brows. "This fucker has been riding my ass for miles. What the hell?" She switched lanes and the car followed. "Oh, fuck me."

I shifted my weight to look behind us. Sure enough, a black sedan was right on top of us. "They found us?"

"Dunno." She sped up.

The highway was empty so there was no reason for the car to be riding our tail like that. When Kay tried to move out of the way again, the sedan came up to her side and rammed into us. Kay swerved out of the lane and was forced to take the exit.

At the end of the ramp, an SUV jackknifed in front of us, and we had to stop.

A man opened the passenger door, fisted my hair, and yanked me out. My body slammed hard on the side of the Prius. "Did you really think you could make a fool of me and then simply go home?" Liam pressed his lips on my cheek.

CHAPTER 24
But You Understand Now

SANTINO

My mother died when I was fourteen-years-old. Ever since I could remember, I knew I would one day take over for Dad and become the next Don of the Buratti family. Every single thing I ever did was for that purpose—special schools, combative training, weapons study, survival skills. But the day my mother was shot and killed in front of me was the day I fully understood the weight that had been placed on my shoulders.

"Mom, do we have to?" I'd asked as she stopped in front of yet another bookstore.

"Santino." She cupped my cheek as if I were a little boy. Even though I was several inches taller than her. "You promised. For my birthday, I got to spend all day with you. I never see you anymore. Always training. Who knew being a mafia member required so much work?" She beamed at me.

"It's my duty." I removed her hand from my face, mostly because she made me feel like a kid, which I wasn't.

227

"Someone has to keep the peace and protect us. That's you."
She hugged me briefly. "But today, it's just us. Come on, this
place assured me they had the collection of poems I've been
looking for."

"Fine." I rolled my eyes and followed her into the alley
where the main entrance was located.

Mom spent most of her days running fundraisers and a
myriad of social events. I never got the sense that she and dad
were madly in love, but they cared about each other. They
understood what it meant to be an integral part of the Society.

When she wasn't throwing fancy parties, she liked to read
poems more than anything. At the other side of the bookstore,
she took a thick book the store attendant was holding behind the
counter for her. Her brown eyes beamed with so much glee, it
was contagious. I chuckled and gave her two thumbs up.

"Happy birthday, Mom," I muttered so she wouldn't
hear me.

I had to admit, when Mom was on a mission, when something made her so happy, I simply couldn't say no. Dad suffered
from the same malady. As ruthless and cruel as he was, he
always had a soft spot for Mom.

"See? That wasn't too bad. Now we can go enjoy our lunch.
And then you're free to go." She ran her hands through my hair
to fix it then gestured for me to get the door.

Outside, her driver waited for us in the SUV. Vehicles were
not allowed in this part of the alley, but he didn't care. Our
safety was more important.

Still smiling, she stepped onto the asphalt and waved at
Frankie, calling for him. When he didn't move, she gripped my
arm as she scanned the deserted alley. "Santino, get back inside.
Call Dad."

We'd trained for this. Many times. But in the heat of the moment, I couldn't leave Mom. I wasted precious seconds trying to get her to come with me. But she insisted on holding them back. "Santino—"

Several shots echoed around us. I dropped to the ground then watched her freefall with her book clutched to her, stained with blood. Blinking fast to clear my vision, I cradled her body to mine. The pelting of bullets around us halted. I only had a second or two to decide if we were being ambushed by a single shooter. If we were, he'd stopped to reload.

"Hold onto me, Mom. I'm getting you out of here."

"No, Santino. Leave me. You're more important."

I had to chance it and get Mom to safety and a doctor. Ignoring her feeble attempts to shoo me away, I picked her up and half-carried, half-dragged her to the SUV. I tapped Frankie on the shoulder to get him to go, but he simply fell limp onto the stirring wheel.

Fuck me.

I shut the door behind me and climbed in the front seat, moving him out of the way in the process. He was already dead. And Mom was running out of time. Tires screeched as I rammed my foot on the gas pedal and careened out of the way. My driving wasn't perfect, and I hit several parked cars once I made it onto the street, but I managed to get us out of there.

By the time I reached the safe house where I was told to drive in case of an emergency, Mom was already dead.

Almost fifteen years had gone by since that day. I still thought of that moment at least once a day. If I had been stronger, faster, smarter, she might still be with us. My life changed after that. Dad had more guards keeping watch. I had to train harder and study every logistical scenario that could get Dad, or me killed. I had to be ready. Every single day, I had to be ready to take over for Dad, to become Don.

For a kid to live waiting for his other parent to pass on was a new breed of torture. I knew the day would come when Dad would die of old age or at the hands of our enemies. But like any other human being, I'd hoped we'd have more time.

"The chopper is here, Sir." Mark, Dad's bodyguard, veered into my line of sight and effectively blocked Dad's body in the middle of the hallway.

"Let's go." I nodded. "You can explain what the fuck happened on the way to the hospital."

A team of paramedics had Dad securely fastened to a gurney. They wheeled him to the elevator at a hurried pace, though they held the door for me, so I could join them. The helicopter ride took all of ten minutes. When we arrived, I waited in my seat until Dad had been unloaded and carried away.

I stayed put because I wasn't ready for answers. I didn't need to be a genius to know that somehow Dad's bullet wounds were my fault. He got shot protecting me—or rather, protecting our legacy, the Society.

"You're more important." Mom's words were on repeat in my head.

I wasn't a kid anymore; I had to face what was coming. Fishing my phone out of the inside of my suit jacket, I called Tommy, the guy I'd left behind to watch Luce, and Mark, Dad's lead bodyguard.

"Meet me in the war room." I hung up.

In the past few years, Dad had been in and out of the hospital so many times, he'd made arrangements to have his own private wing. It made security protocols less of a nightmare and his doctors were on call twenty-four-seven. The room adjacent to his had been turned into a meeting area complete with computers and other gadgets. Something we had set up for the days when he had to work from his hospital bed.

I pushed the door open and slammed it. I was beyond irate. I needed someone to blame, someone other than me. "What the fuck?" I pointed at Mark, Dad's second-in-command. "You start."

When he opened his mouth and the words didn't come out, I pulled out my gun and aimed it at him. "Start talking."

"Don Buratti wanted to see Ms. Luce."

"Why?"

"Erm." He scratched the back of his head. "To relocate her."

"She's gone." I gripped the handle of my weapon tighter to ease the pain in my chest. "He's here. So where did she go?"

"Don Buratti wanted us to wait downstairs. So, we did. When the shooting started, he called me. I showed up and found the same clusterfuck you did."

"And you?" I turned to Tommy. "Why were you not at your post?"

"Sir. Don Buratti asked us to give him a minute."

I placed my weapon on the table. I needed to calm the fuck down before I started shooting my own men. So Dad either went to my penthouse when he knew I wouldn't be there to kill Luce or save her. Something happened in the middle and now he was fighting for his life while Luce was missing.

"Did you check her tracker?" I asked Tommy.

After she shot me, I had Rex's hacker put a chip in Luce's

necklace. Deep down, I knew this day would come. I knew she'd leave me.

"Yes, sir. Just now. The signal is weak, we've been trying to locate it, but it's likely she's underground?" He shrugged as he racked his brain for the right words to pacify me. Red crept up his neck as he cleared his throat. "We'll find her, boss."

"Is she hurt?"

"No." He said it with plenty of conviction, happy to give me some good news.

"And the guy you found?" I braced a hand on the table and glared at Mark. His eyes widened in surprise. The fucker was trying to keep information from me. Why? I slammed my hand on the Formica. "I swear if you lie to me or withhold information..." I let the threat linger in the air. Dad's bodyguard was familiar with my work. He knew what I was capable of when I didn't get my way.

"He's dead. He came at us, we had to shoot him. But he looked like one of Walsh's men." He met my gaze as if that would make his words truer.

He was lying. But there was only one reason he would risk his own life like that. He was protecting Dad. I could stay here and beat the truth out of him or go next door and ask Dad.

"Find her." I pointed at the two of them, then headed for Dad's suite.

His doctor met me at the door with both of his hands up in surrender. If my eyes showed how I felt right now, he no doubt saw blood and murder.

"He's stable. For now," he whispered. "The bullet didn't hit any organs. That's the good news. But he lost a lot of blood, and his heart isn't strong enough for this."

"Can I talk to him?"

"I don't think that's a good idea." He cleared his throat. "Sir."

"Let him in." Dad's smoker voice eased the tension along my back muscles.

"As you wish." The doctor nodded once and scurried out the door.

"Santino." Dad waved me over.

I strode over to the bed and stood by the footboard with my arms over my chest. He looked old and tired—as if he were hanging by a thread. Sheer will kept his defective heart still pumping.

"It was Walsh. His man was on your floor." He inhaled. "He was coming for you."

"You left yourself open when you sent our guys away. You put her in danger too." To my credit, I managed to filter the anger out of my voice. The old man went to my place to meddle in my business. He turned everything to shit. "You better not die on me, old man."

"Is that what you're worried about?" He chuckled. "You ignored your duty to the Society and now here we are. What a fucking mess."

"Oh, I see." I gripped the footboard. "You think this is on me. I'm sick and tired of Walsh. He's nothing. He's a speck on our radar. I should've taken the trash out when he first made a move on Hell's Kitchen. But no, Rex and the board wanted a peaceful resolution."

"Jesus fucking Christ, Santino. Listen to yourself." He waved a hand in my direction, pulling on the tubes and needles stuck in his veins. His machine beeped out of rhythm for a few seconds. The nurses rushed in, but he waved them away. "I'm not dead yet. Give us a minute." He glanced away and took a lungful of air. When he turned to me, his eyes were pools of blue, serene. "Look at what she's done to you. That's not a partner. She could never be. You brought the wrath of the Irish to your own doorstep simply because you couldn't let her go. If you had listened to Rex—"

"It wouldn't have made a difference. She had already spent the night with me. What do you think "the Butcher" would've done to her if I had sent her back? Hmmm. She's an innocent. He would've killed her." In truth, he would've tortured and fucked her until she took her last breath just to make an example out of her.

"An innocent? What the hell are you talking about? She's not some poor child. Who do you think did this to me?" He pointed at his bandages then winced in pain. "She had a phone. I have no doubt she called Walsh and told him where to find her. There was someone else waiting for her. Use your head, Santino."

"What?"

Dad's words had become muffled. I glared at the screen and the heart rate line going up and down, slower than it should. If Dad didn't survive this, neither would Luce. How could she be so stupid as to shoot at a Don? When she shot me, she didn't know who I was? But she knew who Dad was.

"That doesn't make any sense. She has a temper, sure. But she's smart. Only a person with a death wish would pull the trigger."

"Maybe she's not as smart as you think."

"You're lying." I inhaled. "You're lying because you want me to send her away. I can't do that."

"If I don't make it." His eyes fluttered closed as he breathed evenly. A few beats later, he recovered and glanced at me. "You'll have no choice but to let her go. Santino, you know the by-laws."

"I do. The punishment for killing a Don is death."

"You're my only son. You'll have to do it."

My chest tightened. "You can't ask me that."

"I have no one else. It has to be you." He extended his hand toward me. "You're too important."

In a trance, I shuffled over to him and placed my palm over his. Dad had always been a force to be reckoned with, bigger than life. I had no delusional notions that this was all about fatherly love. No, his concern, his obligation was only to the Society. He owed them an heir, someone to take his seat when the time came. Everything he ever did was to honor the legacy his father entrusted him with. Still, seeing him like this pained me, knowing that the reason for it was Luce—me—broke me.

"I think it would be best if you let him rest." The doctor offered me a kind smile. "I'll let you know if anything changes. For now, he needs to sleep."

I braced my hand on Dad's shoulder, but he didn't notice. His features had softened and his body relaxed as he fell into a deep slumber. With a nod, I stepped away from the bed to let the doctor make Dad comfortable.

The old man was right. I forgot about my duty to the Society, and in the process, I made a big mess of things. I implicated an innocent. My desire for her had started as a wicked game that now had turned lethal. I pushed Luce too far. She pulled the trigger, but it might as well have been me. I rubbed a hand over my chest—with every beat, thorns dug deeper into my heart, turning it into something dark and evil.

If I ever thought I had feelings for her, it had to be over now. I could only have hatred for her. Even if right now hate was the last thing I felt when I thought of Luce, eventually, I had to teach myself to feel nothing but loathing. How else would I be able to carry out my mandate?

"Don't die old man." I called over my shoulder and sauntered out.

In the hallway, Joey caught up to me. "We found her."

Those three little words made my whole body stand at attention. I'd gotten used to coming home to see her and talk to her. In the time she spent with me, I found myself leaving the office earlier and earlier. The last few days, I hadn't even bothered to go in. I hadn't realized how addicted I had become to her presence and her energy. Now that she had taken it away, I couldn't breathe.

"Where is she?"

"She went back to Walsh." He sucked in air and stalked away from me.

A flash of red sparked in front of my eyes. Why him? Why did she think he was the only one who could do something for her? She wanted an army? I could've given her a hundred men —if she'd asked—I would've done anything for her.

Fisting my hands, I blinked fast to erase the images flitting through my mind. Luce on Walsh's arm everywhere he went, in his house, and in his bed. My stomach twisted into a painful knot when I saw them clearly in my head—the old man kissing and playing with her pussy—my pussy—she was mine.

I pressed my index finger and thumb to my eyes to rub the sting of my tears off. Luce wasn't mine. She never was. She was my captive, and now my prey.

"Sir?" Joey's Adam's apple bobbed before he spoke again. "They're in a factory outside of Harlem."

I met his gaze, and he stepped back. Joey wasn't afraid of me. That was pity written all over his face.

The poor little prince lost his princess.

Of course my men, like Dad, knew how far down the rabbit hole I had gone with Luce. I'd never fallen for anyone before. Between school and tactical training, I had no time to get to know anyone. I didn't want to. What was the point? In my world, the innocent never lived long. So yeah, it took me a minute to see our relationship for what it was. And for the same reason, I failed to see that as much as Luce desired me, no matter how many times she came undone in my hands, she still couldn't love me back.

"Did you see who shot Dad?"

"No." He shook his head. "Luce and the Irishman were alone with him. When we got there, Don Buratti was down. Luce was with him, so we rushed the other guy."

"So, no one saw anything?"

"No, sir."

I glared at him, trying to find the truth in his eyes. But it would seem he truly didn't know who shot Dad. "Let's go. I want Walsh alive. I want to be the last person he sees before he dies."

CHAPTER 25
We're On Our Own

LUCE

"You're still thinking your family wants to hear from you?" Liam peeled the burner phone from my grip and smacked me across the face with it.

I had tried to hold on to it, but it was no use. He was stronger than me, and way more lethal. My cheek exploded in pain. On instinct, I clenched my jaw, which caused me to bite my tongue. I tasted metal as I glared at him.

He laughed, a vicious sound that made my insides twist in panic. I wanted to run and put as much distance between us. His breath on me repulsed me. I couldn't stand him being so close to me. But his men had us surrounded. They had Kay in a headlock on the asphalt. No way in hell I was leaving her behind.

"And they said you were the smart one." He smirked and gestured to the men holding Kay down.

They reached for her pocket. She kicked one of them in the shin and shoved the other one. That earned her a punch in the stomach. She fell to the ground, gasping. While she tried to recover, the guy who was as wide as a fridge removed her jacket and retrieved her other burner phone.

When they did, Liam turned to me with a satisfied grin on his face. "If they wanted you, they'd be here by now."

He wasn't entirely wrong. The night Kay had given me her mobile, I hid in Santino's powder room and tried calling every number I could remember, including Ronan's. I left him several messages. Wherever he was, he either didn't have access or he wasn't ready to hear from me. Regardless, the burner was useless to me at this point.

Kay and I had managed to escape Santino's penthouse but couldn't avoid getting caught by Liam. We had no one to call.

"Load 'em up." He let go of my wrist.

Kay had said Liam was furious with me because I left him. He'd told her dad he had plans to make me pay. I didn't have my family's backing. All I could do was hope he would be forgiving, or at least, lenient in his punishment of me.

"This is between you and me. Please let her go."

"Is that what you think? That this is just between us. Wake up already." He shoved me into the back seat of a black sedan where one of his men had already settled in.

I shifted my body to find Kay pressed against the hood of her Prius. All I could see was her slender body struggling as a bigger shadow forced her into another vehicle. Liam got into the third car. As soon as he did, the exit ramp was lit up in red from the taillights. Our driver jerked into action, started the engine, and fell in line behind Liam.

Dread oozed into my chest as the tires crunched on the gravel and slowly bumped back onto the road. I was going back to the dungeon. I was sure of that. Why did I think that begging would get me anywhere? Liam was the Butcher. He certainly hadn't earned that title because of his merciful nature.

We drove for more than an hour. As I looked out the window, I could tell we were not headed to his apartment. The car stopped in front of what looked like an abandoned warehouse. His men ushered us into the elevator and hit the call button for the top floor. Mrs. Jones waited for us out in the hallway, as if the time I had been gone hadn't happened, as if Santino never existed.

For a split second, I had the feeling that maybe I never escaped, that it was all in my head to make me feel better.

"Get them ready." Liam spoke to Mrs. Jones in a gentle tone as he shoved Kay and me inside.

Like his place in the city, the apartment didn't have much furnishing. The floor plan was similar with a living area, a study, and an upstairs. How many of these places did he have?

"You asshole." Kay rounded on him. "I know what you do here. I won't let you do that to her again."

I shook my head at Kay. In the next breath, the wind got knocked out of me. I dropped to the hardwood floor, gasping for air. I glanced up expecting to see Liam's cruel eyes, but instead met Mrs. Jones' icy glower.

"You got me by surprise the first time because I thought we had already become a family. But no more." She turned to Kay. "Your disobedience will cost her dearly. So, tell me again what you're willing and not willing to let us do."

Kay blinked fast as understanding washed over her. Every time she refused to do as she was told, I would be punished. Her gaze shifted from Liam to Mrs. Jones several times before she finally conceded. "I won't give you any trouble."

"You can handle it from here?" Liam stopped in front of Mrs. Jones on his way to his office.

"Of course, sir." She smiled at him so pleasantly, I had to wonder if they were lovers, the sick kind, but still. When he shut the door behind him, Mrs. Jones gripped my elbow, digging her nails into the soft flesh. "Up you go."

As I climbed the steps, my mind escaped to the last place where I felt safe. To my surprise, I didn't dream of home. I thought of Santino and all the times he refused to let me go, all the times he held me tightly in his arms, and all the nights I fell asleep to his sad lullaby.

She pushed open a hidden panel and revealed an exact replica of the dungeon she kept me in before. The first time I was in a place like this, I was too numb to fully understand what Liam planned to do with me. I had never even heard the word *pet*. I wasn't an innocent bride anymore.

Liam never asked me if I wanted to be part of his BDSM world. He imposed that on me. They dressed me up and pulled my strings like I was a lifeless puppet. And now he was about to do the same to Kay. She left home because of me. She was Liam's prisoner because of me.

Mrs. Jones ushered me to the sex wheel in the middle of the room. Like in the other room, it faced the cage in the far corner and the front entrance.

Keeping her gaze on Kay, she tied both my wrists to the top of the wheel. She had me widen my stance until I could barely stand, and then, tied my ankles to the bottom posts on either side of me. She yanked at the rope holding my arms up, and I came up onto my tiptoes. Of course, she had plans to make me pay for knocking her unconscious the night I escaped. She acted as if I had broken her trust and hurt her feelings.

The strain on my legs and arms shot like hot pokers down my spine. It made it hard to breathe and speak. I panted a few puffs of air. And just when I thought I was going to scream, she let go.

"Go into the bathroom and remove all your clothes." She gestured toward the door to the right.

Kay's eyes went wide. In the car ride on our way to Chicago, I had told her everything that Mrs. Jones put me through, but I left out a few details, like how I was half naked the entire time.

"I'm sorry." I mouthed to her. "I'm so sorry."

When she didn't move, Mrs. Jones removed a pocketknife and released the blade, angling it on my inner thigh. "I don't have all day, you stupid girl."

"No. Please don't hurt her. I'll go." She put up her hands and hurried to the en-suite bathroom.

"You don't need her. Let her go." I had a feeling begging wouldn't work on her either, but I had to try. "I'll stay. I won't fight you. I promise."

"No, you won't." She pressed the blade against my flesh until red droplets ran down my leg.

"Ahh." I bit my lip to keep quiet. If Kay tried to help me, I was sure Mrs. Jones would do more than prick her leg.

"You could've been the best of all of them." Tears brimmed Mrs. Jones' eyes before she glanced away and made her way to Kay.

Omigod. She wasn't all there. How did I not see that before? How many women had gone through this dungeon before me? How many of them had agreed to be here? My guess would be zero. She hadn't shown a modicum of remorse when Kay's bravado turned to pure trepidation. Her job was to break Kay, like she did me.

If Dad hadn't gotten killed, I probably never would have snapped. I never would've tried to escape or even thought about it. But then, Dad and my family were the reason I had come here to begin with. Liam and Mrs. Jones were doing the same to Kay. They were using me to get to her.

I squeezed my eyes shut and inhaled. No, I couldn't let this happen to her. We had to figure a way out.

When Kay came out, her eyes zeroed in on me and the blood pooled at my feet. A small gasp escaped her lips as she let Mrs. Jones escort her to the five by three cage on the opposite end of the room, where she had a direct line of sight to me. She was dressed in Liam's choice of costume for his pets—a sheer white leotard and glittered nipples.

Mrs. Jones scanned the room with a deep scowl between her brows. I'd seen that look before on her. She wanted everything to be perfect. When she turned her attention toward me, she rolled her eyes and her smile faded.

I supposed everything in the dungeon was as it should be, except me with my dirty camisole, shorts, and bedroom slippers —the outfit I was wearing when Don Buratti came to see me. The clothes Santino helped me with after we had sex this morning. I felt like that time had happened months ago and not hours.

She glanced at her watch. After a few beats, she headed back to the bathroom and returned with Kay's jeans and top all bundled under her arm. "Mr. Walsh will be here shortly." She beamed at me then at Kay. "But we have time to dress you properly."

Hot blood rushed through like tiny pricks as soon as she

released my arms and legs from the sex wheel. I dropped to the floor because I hadn't realized how tight my muscles had become. Mrs. Jones gripped my elbow and helped me up. I trudged to the bathroom, let her remove my sleep clothes, and usher me into the shower. My arms hurt from the poor circulation, but I did my best to wash up.

Before I was finished, she opened the glass door and shut off the water. She worked fast while I dried off—powdering my nipples and then slipping the leotard over my head. I hated that this part felt familiar, that I knew what she'd do next. The hair and make-up came next. The whole time I sat still, not really seeing my reflection in the mirror.

Then, it was time to go back out. Shame and guilt punched a hole in my gut as I padded out of the bathroom and back to the wheel. I tried to cover my breasts and pussy when I knew I was in Kay's line of sight, but Mrs. Jones slapped my hands away.

"There's no room for that here."

When I turned to face Kay, she was in a fetal position facing away from me. She stayed like that while Mrs. Jones tied me up again. She was my best friend, and I let her down. I did this to her.

As soon as Mrs. Jones shut the door behind her, I called for Kay. She was about twelve feet away, so I was sure she had heard me. I tried again. "Kay, I'm sorry. Please don't be mad at me."

"I'm not." Her body trembled like she was crying. "I'm the one who should be apologizing."

"What?" I pulled at the jute binding one of my wrists.

Slowly, she came up to a sitting position and turned around with her legs tucked under her butt. Her brown hair was pulled back into a messy French braid. When she lifted her head, tears streamed down her cheeks.

"I was supposed to take care of you, and I failed." She shrugged. "Just like everyone said I would."

"You're my best friend. It meant the world to me that you stayed behind. But that's not your job."

"Don't you get it, Luce. I'm your bodyguard. For real. I was trained to do this job." She huffed. "I wanted to contribute, you know. You went to nursing school. I had to do something. I was good with guns, so I thought I could join the team. It was so stupid of me."

"It wasn't. You came for me when no one else would."

"Yeah, but I let pride get the best of me." She wiped her face with the back of her hand. "I didn't ask for help. Not even when I realized that the Italians had you. We're in this deep shit because of me."

"Don't say that. I think it's safe to say we were both guilty of hubris."

I thought of Santino's words. *"In my world, you play the game and hope to stay alive."* I didn't understand what his words meant—not really. I walked into Liam's contract, thinking he was the answer to our problems, that I could fix everything. But I was no more than a pawn on Liam's board. Pawns never survived.

"Why didn't you tell me you were working for dad?"

"Because your dad didn't want you to know. When we were in high school, someone tried to kill you. After that, he panicked and decided to have someone with you twenty-four-seven. That's when I volunteered." Her cheeks turned red as she raised her hand.

"I think I would remember something as big as that. When was it?"

"Prom night. But Ronan got there in time and diffused the situation. Everyone decided not to tell you. So you wouldn't worry."

"Kay, I'm the daughter of a Boss. I should be worried about getting shot or stabbed, or whatever that person tried to do."

"Bomb."

"Or that."

"Some bodyguard, eh? I mean even Liam didn't believe it when we told him I was here to protect you."

"He was never going to let you stay, Kay. Don't beat yourself up over that. You came for me. That's all that matters."

I had spent all my life being coddled by Dad and everyone in the crew. The world could be a cruel place. I knew that. But I never truly understood how much until I came to New York. If I had known, would I have agreed to a marriage contract with Liam? Probably not. I agreed to it because I didn't fully recognize what was at stake. My body and soul weren't something I could give away freely to someone as sinister as Liam, the Butcher.

"It was very stupid of me to think I could save my family."

"No, don't say that. You had to try." She pressed her face to the side of the cage. "One thing is for sure Luce. We're on our own here."

"I know." I swallowed my tears. No one was coming to save us. We had to do whatever it took to survive. "How are we going to get out?"

Before, Mrs. Jones didn't bother locking the doors because she knew I wouldn't do anything to put my family in danger. She was using the same tactic now. If Kay disobeyed, I would get punished. If I did the same, Kay would pay the price. She had gone above and beyond what any bodyguard would do. I couldn't let her get hurt.

"Is the cage locked?"

She wiggled around and tried the top latch. It opened, and she stood. Her eyes went wide as she glanced around the room. Knowing her, she was for sure looking for weapons. I turned toward the north wall where Mrs. Jones kept a bunch of sex toys in the other dungeon. The last time I was there, I used a huge dildo to knock her out. Of course all the dangerous gadgets were gone.

When she bent down to climb out, she froze with her eyes fixed on the door. She brought her fingers to her lips then mouthed. "Camera. It just turned on."

I followed her line of sight and, sure enough, the red dot over the threshold stood out. Did the other room have cameras too? Someone like Liam, and even Mrs. Jones, would want to keep a close watch on their pets. Did they do that? Did Liam sit in his office and watch me while I sat in the cage, day in and day out?

At this point, it didn't matter really. But a cold shiver ran up my spine to think that Liam had seen me naked many times, that he saw me pee my pants the first night, or that he watched me while I fantasized about the stranger from the airport. I struggled against the ropes. He had taken more than what I was willing to give. He had to pay for that. One day, he would have to answer for what he did to me and my family.

And for what? What did Liam want? A plaything? It seemed too simple of an answer. He was a proud man, so the punishment bit made sense—as fucked up as that was—but what did he want with me before? Why risk doing this to the daughter of a boss?

"Untie me." I wiggled my fingers.

"I'm sorry, Luce. I can't risk it." She sat back down and shut the gate.

"That's okay." I released a breath. "We wouldn't make it past the guards in the hallway anyway. We'll find another way. I promise. We'll never stop trying."

"Agreed."

CHAPTER 26
Kill the Girl, Kill His Plans?

SANTINO

I climbed in the back seat of my SUV and sank into the soft leather. Between work and the hospital, I was beat. But this business with Liam couldn't wait. The asshole knew where I lived. I let my head fall back and chased away the images of him and Luce together. She'd been with him all day. A lump churned in my stomach, and I hit the seat in front of me.

"Why the hell are we not moving?" I asked when Tommy shifted his body to meet my gaze from behind the stirring wheel.

"Don Valentino is here."

"What? Fuck me. Go." I tapped him on the shoulder.

He nodded and moved to start the ignition. But then the door opened, Rex climbed inside and sat next to me. "Going somewhere?"

"You know I am." I met his gaze. "He came after me. He knows where I live. I can't have that."

249

"I get that."

"I don't have time to sit here and chitchat."

He leaned forward. "Drive."

"Okay. So you're not here to tell me not to go. What do you want?" I placed a hand over my chest. "You never just visit anymore."

"I'm busy." He cocked an eyebrow.

"Right. Running an empire no one knows about."

"Yeah, that's the one. Walsh thinks we're with the New York Faction. And I'd like to keep it that way. You can't tell him about the Society, or what we're here to do." He unbuttoned his jacket and settled in.

Fuck this was going to take a while.

"What's the point of being us? All this sneaking around is giving me whiplash. Besides, we tried your way, and it got us nowhere."

I rambled on about his failed methods for a whole two minutes without him interrupting. Then I realized Rex was letting me vent. I didn't like being handled. Jesus, I wanted to punch Liam in his smug face and let all this pent-up anger out of my system.

"Whatever you have to say, say it." I glared at him.

"How's he holding up?"

"You know the old man, he's stubborn as fuck. His heart is another matter. He lost a lot of blood." I shrugged.

What else could I say? The man got shot. And his body was too weak to come back from it. Or who knew, maybe he would. Over the years, Dad had survived plenty of attacks. Many, including me, were convinced he had made a deal with the devil.

"You're angry. I get it." Rex leaned back, as if considering something. "If your dad doesn't make it, all bets will be off. I will help you nail that asshole to the wall and make sure he pays. That's your right. But for now, I would advise you not to go in there with guns blazing. There's a better way to deal with him than this old-school bullshit that's only going to implicate the New York Faction. We don't want gang fights on the streets of New York or Chicago."

"You forget Walsh has footage of me blowing up the Irish pub?"

"I already took care of that. He no longer has proof we were there that night."

My heart drummed so hard in my chest I could feel my pulse on my neck. For a second, I thought Rex was here to make sure Luce didn't live past tonight. In our circle, information traveled fast. If Rex didn't know Luce shot Dad, it was because Dad wanted me to be the one to tell Rex. He was sure I would choose duty over whatever the hell this thing with Luce and me was.

"What do you suggest we do? You came here with a plan."

"Not a plan. Information." He looked pleased with himself. "My hackers figured out what he wanted with the woman."

"What woman?"

"Lucinda O'Brien. You met her." His tone was laced with sarcasm.

"She's back with him. Just like you wanted."

"I know. She's the reason he came after you. Why he showed up at your doorstep. I told you your security was shit."

"Dad had something to do with it. He sent my men away, left the door wide open for them to come in."

"Yeah, I'm aware. It wasn't a smart move. But I see why he

wanted her gone. You don't need that kind of trouble, Santino."

"You don't know what I need." I exhaled loudly. "So, what does he want with her?"

"Right." Rex gave me a knowing smile. He knew I'd listen to anything that had to do with Luce. "She's next in line to lead the Red Wolves, the Irish gang in South Chicago."

"Yeah, I know who they are. A lady boss?"

"Not exactly, her marriage to Liam gave him leadership rights. According to what we were able to put together, he plans to take over the gang and then expand to other territories. He has the manpower and the money to do it. He wants his Irish version of the Society."

"Luce was a means to an end. The first move on the chess board."

"Exactly."

"Lucky bastard. When he saw our guys in Chicago make a move on Luce's crew, he saw an opportunity to cash in."

"Not luck at all. The Chicago Boss didn't authorize the looting and vandalizing, just like he said to you when you were there last month." He raised both eyebrows and gave me a minute to put the pieces together.

"He got to one of our own."

He nodded once.

"Tell me you already have that traitor and that you're dealing with him—old-school style."

"Of course, I flew to Chicago myself to make sure of it. Between the information my hacker was able to gather and my interview with him, we were able to figure out what Walsh was up to and why he was so desperate to get Luce back."

I fisted my hands. I didn't like having that picture in my

head—Walsh and Luce together.

"I think she could be useful to us."

"What?" I squinted at him. "She's innocent in all this." Well not entirely, but Rex didn't need to know that right now. "Kill the girl, kill his plans? Is that your angle?"

"I didn't say kill."

No, he hadn't, but recently, it felt like everyone wanted a piece of her—Dad, Walsh, and now Rex. And if I were being honest, me.

"Did your hacker tell you what he found out about Luce's dad?"

"He did. Walsh tried to pin that body on us." He tapped a finger on his thigh as red crept up his neck.

"He sure as fuck did."

"If I could axe him and be done with it, I would."

"You have no idea how good it feels for you to say that." I pressed my hand to my chest in a sardonic gesture. "The question is why? Why kill a boss, then go through a convoluted plan to blame it on us? It doesn't seem like a very smart move."

"No, it doesn't. We still don't have anything solid on that." He glanced out the window.

We were almost to Walsh's building in Harlem. My insides stirred with a mix of anticipation and desire. I had this incessant need to ring Walsh's neck...and see Luce. She'd turned me into a complete idiot. Dad told me she was the one who put him in the hospital, and I still couldn't stop this ache, this need, to be with her again.

Tommy touched his index finger to his earpiece, then nodded. "They're in. Security was minimal. There's a team in the alleyway waiting for you."

"Should I be insulted?" I glanced at Rex.

253

"I'm so fucking tired of the balls on that guy."

"Go home. I got this."

The information Rex shared with me was invaluable. Now I knew how much Luce meant to Walsh. I knew this wasn't a matter of honor or love. It was his own greed. I could deal with him on my own. Rex had an empire to run. He didn't need to be mixed up in gang stuff.

"Don't do anything stupid."

"Sure thing." I climbed out of the SUV.

He did the same, and immediately jumped into his own vehicle. I put him out of my mind and focused on my surroundings. Did Walsh not think I'd come after him tonight? I rushed to the alley where I met ten of my men.

Did he live here? The place was adequate, but it didn't suit what I now knew of him. That struck me as odd, given how much effort he'd spent during our meeting, trying to impress us with his money. The first floor looked like some sort of warehouse or a factory. The rest of the floors looked like abandoned office space.

"Where is he?" I reached inside my suit jacket and unholstered my handgun. With any luck, the asshole might give me a reason to shoot him tonight.

"Top floor, sir." Tommy gestured toward the back entrance of the building.

I nodded and motioned for him to lead the way. We rode the elevator to the floor below Walsh's, then took the stairwell. Outside the door, several men lay unconscious, not mine, but his. Before we came here, I had told Joey I wanted Walsh alive, and he delivered.

"Go."

Five of my guys filed along the wall and sprinted to the

end of the hallway ahead of me. They broke down the door and barged in. Adrenaline pumped through me like oxygen. I rushed inside and stopped to take in the empty space.

"Are you sure he's here?" I went left into a room that looked like an office, where he had a few scattered pictures and two chairs. "The fucker's gone." I braced my hands on my hips and inhaled. "That's why the security was minimal. He took off. Check every nook and cranny." I pointed at Joey.

"If he's here, we'll find him."

Fuming, I sat on the chair behind his desk and waited until my guys checked every room in the lower and upper levels. When they returned, they confirmed this was the right apartment and that he had left recently.

"What about Luce's tracker?"

"We found the necklace in the laundry room upstairs." Joey placed the Celtic Cross pendant in front of me. "What now, sir?"

Shooting and punching were no longer an option, so I went with the next best thing. "We leave him a souvenir. This is his building, right?"

"Yeah, the factory is closed and so are the offices. We checked. No one's here."

"Blow the fucking place up."

"With pleasure." He beamed at me and signaled for the rest of the guys to follow him.

When everyone left, I couldn't resist the urge to look around his study. He had a few books on the shelves. The apartment looked lived-in, but he didn't have a lot of furniture. Maybe this was his second home or main place of business. Either way, I wasn't impressed. I pulled out the top drawer and found a remote, though there were no screens anywhere.

I pressed the on button, then followed the whirring noise to one of the bookshelves. When I opened a door, I found surveillance equipment. Blood pulsed through me. I squeezed the remote so hard, the battery cover popped off. There, on four separate screens, was Luce on display, tied up to a device, wearing a leotard I knew well.

"Fuck me. She was in the dungeon she told me about." Was this here? Was this today? I scanned the information on the feeds. The date and time were right now. "Luce," I called out as I rushed out into the living room and up the stairs.

My phone buzzed in my pocket. I dug it out and glanced at Joey's message warning me I had ten minutes to get out. I tapped on the screen and called him. "Shut it down. I think Luce is still in the apartment."

"She can't be. We checked every room."

"There's a camera feed. I'm taking a second look."

"Boss, I did a quick and dirty. I can't stop it. The one in the factory will burn fast. I jacked up the electrical wiring. Shit. I could go back and see what I can do, but—"

"Shit, no. Leave it. It's too late. Get everyone out and then come help me." I tapped the phone to my forehead then hung up. "Luce." I kicked the first door off the landing. Sure as fuck, no one was there.

The two other bedrooms were just as the guys had said... empty. Where the hell was she? I seeped through all the details of what she had shared with me about Walsh and his sex room. But nothing was useful. On my way back, I stopped to stare at the bottom of the stairs.

After Mom was shot, Dad lost it for a while. He became obsessed with my security detail. He even built a panic room next to my suite. Was that why Luce's tracker was glitching? It was in a soundproof area? Why did Walsh need a room with padded walls?

Luce had seemed ashamed when I asked if she was Walsh's pet. Was it because she didn't want to be?

"Luce," I called for her again, then rammed my fist on the wall, listening for any hollow sounds. I kept going until I hit the right panel that opened to reveal a door. The BDSM scene wasn't new to me. I'd been to a few dungeons in the city. But still, it shocked me to see Luce half-conscious, hanging by her wrists.

"Jesus Christ." I ran to her, shouldering off my jacket.

"No," she whispered, shaking her head.

"It's me. You're safe." I untied her hands and feet, and she crumbled into my arms.

"We gotta get out of here. This place is going to blow up in about five minutes." I wrapped the coat around her shoulders.

"Kay is here too. She's my friend."

"He's with the Italians, Luce. He's no better than Walsh." Kay flipped open the gate but stayed inside it.

"He's all we've got." She limped to the cage on the opposite end and removed her jacket to give it to Kay.

"Are we seriously having this conversation right now?" I took off my button-down shirt and helped her into it. "The place is about to blow up. We have to go. Now."

"What the hell? Liam and his minion left us here to die?" Kay's cheeks turned bright red. Even dressed in an oversized jacket, she looked like she could do some serious damage.

"It wasn't him. I ordered my men to blow up the joint." I turned to Luce as she backed away from me. "That was before I knew you were here. Why are we still talking?"

I bent down and hoisted Luce on my shoulder. If Kay was

a true friend, like Luce had said, she'd follow and keep up with my pace. Joey met us outside in the hallway, with his face and clothes covered in soot.

He panted a breath of relief and then furrowed his brows. "Oh fuck."

"Yeah, we'll talk about that later." I headed for the stairs. Given the impending fire, I didn't think the elevator would be safe.

I raced down the ten flights of stairs until we reached the lobby. Somewhere in the factory section, detonations sounded off in succession. Luce's entire body beat hard against me. If she hadn't moved, it had to be because she was scared. After the explosion though, her body jolted in response and her thigh rubbed against my cheek.

Fuck me if that didn't get my attention. I set her down because right now wasn't the time to act like a horny teenager. She let me take her hand and pull her across the street.

Since I left the penthouse this morning, after a few rounds of sex with Luce, my day had gone from shitty, to fucking shitty in a matter of hours. Another blast sounded behind us, a bigger one this time. It set off the alarms and all hell broke loose. I pinned Luce to the brick wall of the building across the way and shielded her with my body.

She ran her hands up my chest and around my neck as she glanced up at me with those green eyes. Her soft skin, her scent, her hair—it all felt like home. I opened my mouth to apologize, to tell her I was glad she was alive, but instead, I pressed my lips to hers. She parted them for me, and the rest of the world fell away.

CHAPTER 27
Pray He Doesn't Die

LUCE

The world was literally on fire, and all I wanted to do was kiss Santino. I wanted to stay in his arms and forget about everything that happened today after he left the penthouse. I ran my hands over his bare chest and buried my face in the safety of his smooth skin and the thumping of his heart against my cheek. He held me tightly as he barked orders at his men. Tires screeched in the distance as smaller explosions detonated inside the factory.

I glanced up to watch the building burn. Bile rose in my throat when I thought about what almost happened. Santino cocked his head to meet my eyes. When I kept my gaze fixed on the tall flames, he kissed the top of my head, bringing me closer to him. That act alone stirred tiny sparks of yearning in my core.

But even his warmth and my desire couldn't erase my time in the dungeon. I hated how much Kay and I had given up, how we'd agreed to do anything Liam said just to keep each other alive.

"I used to have a pet who liked getting cut." His words echoed in my head.

I vividly saw him entering the room, removing his dress shirt, and licking his lips like I was something to eat. His white belly bulged over his brown leather belt. For whatever reason, he looked older half naked like that. To my relief, he wasn't erect. If sex was his end game, I had a feeling he planned to toy with us for a while.

"We'd played this game where I would do tiny scratches on her peachy skin until she'd scream. She had the most delicious screams." He gripped my braid and took a waft of it. "I want to hear you scream. So, what would it be?" He turned to Mrs. Jones who stood a few feet away, as if supervising our interaction.

"Sir." She offered him a pleasant smile and then placed a crop in his hand.

Before my brain could register what was going on, he snapped the outside of my thigh. I bit my lip in surprise, but no sound came out of me. This day had been so long and strenuous, I was out of tears and yelps.

"No." Kay banged on the cage.

I shook my head at her to urge to keep quiet. If Liam had his attention on me, he wouldn't touch her.

"Be patient." He smirked at her. "You'll join us soon. Luce and I have a conversation pending."

"I left because my father's killer deserved to be punished." I pursed my lips to keep them from trembling. I didn't want Liam to see how much he terrified me. Pain didn't scare me. "That's on me. Please leave her alone."

What did he plan to do? Not knowing was killing me. Maybe that was part of his torture—to let us imagine the worse.

"I thought you understood how this works." *He whipped me just below my navel.* "She pays for your sins." *He bent down and licked my neck, leaving a wet trail that reeked of booze.* "I want to see the two of you play together. But first, I want to hear you scream."

He delivered another swat on my other thigh. To his left, Mrs. Jones regarded us with a grin on her face. If anything, she looked more turned on than he did. In all the times she saw me naked and watched me in the shower, she never seemed this much interested in me.

"Go ahead," *he called over his shoulder.*

Mrs. Jones left the room then came back with a camera and a tripod. She set it in front of me and then glanced up at Liam. "Whenever you're ready, sir."

What a fucked-up duo.

He hit me again over my quads. And then I realized the pattern. He was working his way toward my pussy. The idea appeared in my head and then it was all I could think of. I didn't want him to hit me there. My pulse spiked and knocked the wind out of me.

When his phone rang in the pocket of his trousers, I let out a small sigh. He glared at me as he retrieved it. "This better be important."

I panted with my whole-body trembling as he stood there listening to whomever had called. After a couple of minutes, something in his demeanor shifted. His shoulders slumped while his eyebrows shot up. Was he surprised or in panic mode? I couldn't tell.

"*Fuck. Meet me in the garage.*" *He hung up and turned to* Mrs. Jones. "*We have to go.*"

"*What happened?*"

"*Leave them here.*" *He grabbed his shirt and met my gaze.* "*We'll be back soon. Don't try anything. My guys will be just outside the door.*"

With that, he gestured for Mrs. Jones to follow him, and they walked out.

"*Are you okay?*"

"Are you okay?" The words were louder. Santino cupped my cheek and tilted my face toward him. "You're trembling. It's okay. You're safe. Get in the car."

I did as he asked because I wanted nothing more than to get as far away as possible from this place. I scooted all the way to the other side. "Where's Kay?"

"She's in the car behind us." Santino tapped his driver on the shoulder. "Let's go."

"Home, sir?"

Santino met my gaze. The pain in his eyes cut me deep. And I knew why. When I left his penthouse this morning, his dad had been injured. How was he doing? Did he die? I couldn't ask him that. Don Buratti had gone to his son's penthouse to get me out and away from his son for good. Why did O'Malley have to shoot him? He didn't even give Don Buratti a chance to tell him that he was letting me go. Maybe that had been his directive—kill as many Italians as possible.

"Just drive for now."

"Thank you for finding us."

He cradled my cheek then pulled me toward him to capture my mouth with his. I half-landed on his lap. For a fleeting second, I considered how this would look to the other person in the SUV with us. But then Santino's tongue collided with mine, and I forgot about everything else.

Since the day I met him, Santino has had this effect on me. He had the ability to make all the bad in my life go away. I tunneled my fingers through his soft hair and deepened the kiss. He groaned and squeezed my ass with his strong hands.

He pulled away first. I gasped as he gripped my French braid and tugged on it until I let go of his chest to brace my hand on his thigh. "Does he kiss you like I do?"

I shook my head once. Liam had tried that once the very night I met Santino, the same night I let him eat my pussy in a private room of the Crucible. He ruined me for everyone else that day. When Liam's lips brushed mine, I knew I would never feel the way I felt when Santino kissed me.

With ragged breaths, he unbuttoned my shirt and let the fabric fall to my sides. "Did he fuck you?" He ran his hands over my glittered nipples.

If I didn't know any better, I'd think Santino was jealous of Liam. Why would he think I wanted Liam?

"No."

Liam had been so set on punishing me with his whip first, he didn't get to that part. What would he do now? Who would he go after once he realized I had managed to escape again? For sure he would start with my family. I was slow to recognize that Liam wasn't the answer to our problems. We would have to figure something else out because there was no way in hell, I was going back to him, no matter how many men he promised to send to help us. We would deal with the Italians ourselves.

"Don't lie." He pinched one pebbled bud and then the

other. "I feel like punching a wall every time I think of him touching you."

I squeezed my legs together to ease my throbbing clit. "I'm not lying. He didn't touch me."

He glanced down at my pussy and the wet seeping through the sheer fabric. The smirk on his face made me struggle to break free from his hold. But he held me tighter. He enjoyed having me like this—under his control and burning with lust for him. This was his wicked game, and I loved it. I craved it. So much so that I didn't care if we were not alone.

"What do you want from me, Santino?"

"The same thing you do."

"Then do it. Fuck my pussy," I whispered. "I know you want to."

The ribbons of raw energy coiling in my core were putting words in my mouth. Right now, I would say anything to have Santino again. My body trembled in anticipation. I wanted to feel his cock inside me. A whole day had gone by since the last time I felt him. I needed a hit. Santino had become my drug. What was he waiting for?

He licked his lips while he studied all of me. "Did you know your dad officially named you his successor? That in the marriage contract, he basically left Liam in charge of the Red Wolves."

"What?"

"Answer."

"I didn't know about the contract. I never got to read it."

Ronan was the natural choice since he was male. But he didn't have the leadership skills to do it. He was hot-headed and impulsive—a wildcard. Dad figured that if I married a powerful man, the crew would listen to me and let me lead them. The big assumption here was that my husband would allow such a thing. Liam didn't even think of me as a person, let alone a leader.

"So, Liam is now the boss?"

"No, he's not. The marriage hasn't happened." He gripped me tighter. "Are you still thinking about going back to him? He's not the answer, Red."

"Of course not."

"What happens now?"

"I don't know." I chose not to mention the fact that a few hours ago, my plan had been to go home and find a way to convince Liam to make good on his promise to help us. That my plan had still been to use my virginity to buy us men. "All I know is that I can't be with him. He's cruel. He disgusts me."

He's not you.

"Help us." The words spilled out of my mouth before I could fully process the implication of what I was asking for.

"In exchange for what exactly?" He cupped my pussy, running his thumb over my swollen clit. "Is it back on the market?" He applied more pressure to make sure I knew what the "it" was. My eyes fluttered closed with the sweet relief his fingers offered. I bit my bottom lip and swallowed a moan. With a knowing smile, he palmed me until my body tensed. I was about to orgasm. "Well, is it?"

He stilled his hand. I let out a breath and his face came back into focus. Jesus, how did he do that? How did he make me lose myself like that?

"No, it's not." I hated that he knew that about me. In his eyes, I was the woman who sold her virginity to the highest bidder.

"Your deal fell through so now you're looking for a new buyer." His intense gaze bore into mine.

"Don't be cruel. I did what I thought was the best thing for my family." I inhaled and braced my hand on his chest, right over his drumming heart. "You offered before. So, I'm asking now. Please help us. Liam will not stop looking for me. Today, he found me so easily."

"You mean you didn't go to him?" His features softened.

"No, I knew he would be angry at me for leaving. Kay and I were on our way to Chicago when he intercepted us and brought us back to the dungeon. Help me. Please." The begging no longer bothered me. I no longer had any pride left in me. Liam saw to that.

"It's too late, Red." He released my hair and pressed his forehead to mine. "My hands are tied."

"What does that mean?"

"It means you killed a Don. And now my entire organization is after you. Believe me when I tell you that Liam is the least of your problems right now."

"Your father's dead?" I placed a hand over my mouth. "I'm so sorry."

Regardless of how ruthless and cruel Don Buratti was when he was alive, he was still Santino's dad. The pain of losing a parent was something I was familiar with. Wait? What did he say? I killed a Don?

"He's not dead. Not yet anyway." He rubbed his temple, looking utterly exhausted and beautiful.

"I didn't shoot him if that's what you think." My chest tightened. I didn't want him to think I would wish that kind of suffering on him.

"It's what he thinks. And that's all that matters." He released me and set me down on the seat.

"What? He's blaming me for it?" I cradled his cheek to make him look me in the eye. "Santino, you have to believe me. I didn't do it."

"Like I said, my hands are tied." He tapped his driver on the shoulder. When he pulled out his earpiece, Santino spoke again. "Pull over."

"I didn't shoot him. It was the other guy that was there, O'Malley. Your dad's men got to him. Ask him."

"Red, you let the enemy into my home. Do you understand the gravity of what you did? I can't help you."

"Santino."

"Listen to me very carefully." He gripped both my wrists. "The punishment for killing a Don is death. So run, Red. Run and pray he doesn't die. Because if Don Buratti dies, I will have no choice but to come after you."

He nodded once at his driver, then they both climbed out of the car. I made to follow him, but he shut the door in my face. I shifted my body to see out the back window. Kay was yanked out of the back seat of the SUV behind us and shoved toward me. As soon as Santino got inside, the car peeled off the curb and took off.

I covered my face and wept because deep in my gut, I knew I would never see him again. At least, not this version of Santino, the one who could make my body tremble with desire, the one who risked the fire to save me from Liam's dungeon— the one I loved.

My life was tethered to his father's. The old man had found a way to get me out of the way for good. He found a way to get

Santino to hate me. I touched my fingers to my lips. Santino didn't hate me. The desire I felt in his kiss and his touch were real. How long before that faded into something dark?

But even if Santino still wanted me, I was one hundred percent sure he would go after his father's killer—me. How could I prove to him that he had the wrong person?

It was my word against the word of a Don.

CHAPTER 28
Luce O'Brien

SANTINO

I landed another punch straight on his nose. It wheezed as Tino struggled to catch his breath. My raw knuckles throbbed from the beating I'd given him. No matter how much of my anger I unleashed on him, it wasn't enough to make the crushing weight in my chest go away.

"Where the fuck is he?"

Maybe my mood wasn't improving because I had the wrong guy. I would give anything right about now to have Walsh in my grasp. I bent down and fisted the front of Tino's shirt. Tino was one of us from Chicago. He was also a traitor. The son of a second-in-command who thought he wasn't getting what he was owed.

He'd made a deal with Walsh. Between him and his little group of petty ingrates, they had raided the Red Wolves for almost a year. Little by little, they brought Luce's family to its knees. The fuckers had nothing to lose. They had all the time in the world, and their father's resources.

When I made my trip to Chicago last month, his dad Joseph had assured me the Chicago Outfit had nothing to do with the attacks. What he didn't know was that his own son had orchestrated the whole thing. To prove his loyalty to the Society, he delivered his son himself. Rex decided I should be the one to handle him. Fair was fair.

"I don't know. I swear." He cowered away from me until he bumped against the wall.

We were in the basement of the Crucible. A perfect place to keep assholes like Tino. This was a fortress. No one came in or out unless we said so.

"How did you get your orders?"

"He usually sent someone. I never actually met the guy." He wiped his nose and more blood oozed out of it.

"What did Walsh want with the Red Wolf gang?" I asked for the fifth time tonight. Tino had already answered the same question a few times when Rex asked. Thing was, his memory had gotten better since I showed up. "Take it from the top."

"He wanted the territory." His eyes shifted away from the single light bulb hanging from the ceiling. He blinked as if the brightness hurt his eyes. It should, given how he hadn't seen the sun in almost a week. "He figured from there he could take over the other crews."

"What else? Think Tino. My fists are tired. It's time to bring out the tools."

"No. Wait. He also, um. He had a new business idea to bring in more money. He said he had girls, you know. Enough to start a club."

"Where are these girls from?"

"I don't know."

I inhaled deeply.

"One of his guys mentioned Venezuela. They're getting people from there for a bunch of things, sweatshops, brothels, whatever we want."

I clocked him, and his jaw made a satisfying crack. I got that we were not the good guys here. But human trafficking was where I drew the line. "Whatever we want? We're not animals. You fucking fuck."

"It's what he said."

Tino's words made a lot of things fall into place. For example, why would Walsh want to have absolute control over the Red Wolf gang? With Luce's dad out of the picture, Luce was the new boss. But if he controlled her, then he could do whatever he wanted with the territory and its people. A brothel with women who had been plucked from their homes in Venezuela would be something Luce would not tolerate—unless she'd been broken too.

If I had to guess, based on what I saw in his dungeon, that was his plan for Luce. He wanted to break her until she lost all hope, and he became her master. All he had to do to kickstart his plan was lure one of our guys into doing his dirty work. Tino was promised money, but more than that, he was sure Walsh could help him rise to power within his own crew.

Hell, if Rex and I would allow a punk like this to have any kind of say in how the Chicago outfit was run. We had by-laws for a reason—Tino's greed being one of them.

"I'm going to let you go. But you have to deliver a message for me." When he didn't move, I slapped him, not hard, just enough to wake him up. "Did you hear me?"

"Yes, a message."

"Right. You're going to go home, wait for Walsh and tell

him that the Red Wolves are, as of right now, under my protection."

"Why do we care about the Irish pigs?"

I smacked him again. Was this the kind of men we had coming up the ranks? "You're just an idiot, aren't you? What is the message? Say it, I want to make sure your little brain understood."

"The Red Wolves are under your protection."

By now, Walsh had a pretty good idea of who I was and who was backing me up. I knew this because, the minute he saw me coming for him, he fled. Walsh was smart. If he had stayed in his apartment, it would've been a bloodbath. And he would've lost.

"You leave in the morning." I glanced down at my bloody knuckles.

"He'll kill me. If he finds out I talked to you, he'll kill me."

"If you don't deliver my message, I will kill you."

I sauntered out of the room, still feeling like shit, but at least the plan to get to Walsh had been set in motion. Fisting my hand several times to get the aches out, I strode down the long corridor. When I reached the end of it, the elevator doors slid open.

"You look like shit." Rex stuffed his hands in the pockets of his trousers. His hair was perfectly combed, and he wore a fresh tuxedo.

"You going somewhere?" I stepped inside the elevator car and pressed the lobby call button.

"We both are." He leaned forward and inserted his key in the slot and the light for the forty-third floor came on. "I called for an emergency meeting. Everyone's already here."

"Fuck me. Can't this wait until tomorrow?"

"You know it can't." He exhaled then shrugged. "And you're already here."

"I need a shower."

"You have twenty minutes."

Rex dropped me off on the twentieth floor where clients kept private suites. The Crucible wasn't just a high-end sex club, it was also a casino, headquarters for the Society, and a prison for our enemies.

I quickly showered and put on a fresh tailored suit. The entire time I tried not to think about Luce and how much she would've enjoyed being here—how much I would've loved fucking her brains out in this room. I needed to stop thinking about her. Letting her go was the best thing for all of us. If Dad died, I didn't want to know where she'd gone. Because if I did, I'd have to do the unthinkable.

Fuck my life. Why did she have to shoot him? Anyone else, I could've looked the other way, but not with Dad.

The by-laws were clear on this.

I hopped on the elevator and rode it to the forty-third floor. When the doors slid open, I was greeted by the mild scent of a bygone and vintage furnishings. While Rex had spent a great deal of time updating the building, this floor remained pretty much the way it had always been. He'd replaced the frayed carpet and silk carmine wallpaper, but the new coverings were basically a replica of the old.

At the end of the corridor, where it opened up into a vestibule lined with more artifacts like statues and gold vases, I spotted Donata's slender frame and bouncy blonde hair. She was all smiles, talking to the Alfera brothers—Enzo and Massimo. Not too long ago, we were all friends. Then, Rex's dad died, and it all went to shit.

Like this building, with its old and new, the Society was in transition.

Dad and Signora Vittoria were the last sitting Dons from the previous generation. Enzo Alfera had finally taken over for Michael as the new Don. Something that would never have happened if Rex weren't so in love with his bride, Caterina Alfera. For her, he let the Alferas back into the fold.

The Gallos were all but gone. Every single member gone —thanks to the FBI. Another reason why we didn't want them up in our business. So that only left Vittoria, but she wasn't going anywhere anytime soon—she was fierce and unyielding. Donata would never move a finger to try and unseat her aunt.

But Signoria Vittoria wasn't the reason for our emergency meeting. The board was gathering tonight because Dad's life hung in the balance. Because soon, I'd have to take his seat at the table.

"Santino." Donata turned to face me as soon as I was within earshot, which told me she'd seen me when the elevator doors opened. She hugged me. "How are you doing?"

"Peachy."

"You remember Enzo and Massimo." She gestured toward her escorts.

"I do." I shook their hands.

To their credit, both brothers seemed happy to see me. Fuck me. This was going to be a long night.

"How's the old man doing?"

"As expected." I shrugged. "He got shot, and his heart didn't like it. But don't worry. He's too stubborn to die on Rex's schedule."

"Let's get the man a drink." Enzo wrapped his arm around

my shoulder and ushered me past the vestibule and into the board room. "Pappy?"

Ignoring the long table to my left, I went right and took one of the club chairs facing the fireplace and the built-in bookcases. The crackling flames reminded me of Luce and her fiery hair. *Damn her.* If she had listened to me, if she had stayed, if she hadn't betrayed me, none of us would be here right now. Dad wouldn't be in the hospital, dying.

"Drink fast. They're both for you." Enzo set two tumblers on the side table. "Cheers."

"Thanks." I took a long swig of whiskey.

The second my body relaxed, the piano tune I'd been tinkering with began to play in my head. Along with it, the images of the few days I spent with Luce unfurled like an old movie. I saw her in the study, reading Mom's book of poems, in my shower, and in my bed.

"I'm not saying it gets better." Enzo glanced down at his drink. "But you get used it."

"Great advice, man." I chuckled.

Enzo's dad passed away last year. Again, something we owed to the FBI. I supposed he knew what he was talking about. He hadn't meant I'd get used to being without a dad. He meant, I'd get used to being a Don.

"Tino is on his way to Chicago." Rex sat on the chair next to me. "He's agreed to play bait for us. We'll get Walsh. It's just a matter of time."

"That asshole better deliver." I drank some more. The mere mention of Walsh's name put me on edge. "And we need to have a talk with his dad. That boy's got birds for brains."

"He's aware." Rex sipped from his glass and glanced behind him.

When he did a double take, both Enzo and I rolled our eyes. Caterina was in the room.

"Shall we get started?" He rose to his feet and went to meet her.

"How do you stand being related to Rex?" I stood shaking my head.

"Barely."

I gestured for Enzo to go ahead then started on my second Pappy. Slowly, the board members filed into the room. At the head of the table was Rex, in his freaky chair with a head of a lion carved into the backrest. To his left, he had Caterina and her two brothers, Enzo and Massimo. At the other end of the table, Signoria Vittoria and Donata took their seats. Because the Gallos were now gone, the chair to the right of Rex was empty as was the one next to it—Dad's chair.

This wasn't my first board meeting. In the past two years, I'd attended several meetings when Dad's illness prevented him from making an appearance. Tonight, it was different. Because this gnawing feeling in my chest told me that Dad would never sit there again.

"Santino." Rex called for me, clutching his phone in his hand.

When I glanced up, everyone's eyes were on me. I'd missed what he'd said before. Though, looking around at the pity in everyone's faces, it could only be one thing.

"Don Buratti passed away."

I nodded once, staring at Dad's old place. After a few beats, I released a breath and made my way to it. The worn-out upholstered armrest molded to my hand, as I was sure it had done for Dad and his dad, and his dad's dad.

Ever since I could remember, I knew I was always meant

to take over. I just never imagined it would hurt like this. Was Enzo right? Would I get used to the pain and everything else this chair represented?

"I called this ascension meeting to offer special permission to induct Santino as a Don. It seems we're a bit late." He dipped his head in my direction. Rex wasn't into the whole "sorry for your loss" bullshit. Nothing he could say would change the course of my life now. "The Society now recognizes Santino as the new Don Buratti."

Donata smiled at me, a sad but genuine smile. I pressed my lips together and accepted my new charge. So be it. As much as I didn't like things changing, life had a way to tug and pull until nothing was the same.

"Don Buratti." Signoria Vittoria dipped her head in my direction.

One by one, everyone paid their respects with a nod, as "congratulations" wasn't the right word to use. What would they say? Sorry your dad died, congratulations on your ascension. A simple acknowledgement was all that was required.

"Now that everyone is here, we can move to the next order of business." Rex glanced over at Caterina, exchanging a meaningful look.

"This part is simple." Signoria Vittoria spoke first in her usual smoker's voice.

Whenever there was a need for blood, she was the first one to point it out.

"Someone killed a Don. I want to see at least one head roll." She met Rex's gaze across the table.

My heart rate spiked because the old lady was talking about Luce. I kept my emotions in check and sat back, playing with the ring on my finger. "Is there a specific head you have in mind, Vittoria?"

"That's Rex's area of expertise." She sat forward in that regal way of hers that screamed old money. "I hope you have a name."

"I have two. The late Don Frances Buratti identified his shooters." Rex sipped from his glass. "O'Malley died on the scene earlier today."

"And the other?" Vittoria pressed on.

"Luce O'Brien." Rex made eye contact with everyone but me.

I appreciated him not putting me on the spot. Though it begged the question. How many members knew I had Luce sequestered in my penthouse for the last two weeks? That she killed Dad while trying to escape me. If they knew, they didn't show it. Worst part was they didn't blame me for it. Other heads needed to roll, but not mine, though I was just as guilty. My hubris and my lust for her led us to this point.

"Well, it's as they say. Away with her head. And let's be done with this." Signoria Vittoria shrugged as if Luce's life was nothing.

"I thought we had gotten smarter." I glared at Rex.

I should've put Liam Walsh in his place when I had the chance. Back then, Rex wanted to play it smart and simply help Walsh hang himself. Now Dad was gone, and the Dons were calling for Luce's head. How the hell was that being better than our forefathers?

"Certain sins can only be washed with blood."

The old woman was getting on my nerves.

"She's an innocent girl," I said through gritted teeth.

"Tell that to your father." She fired back with a murderous gleam in her eyes.

"Enough." Rex shot to his feet and slammed his hand on the table. "If it's blood you wanted, Vittoria, you got it. O'Malley was executed on site, which is lucky because now we have leeway. We got our blood for blood. It ends here."

"Jesus Christ." Vittoria sat back.

"Think about what would happen if we went after Luce *Al Capone style*—old school."

"You know, the way you like it." I smirked at Vittoria.

Her gaze shifted between Rex and me. Why was she in such a hurry to get rid of a woman she'd never even met?

"Luce is the daughter of the late Patrick O'Brien, the leader of the Red Wolves gang in Chicago. Not a big group, but very Irish and very proud. If we kill her, Walsh will have an excuse to go after the New York Faction. Our job is to protect our own, not incite a war on the streets. It's not our lives on the line, it's our people's."

"What do you propose we do?" I liked that Luce's head was no longer on the chopping block. Rex had my full attention.

"Exactly that. A proposal." He smiled at Caterina as he lowered himself to his seat. "Enzo has been Don for almost a year. He needs a wife. He could marry Luce. Make sure she's punished for what she did."

"Come again." It was my turn to shoot to my feet. "A marriage proposal?"

"Yes, we'll have her under surveillance. No need for more bloodshed."

"Well, as long as she gets a beating once a week, I suppose I'm fine with it." Signoria Vittoria smiled sweetly at Enzo.

"You know that whole thing where Dons need a wife, it's more of a guideline than a rule of law." Enzo furrowed his brows, clearly not happy to be told what to do.

What was Rex thinking? No, this had to be Caterina's idea. She thought too highly of her brothers. Enzo was no match for Luce. I thought of Enzo and Luce together on their wedding night, and stars exploded in front of my eyes.

"No."

"No, what?" Rex's attention flitted to me. "It's better than the alternative. It'll show good faith on our part. Who knows, maybe this will improve our relations with the Irish?"

Vittoria scoffed.

"It's the best solution for all of us." He met my gaze and nodded once, as if saying, "now you don't have to feel guilty or responsible for her."

"Enzo can't marry her."

"Well, let me think about it." He leaned forward. "I'd like to meet her first. Then I'll decide."

"Fuck off." I braced a hand on the table as my gaze shifted from Enzo to Rex. And before I could question my resolve, I let the words I never thought I'd say fly out of my mouth. "I'll marry her."

CHAPTER 29
Code Red

LUCE

"I still think we should've kept Santino's SUV." Kay adjusted the passenger seat, so she could lay back some more.

"You don't think he has his car bugged? He only gave it to us so he could keep tabs on me." Gripping the steering wheel, I checked the rearview mirror and took notice of every driver around us.

After Santino dropped us off on the side of the road like we were nothing, we decided it would best if we went back for Kay's Prius. As luck would have it, the little car was still there.

Fuck Santino Buratti.

"If he wanted to help us, he would've let us stay at his place for the night. Or, at least flown us home. I don't know. He flat-out refused."

"I'm sorry. But it's probably for the best, Luce. Getting involved with the Italians never ends well." She rubbed my back. "This Santino sounds like a royal jerk."

"I hate him."

"I know. But we'll be home soon. We'll find Ronan. And then Dad, Ronan, you, and me, we can start thinking about rebuilding. We'll figure out a way to kick the Italian bastards off our streets. Yeah?"

I wiped my cheek and then checked the mirrors again. "It's so late, we shouldn't be out here."

"I know. I'm going to call Dad. Maybe he can meet us halfway. We can't drive all night."

"Yeah, do that."

She fished her phone from under my seat. When Liam's men found us earlier tonight, she had the sense to hide her personal mobile. At least one thing had gone in our favor tonight.

"What is it?" I slanted a glance toward her. "What did he say?"

"It went to voicemail. But now I have a text from a private number." She shifted her body to face me. "Luce, it's code red."

A shot of adrenaline rushed through me. I tightened my grip and veered off the road. Cars honked at me, but I couldn't see in front of me anymore, and I couldn't hold my hands steady.

Code red meant go underground.

Things were so bad at home, Kay's dad had decided to call code red.

"We have to do it, Luce. Just like we practiced."

"Fuck." I hit the steering wheel with my palm. "For how long?"

"Until Dad comes for us."

"I'm not in the mood for telling stories to strangers."

"Are you kidding me?" She scoffed. "Look at our clothes? One look at us and they'll know we're for real. Come on. There's a gas station up ahead. We're gonna need a lot of booze for this."

"Actually, I could use a drink." I put the Prius in gear and drove two miles to the next exit.

Kay reached under the seat and removed her wallet. Fixing her jacket, she went into the liquor store. At least one of us had her head in the game.

Before Liam came for us, all I could think about was how I was never going to see Santino again. I wished that had been true. Because now I knew I meant nothing to him. I was so stupid to think that we had a real connection. Why would I even think that? The man kidnapped me. He fucked me as punishment, nothing more. I made it all up in my head. His touch and those all-consuming kisses, that was all me. He used me. And I was too stupid and too naive to see him for what he was.

"Okay." Kay opened the driver's door. "Scoot. You drink, I drive."

Blowing out a breath, I did as she asked and popped over to the passenger seat.

She handed me a bottle of Vodka and one of juice. "Start mixing. And tell me your name."

"My name is Parker Williams, I'm twenty-one years old." I skipped the cocktail and drank straight from the bottle. "I was born in Las Vegas. I live with my mom, well I used to, before she kicked me out."

Thank you so much for reading Big Bad Wolf, Book 1. I hope you enjoyed Santino and Luce's forbidden love story. Their wild ride concludes in Big Bad Wolf (Wolf Duet, #2), where Luce is forced to accept Santino's marriage proposal.

I have to find Luce before our enemies do, and I lose her forever.
She thinks she can hide from me. But I don't care if I have to go to the ends of the world to get her back. One way or another, Luce O'Brien has to understand that I'm not letting her go. She's mine to keep, mine to protect.

Download Big Bad Wolf (Wolf Duet, #2)

I've included the first chapter of Big Bad Wolf (Wolf Duet #2) so can you can try it for FREE. Go ahead, you know you want to. :-)

Do you want more Dark Mafia Romance? If you enjoy steamy reads, please do consider leaving a kind review. It lets me know you'd like to see more books like this one.

Big Bad Wolf

WOLF DUET, BOOK 2

CHAPTER 1

CHAPTER 1
The Wrong Woman

SANTINO

How was it possible for a person to completely disappear off the face of the Earth? I had never spent this much time and effort trying to locate someone. And I had never been so desperate to find a woman—Luce O'Brien, my soon-to-be-wife, who had been missing for over three months.

I slid back into the usual rabbit hole of scenarios, where I saw Luce in Liam's surveillance screens with her wrists and ankles tied to a sex wheel in his dungeon. I let anger pool and simmer in my stomach. Worst part was that I had no one to blame for what happened but myself. When Dad accused her of shooting him, I knew the only way to keep her alive was for me to let her go so the Society wouldn't find her.

That night, I left her on the side of the road, like she didn't mean anything to me—as if the time we had spent together hadn't seeped into my heart and soul. She seemed so hurt. But the truth was, I had fallen for Luce. I'd never been the type to form attachments. So, when Luce showed up and tore down my walls, I didn't recognize my feelings for what they were. I was in love with her. All those times when I couldn't bear to see her go, now I understood why. She'd gotten under my skin.

But was it too late? Did Liam get to her? Was she even alive?

She had to be. Even if Liam had her, he couldn't kill her. Not if he wanted to rightfully takeover the Red Wolves. Luce's crew was a proud bunch. They would never follow someone who hurt one of their own. Liam was a lot of vile things, but he wasn't a fool.

I paced the length of my office. I was tired of waiting for news, for my guys to give me something I could work with. I had already exhausted all my leads. But I wasn't ready to give up on her. Wherever she was, I hoped she didn't hate me. Though, she had every reason to.

I let her go.

This one was on me.

"Sir."

"What?" Even I heard the edginess of my tone.

My assistant Lia took two steps back, toward the door, with her eyes wide. "Erm, Mr. Joey is here. He says he has information for you."

"Let him in."

I leaned on the edge of my desk, tapping my fingers. My second-in-command strode in. His sense of urgency appeased my bad mood. "Don Buratti." He nodded once.

I started to say, "Don Buratti is my dad," but that was no longer the case. Dad was gone, which made me the new Don Buratti. "Santino is fine, Joey. We've known each other for years."

Joey was much older than me, closer to Dad's age. The

stuffy reverence between us was more for his benefit than mine. I was sure he still saw me as the little punk who had zero respect for his dad and everything he represented within the Society. Had I made a mistake keeping him on as my second? Rex thought so. But I figured if Joey stuck around, maybe the empty space Dad left wouldn't seem so dark. Joey had smarts, the kind one could only acquire with years and years of service.

"Tell me you have something."

"I do." He set his iPad on my desk. "We missed a warehouse. This one." He pointed at the screen. "The one we blew up about four months ago in Hell's Kitchen. You know, when Walsh tried to move in on our territory?"

"Yeah, I remember. Rossi set off a pipe bomb. He didn't leave much behind."

"Right. Well, Walsh didn't bother fixing it up. He's got one room in the back that's still active."

"Drugs."

"Yeah, mostly. He has a few women working there. One fits her description."

Her.

He wouldn't even say Luce's name in front of me. Needless to say, I'd been a real asshole these past few months. I glanced down at my watch. "Are they working right now?"

"They cook late at night."

"I want to be on site when Walsh's crew shows up. I want to see her for myself." I didn't care if I had to sit outside the building until dawn. Luce was coming home with me tonight. "Get Tommy and the others and meet me in the garage."

"On it." He nodded and rushed out.

I stayed and took a moment to calm the fuck down. But

instead, my mind conjured a myriad of images of Luce wasted out of her mind, doing Liam's bidding. This was my punishment for leaving her. I was so angry at her that day. To be honest, I still was.

She killed my father, for fuck's sake—while trying to escape from me.

As soon as the elevator door opened in the garage level, I knew this night would get much worse before it got better. "You gotta be fucking kidding me." I ambled toward Rex, the current sitting king of the Society, and Enzo Alfera, the new Don Alfera and Rex's brother-in-law.

Our one-hundred-year-old criminal enclave consisted of five founding families. Since the beginning, marriage between us was frowned upon. And this right here was the reason. Caterina had a lot of influence over Rex, which in turn meant the Alfera brothers got to do whatever the hell they wanted.

"If it helps," Enzo leaned against my SUV, "I didn't want to come either. My sister insisted."

"Let me guess. She wants you to spend some quality time with her husband. Just like old times." I was wrong. The Alfera brothers were also under Caterina's control.

"Something like that." He shrugged. "Word of advice. Never get married. Oh wait." He chuckled. "Too late for that."

"I'm not married yet," I grumbled.

"You gave me your word." Rex met my gaze, as if daring me to back out of the deal I made with him and the entire board. Though he knew I wasn't about to put Luce's life in danger by not going through with the wedding.

"Is that why you're here? To make sure I don't bail and kill Luce myself."

"I don't think that's what you want." Rex nodded at my guys. "We're here to help."

Tommy put his phone away and moved to open the door for me, while Joey went around and opened the doors on the other side. Rex unbuttoned his suit jacket as he ambled around the vehicle. With a smirk, Enzo followed behind him. I considered my options for a moment, which of course, were none. Then, I climbed into the back seat and settled in.

"This is going to be a long night."

"You're telling me." Enzo shifted his body in the passenger seat to look at me. "I don't think Walsh is stupid enough to keep your fiancée right under our noses. I'd bet she's miles away."

"I know." I shook my head. "But it's all we've got. And honestly, Liam Walsh would be the type to do something like this. Just to prove how clever he is. We can't leave any stone unturned."

"Well, if you insist."

"That reminds me. I have something for you." Rex smiled, and the way his features relaxed told me whatever he had for me, came from his Caterina. He handed me a silver flask. "Pappy. Caterina thought it would make the stake out more bearable."

I grabbed the container from him and took a long swig from it. Enzo wiggled his fingers at me and waited until I placed the whiskey in his hand. Just like that, it felt as if we were back in high school—before our families went at each other's throats over Michael Alfera's decision to defect from the Society. In one fell swoop, the three of us went from best friends to mortal enemies. Enzo found out he could've been king. And that the one taking his seat at the head of the table was Rex. The whole thing was a mindfuck for all of us.

Rex's marriage to Caterina last year had been the catalyst in reuniting the families and working together like we used to when our grandparents were still alive. But was it enough? Even if I didn't feel like Rex stole his title anymore, I still had a hard time trusting his motives. His Machiavellian methods were enough to give me whiplash. Dad used to follow Michael Alfera's orders blindly. Together with Rex's dad, they were a formidable team. Nothing could touch the three of them.

But looking at Enzo and Rex in the vehicle with me, I didn't think we had that. Our friendship was fractured over a decade ago, along with our trust. Too much had happened between us.

"That's better than the shit you used to steal from your dad," I said to Rex as I leaned forward to tap Joey's shoulder. "Let's go."

"Yes, sir." He started the ignition. As soon as he did, the engines in the three SUVs behind us rumbled to life in unison.

"Yeah. Dad didn't care for good liquor."

"So, does Caterina really think this is going to work?" I pointed at Enzo in the front seat.

"She actually does."

"And you?"

"I don't know. We have a lot of unfinished business." He glared at the back of Enzo's head. "One problem at a time, eh?"

"Yeah, I suppose."

Twenty minutes later, the car stopped in front of a dilapidated building. I thought of Luce working in those conditions. The place could crumble at any moment. Not to mention, the air inside couldn't possibly be safe to breathe.

I kept my gaze fixed on the side entrance. From this angle, I could see my guys had already set up a perimeter. Liam's people were surrounded. Or they would be as soon as we entered. My heart thumped hard against my ribs. For one, I wanted to get this goddamn womanhunt over with. But also, because I wanted to see Luce again.

I wanted to make sure she was okay. I wanted to apologize, and fuck her into oblivion, until neither one of us remembered our names.

"Like I said, I don't think I ever had a chance there." Enzo pointed a finger at me with a big knowing smirk on his face.

"What?" I'd completely missed whatever conversation they were having.

"Rex still thinks I would make a better husband for sweet Luce. But obviously, you're not ready to let her go."

"No, I'm not."

"I don't understand what the big deal is with you and this Irish girl. They're a dime a dozen."

"Fuck off." I tapped my fingers on my thigh, anxious to make a move already. "And she's not a girl."

"Isn't she like twenty-three. How old are you? Thirty?"

"She's twenty-five. And no, I'm not thirty yet, old man."

Enzo was the oldest of the three of us. He was about to hit the big three-o, so naturally, he wanted the rest of us to go down with him.

"What is taking so long? They should be here by now." I leaned forward to get a better view of the entire street ahead of us. "Are you sure this site is operational?" I met Joey's gaze in the rearview mirror.

"Yes, sir. I confirmed the information myself."

"Look." Rex hit my arm with the back of his hand. "There."

First, one man appeared at the corner and then another. They filed inside. A minute later, another guy and a woman showed up. She wore a hoodie, but even in the dark, her red hair stood out.

When I made to move, Enzo reached over and grabbed my shirt sleeve to stop me. "We're not teenagers anymore, Santino. You can't go in there like you're bulletproof."

"They're cooks, not professional assassins." I counted to three in my head while I scanned the area for men with guns.

The minute she was out of sight, I yanked my arm away and bolted. The deserted street was eerily quiet and dark as fuck; I picked up the pace and crossed it.

By the time I reached the entrance, the screaming had already started. Apparently, there were more people inside. As soon as my guys moved in, they all scattered. But this door was the only way in and out, and we had them surrounded. Luce would have to go through me to get away.

I stood in the shadows, among the wreckage, in what used to be the lobby, and waited for her to leave the way she came in. At the far end of the main floor, a room had been set up with chairs, tables, and shelving units. They weren't cooking anything, merely packaging powder and pills.

My guys stuck to the plan and made it look like a raid. I didn't give a shit about their product. But I didn't want Liam to know I was looking for Luce, which meant, I couldn't grab anyone and flat out ask for her.

I glanced back to see if Rex or Enzo had followed me inside. In that one second, I looked away, and someone hit me over the head with a pipe.

"Son of a bitch." I turned around and the last thing I saw was the glint of red. "Luce." I chased after her.

The nape of my neck throbbed something fierce. I couldn't see straight. But I couldn't let her get away. Not now when I was so close to getting her back.

She headed straight into the next alley. Sheer will made me get over my possible concussion and run faster. I took three long strides and hooked my arm around her waist. She fought me, but I pressed her hard against the brick wall and knocked the wind out of her.

When I pulled down her hoodie, my stomach dropped. I had the wrong woman. I stepped back, and she dropped to her knees, begging in a language I didn't understand.

"I'm sorry. You're not who I thought. You can go." I pointed toward the street. "Go."

She wiped her tears, looking at me with pure terror in her eyes. She panted and slowly moved her foot to the right. What did she think I was going to do? Let her go, only to chase her again? For sport?

"Go," I said again.

Her body jerked in surprise, but she recovered quickly. She wiped her cheek and took off.

I made my way back to the SUV, where Enzo and Rex waited for me. The fuckers hadn't come along to help me. They were here purely for the entertainment factor. I climbed in the back seat while my guys ransacked the place to make it look like we were there for the drugs.

"It wasn't her." I panted a breath.

"What now?" Rex surveyed the side of my head.

"I keep looking."

"You better do it quick." Enzo opened his door, then

turned around to face me. "Signoria Vittoria might've agreed to this ridiculous wedding, but don't think for a second that her men aren't out there looking for the girl. If you don't find her fast, they will." He climbed out.

"Enzo," Rex called after him, "Caterina is expecting us for dinner."

"I'm done with this charade. Tell her I had something come up." He shut the door. Out of the alley behind us, another SUV swung around and picked him up.

"What charade?" I pressed my palm over the nape of my neck.

"Caterina wants us to be friends again." He rolled his eyes, bracing his elbow on the window.

"Does she know what happened with you two?"

"No. And I'd like to keep it that way."

"Jesus. Just tell Enzo the truth—that you were a petty little punk when you were eighteen—and move on." I tapped Joey on the shoulder. "Let's go home."

Rex and Enzo's situation wasn't life or death, like it was with Luce. Mine was a race against Signoria Vittoria. And all I could do was hope that my resources had better reach than hers. Or that Luce would come to me of her own accord.

"Enzo is right." Rex cocked an eyebrow. "If you don't get to Luce first, Vittoria will, and it won't be pretty. She's old school. She hates the idea of an Irish woman in our midst. She's not the only one."

"You don't think I fucking know that?" I rubbed the ache in my chest. It was like a warning. As if my body knew how much trouble she was in, and how much she needed my help. I couldn't let Liam or Vittoria find her before I did.

Luce belonged with me.

"You've dropped everything to find Luce. I get that she's a priority, but your flock needs tending." He cut a glance over to Joey. "Anything on Walsh yet?"

"No, nothing on him either. But I have a small army looking for him. I want that asshole dead, sooner rather than later."

The tires slowly rolled away from the dilapidated building, while I sat there and pretended I didn't have this huge hole in my heart and a goddamn splitting headache.

Luce, where the hell are you?

Santino and Luce's forbidden love story concludes in Big Bad Wolf (Wolf Duet, Book 2)